WHERE THE HOWL ARE YOU?

ASHLYN CHASE

Cover by Emma Hartley
© Ashlyn Chase 2019, for Imagination Unlimited
Edited by Gerry Russell,
Proofread by Dianne Donovan

Note: This book is the rewritten and republished version of Surviving Mortality by Ashlyn Chase under her previous pen name, Cyndi Redding. The names, places and genre of the story have changed, but if you recognize parts of it, you may have bought the original published by Liquid Silver Books ten years ago. If so, you're one of about fifty people. Thank you!

To my husband for sticking with me through everything.

ACKNOWLEDGMENTS

Special thanks to Kurt Moses of the Kennebunkport Police Department for checking my factual information re: police procedures, to Mark McGuire, who told me what life as a truck driver was like, and to a PI, who asked to remain nameless, because he's a relative and kind of embarrassed by what I write.
Hey—it's not every guy who'll admit he likes romance unless it's part of an action movie. To those few I say, Hurrah! This world needs more lovers of love.

PROLOGUE: TWO YEARS AGO

THE SUMMONING

"I'm so embarrassed, I could die!" Ronda grabbed her bra off the branch and slipped it back on. She had a hard time with the clasp and slurred curses under her breath. "Maura, are you one hunnered percent sure you knew what you were doing?"

Maura steadied herself as she stepped into her panties. "Shhh. Don't talk so loud. At least not until we get dressed and out of these woods."

Yeah, right. She might as well tell seagulls not to circle fishing boats as tell her drunken friends not to talk too loud.

Despite their inebriated agreement earlier, the four friends had suddenly freaked out when a bolt of lightning split the clear, black night. Maybe they didn't believe in Maura's ability to summon immortals, but they went along with it.

Barb let out a huff, then whispered loudly. "A lightning bolt came out of the cloudless sky and could've fried us. That was weird and everything, but no immortals were riding it to earth. Couldn't you have screwed up?"

Haley pulled her tummy slimmer halfway up and staggered, barely staying upright. "I can't believe you made us get naked and dance under the moon. What kind of dumb ceremony is that?"

Ronda added, "I think you just wanted to see how far we'd go to find decent men at our *ahem* age."

Maura snapped. "I'm not sure of anything except that mortal men are not worth the trouble and heartache anymore. If you think immortals might appreciate an older, wiser woman and want to date one, you have to summon one. And I tried to do it—for all of us."

Barb snorted. "Is that what you call summoning? To face in the general direction of Romania and mutter, 'Where the hell are you, damn it?'"

"Look, I tried the nice poetry from my memory of Irish summoning circles, but I was a kid. My grandda made all kinds of magic stuff happen."

"Like pulling a quarter from behind your ear? My grandpa did that," Barb said.

"No, smartass. Things you wouldn't believe—like talking in Gaelic to little people I could swear now were leprechauns."

Ronda had to admit it sounded like blarney. "Irish cele-brations, huh? No wunner. They were prob'bly as shtonkered as we are." Ronda's bra clicked into place. "Ah, I finally got it."

Maura reached for her camisole and swore when it wouldn't fall off the branch where she'd tossed it.

Barb pointed an accusing finger at her. "When I sober up, I'm going to be really embarrassed, not just about the nudity, but for getting suckered into this. Why the Hell did we have to take our clothes off again? We didn't even undress in front of each other in college."

Ronda answered when Maura didn't. "She said we had to come to the high-and-mighty ones pure to show our commim... com... commiment."

"The word is commitment," Haley said. "As in all of us

committed to Bellevue mental hospital if the cops catch us and I'm pretty sure that none of us are pure. Besides, I'm with Barb on dying of embarrassment tomorrow. Commitment's not all we showed by running around buck-naked under the moon."

"No kiddin'." Ronda let out a nervous giggle.

"It's called sky-clad and I'm not exactly proud of my butt without a body shaper, either," Maura said. "Look, I didn't force you to do it, did I? We're all sick of successful men, our equals, going after the little bimbos with the big boobs, leaving us flourishing older women alone, feeling like rejects." Maura couldn't free her camisole from the branch to save her life. She stood there in only her bra and panties frowning at the branch.

"'Flourishing.' Good word," Haley the English professor said.

"Maura's right, everyone." Ronda mumbled the words from under the blouse she had somehow decided to pull over her head instead of unbuttoning it. "She didn't hold a gun to our heads."

"Hey," Barb cried. "That's my blouse!"

Maura stomped her foot. "I'm going to have to climb that friggin' tree."

"Maura, Don't." Barb reached up and touched the branch. "Look, you aren't particularly tall or athletic. Let me do it."

"Is that your way of calling me short and fat?"

"Of course not. I never said that, for god's sake! I'm just trying to help."

"Maura, your body is perfectly normal for a thirty-eight-year-old woman. You have nothing to be ashamed of."

"Thanks, Haley. But I still wish I could find that friggin' fountain of youth."

"Sorry I got mad at you before," Ronda said to Maura. "I just had a bad day at work."

Haley smiled. "Yeah, me too. I really love you, man."

"I really love you, man, too." Barb hugged Maura. "Now let me get your top."

"Well..." Maura eyed the branch. "Are you sure? I mean, I know we're the best of friends and everything, but you don't have to risk your pantyhose for me."

Barb shrugged. "What else is new? Friends to the end, right?"

They attempted a high-five, missed, and wound up pawing the air.

CHAPTER ONE

Ronda couldn't believe she had reiterated the whole story to a complete stranger. A stranger who was now laughing her ass off.

"Hey! I'm glad you find my story entertaining, but I was actually thinking you'd understand."

"Oh, I do..." The clairvoyant sitting across from Ronda Calhoun cleared her throat and tried to compose herself. "Believe me, I understand what you're saying. The older you get the harder it is to find the perfect partner. But immortals? Really? Just because I'm psychic you thought I'd be into all that Woo Woo stuff?"

Ronda jumped up and was about to walk out when the woman grasped her arm.

"No. Don't go. I think I can help."

Ronda wrestled all her angry parting shots into submission and sank down on the chair again. "Fine."

"I'm sorry about laughing. You've lost a lot of loved ones, and they're all shouting at me, desperately trying to get my attention. Let's see if I can get them to shut up and appoint a spokesperson."

Ronda sat on her hands to keep them from trembling,

but she wasn't sure if she was nervous or angry, hopeful or expectant—not that she knew what to expect. She had thought she might find a Bohemian woman working behind a beaded curtain, wearing too much make-up and too much jewelry.

Instead, she had found Janice, a lovely woman so typical of Maine, wearing no make-up, tasteful silver jewelry and a natural fiber skirt with a thick brown wool sweater over it. Gray strands threaded through Janice's brunette hair.

Within the tiny alcove that had been set aside for readings in her home, three white candles burned, lending a comforting glow to the all-white room. The woman closed her eyes, the candles flickered, and she began to speak.

"I have an older woman who is above you, a mother, grandmother or aunt? I see eyes as blue as yours."

"It could be any one of the three," Ronda said, hoping for her mother. Butterflies landed in her stomach as she waited for Janice to tell her more.

"She's showing me a microphone. She loves to sing?"

"That could be my Mom." She held her breath. Six months prior, Ronda's parents had perished in a plane crash, and she missed her mother terribly. Ellen Calhoun was a woman who had known how to let the little things go, but when it mattered, she would stick her neck out and do what she thought was right.

"I'm getting a mothering energy and a name that could be Eileen or Ellen."

"Yes," said Ronda, encouraged. "My mother's name was Ellen."

"Did she sing you a special song when you were young? No, wait. It was something you used to sing together. Is she showing me a barge on the ocean?"

"Yes, that's it! The name of the song was 'Barges'." Her eyes widened in surprise. *Wow*. She could barely stay in her seat. How could anyone but her mother know about that?

Ronda chuckled, and for the first time since she had arrived, she relaxed.

"She wants you to know about something in a box, some article of clothing."

Ronda paused and concentrated. "I don't know what that would be."

"She's showing me a wedding gown. She wants you to know that you'll be wearing it soon."

Ronda shook her head, her dark brown bangs tickling her forehead as she wagged her long ponytail. *Okay, maybe she's good, but she's not perfect.* "You're right about my mother's wedding gown being in a box. I remember that. But there's no wedding."

"She's nodding. She insists you're going to be getting married soon. Say, within seven months. I see the number seven."

Ronda sighed. "Sorry, Mom, it must be your wishful thinking. It isn't likely to happen that way." Unsure if Janice would just start laughing again or not, she forged on. "I just got back from India. I was there twice in six months—attending two of my friends' weddings. They weren't exactly legal though. Neither groom had a birth certificate since they were three hundred year-old shapshifting tigers. My other friend is shacking up in France with a vampire and didn't even bother with a ceremony."

"Hold on, Ronda," Janice said.

She had learned to school her features, because she didn't smile or laugh. She simply changed the subject. Well...fine.

"Your mother wants to tell you something else." Her eyes fluttered, and she continued. "She needs you to know there will be more than one man in your heart. It's crucial that you choose the right one."

"That's weird." From no serious relationships to two men

in seconds flat, but now, beyond curious, she didn't want to interrupt.

"I'm getting another female energy beside you. Your sister? She's showing me a blue hairbrush with a picture of Barbie on it. She's indicating that you used to brush each other's hair."

"Yes, that would be my sister." Seeing in her mind's eye Sarah's long, shiny, blond hair, her throat tightened.

"Now she's showing me a cat. Did your family have a cat?"

"No, we didn't have shedding pets because she and my father were allergic to them."

"Nuisances like allergies don't follow us into the next world. You must look after someone else's cat, then," Janice insisted. "She's telling me to ask you to take good care of the cat, even when..." Janice cocked her head to the side, as if listening. "I don't know what she means by this, but even when your world is turned upside down."

"Nope. No cat. Wait a minute. My world is going to be turned upside down? Is this about the two guys again?"

Janice concentrated once more. "No. I think this is something else, something more ominous, but it could be related. One of the men could be dangerous. On the other hand, it may not be that simple."

She leaned toward Ronda, a serious expression on her face. "Just be careful. They want you to know that they'll be with you and will try to help from the Other Side, but they're concerned about some sort of deceit. Don't do anything drastic or make any major decisions before you know what's going on behind your back."

"What? Someone's stabbing me in the back?" Her anxiety returned and her mouth dried out.

"They're fading." Janice closed her eyes again, and moments later as she opened them, she said, "I'm sorry."

"You've got to be kidding. Get them back!"

"I'm very sorry, it's not like a phone call."

"Wait, I wanted to tell them..." Hold it in, Ronnie, you know how you hate crying in public.

"What did you want to tell them, dear?"

Janice's kind response to her outburst reminded Ronda of her mother. She imagined that Janice must have had to become part-therapist, part surrogate mother over the years, and she'd probably seen any number of reactions.

"I wanted to tell them, to say that ... well, after what happened to Sarah—her kidnapping and murder—my parents couldn't help overprotecting me. Or, they tried to, anyway. I stayed out late, didn't bother to call, ran around with the bad boys. I always had a cigarette in one hand, a beer in the other, and more than my share of one-night stands, all just to prove..." The golf ball sized lump in her throat wouldn't allow her to finish her sentence.

Janice shook her head. "It's all in the past."

"I know." She sniffed. "I only wish I was less wasteful of my parents' love and more compassionate and under-standing of their pain."

"Love is never wasted, and they understand. Honest, they do. It doesn't matter anymore."

"It matters to me," Ronda said, her voice shaking.

Janice walked over and hugged her. "Are you all right?"

She nodded. "I'll be fine. Just fucking fine..."

———

Ronda bought an older Volvo in New York to hold her "worldly possessions" when she moved back to Maine. At the time she remembered an old advertising joke... *Volvo— Boxy but good!*

She drove her used but not *that* good Volvo straight to her temporary home in Old Orchard Beach. She mulled over her messages and her life. *Good Lord, what the hell could my mother and sister have been trying to tell me? And was Janice for real? Maybe she's trying to get me to come back and spend more money. Or that's my leftover New York cynicism.*

She had made contact with her family—she was sure of it. They had identified themselves with obscure details that only members of a close family would know. However, the warnings troubled her. She was going to be deceived and in danger? Plus advised not to do anything drastic. Too late. She already had.

She'd moved back to Maine from New York City, needing time to lick her wounds and think about why all her friends had found love and she hadn't. Her job didn't hold her interest anymore. Nothing did.

If that wasn't upsetting enough, then the spirits disappeared, leaving her alone to figure it out for herself. *How could they leave me like that? Then again, how could they leave me in the first place?*

When she pulled up in front of her cottage her stomach was still too jittery to go inside, so she left her car and began walking off her nervous energy, despite the icy March weather.

How she wished she could be lounging with her parents at their home in Kennebunkport, or maybe walking with her family after a big Sunday dinner, basking in the warmth of their *corporeal* love.

He had driven several miles south on the Maine Turnpike to get to the Calhoun's beautiful home in Kennebunkport. It stood empty and forlorn, but that's exactly how he wanted it. The man and his passenger donned black ski masks and drove over the grass at the end of the driveway to hide the Ford pick-up truck around the back of the large blue-gray estate. Seabirds were the only observers they would have.

Fumbling with a lock on the cellar door he worked diligently. "C'mon. Open."

The other man scanned the grounds and called out, "Are you sure she doesn't ever come here?"

"Will you shut up? I know the car she drives," he snapped. "Do you see a black Volvo anywhere?"

The other intruder shook his head. "But, what if she has another car now?"

"She doesn't. I've kept an eye on her recently. It's in the driveway almost all the time. She must never go much of anywhere."

"Poor kid. She lost her sister, brother, and now her parents are dead."

The lock wouldn't budge. "Yeah, I'm a schmuck. Here, damn it. You try," growled the tall, lanky intruder. "And quit complaining. What good is being an opportunist if you don't take advantage of a golden opportunity? Cut the moralistic crap, will you?"

"Fine. But this better be worth the trouble."

"It will be, believe me."

As Ronda marched over the snow-covered sidewalks of Old Orchard Beach in her mukluks, she pondered all the clairvoyant's messages. She had just turned the slushy corner and was so deep in thought that she didn't hear, and almost didn't see, the car coming toward her.

Not until the car flashed its lights did she startle and snap to attention, only to recognize the driver of the Audi as it slowed to a stop in front of her. The young woman driving it flashed a winning smile.

Marci Jo partially rolled down the window.

"Jump in, woman. I'll drive you to your house. I hope you have heat!"

Ronda grinned. "Don't worry. I paid the bill. Go ahead without me. I'll meet you there in a minute. Oh! Do you know where I'm staying?"

"It wasn't easy, but I tracked you down."

Seeing those twinkling green eyes and bright smile instantly cheered her. When they found out they were both from Maine, her early days in New York became much more fun. Marci Jo was always the life of any party. Right now, in Ronda's life, Marci Jo *was* the party.

As Ronda strolled up her front walk, she watched Marci Jo tromp back down the wooden steps from her screen-porch, spreading her arms wide. She grabbed Ronda and hugged her, hard.

"I know I've been in Costa Rica, but where the hell have *you* been? I've left messages, sent cards—two of 'em, telling you to call me. I was thinking of sending a note on a pigeon."

Ronda chuckled, but said, "Wait until we're inside and I'll explain." Few were privy to her personal business, and her neighbors' homes were close enough to borrow a cup of sugar without leaving the house.

Ronda turned the old key in the rusty lock, and they entered her tiny white cottage with peeling green trim.

After they were inside and had tossed their coats onto the coat rack they shared another hug, and Marci Jo chastised her. "Why didn't you call me? I've been so worried about you. Are you okay?"

"Well, I'm okay now. Up until recently though, I was a mess. I went through shock, disbelief, anger, depression, the gamut—but now I'm finding some equilibrium."

"I tried to call you at your job in New York, and they said you didn't work there anymore. The woman said they tried to keep in touch, but you had just sort of dropped off everyone's radar. What's going on?"

Ronda had been heading toward the kitchen, but she

stopped and faced her friend. "I couldn't concentrate, and I'd burst into tears for little or no reason. Trying to keep everything 'normal' and not worry anyone while going through a huge emotional upheaval was stupid. I eventually had to just get out of there and let myself grieve."

Marci Jo nodded. "Of course. You did the right thing."

"Regular Lipton or raspberry tea?"

"Oh, raspberry, please."

Ronda strolled into the kitchen while her friend flipped through the CD's on a rack near the kitchen door. "You still have these things?"

"Progress is slow up here. I'm renting this place, and those belong to the owner."

Reaching for the tea bags, she continued, "I'd like to get a job soon, but I'm not ready for interviews yet, especially when I'm not sure what to do with myself. If I had to go back to advertising, I'd scream."

"I'll bet. People can be demanding and unreasonable when you're only trying to help."

"Or they can be mean and suck in general." Ronda set the kettle over a flame and crossed her arms. "I've changed my mind about working in New York, probably forever, but I still don't know what I want to be or do."

Marci Jo shrugged. "Hey, so what? Take some time and think about it for a while. Your folks must have left you pretty well off."

"Yeah. I know there were some good-sized assets and my parents' will left everything to me, but their lawyer says I can't touch it for a year."

"What? You're kidding."

"No. Almost everything, including their house in Kennebunkport, has to sit in probate for a year, waiting for someone to contest the will." Ronda leaned against the sink and took in a deep breath, fighting off tears again.

"But you have no family left. I was with you when you

got the news about your older brother dying from his heart condition, and I'll never forget what you told me about your little sister. That's bullshit. That's just lawyers hoping for some illegitimate child to surface so they can earn some more money defending the money." Marci Jo threw her hands up and wandered across the living room to flop into the overstuffed chair.

After setting mugs on the counter, Ronda joined her in the living room. "Well, whatever it is, it seems to be the law."

"Listen, Ronda, I know everyone says, 'Oh, if there's anything I can do...' I mean it, though. Anything. You want to go on a kick-ass vacation and get away from it all? I'll arrange it. Owning a travel agency has its perks."

"I'm not in any position to go away right now. I'm down to my last few thousand in savings and, unfortunately, I'd have to take myself with me." Ronda's lower lip trembled and she sat on the arm of an easy chair.

"I understand, but let me put together a little getaway in a few months. Could you handle, say, Tahiti then?"

"Actually, I'd rather go to Ireland later in the summer, maybe find some distant cousins, but I have to earn some serious cash first."

"Yeah, if you can't get your hands on your own inheritance, I guess you do." Marci Jo scratched her head. "Hey, I know a guy who's been looking for a waitress. They make great tips at his place, and he's a decent guy to work for if it's not beneath you." The teakettle whistled and Marci Jo jumped up. "I'll get it."

Ronda let out a long breath and flopped into the easy chair opposite Marci Jo's spot. The sweet scent of raspberry tea wafted into the living room while Ronda mulled over, out loud, the idea of waiting tables.

"I'd be less isolated. My involvement with people would be casual, and right now, superficiality is a plus. It might even be fun. So where is this establishment?"

Marci Jo returned with two steaming mugs. "Right in Portland, just off the highway—Cousin Tommy's truck stop."

"A truck stop?"

"Yup. I go there once in a while when I want to rub elbows with some real, honest-to-God, earth people. We laugh, tell jokes and enjoy a little break from our boring realities. I walk away well fed and happy."

Perfect, Ronda thought. She inhaled and then tasted the sweet raspberry tea. "Just one thing. I don't feel like going on an interview and hearing, 'I'm sorry, my dear. You're over-qualified.' I hate wasting my time like that."

"Not a problem, my dear," Marci Jo mocked. "I'll call Tommy and fill him in on your situation. He might like to have another college grad around for a while. If I were you, though, I wouldn't let the other staff know about your NYU education and roots in Kennebunkport. They might think you're looking down your aristocratic nose at them."

"Gotcha." Ronda grinned for the first time in quite a while. She could see herself serving up wisecracks with the corned beef hash. Burnt toast and runny eggs were a crisis she could handle.

"So where in Ireland did you want to go?"

Preoccupied, Ronda barely heard Marci Jo. "Huh? Oh, I don't know. Near the western coast, maybe? I'd like to stare back in the opposite direction for a while."

"I'll put something together that I know you'll like." Marci Jo smiled sympathetically. "Let me call Tommy right now and arrange everything. Why don't you go out onto the porch? I know it's cold, but I'm going to talk about you and I'd probably embarrass you to death if you listened. By the way, there's a box on the porch. You might want to open it."

Ronda sighed, grabbed her coat and shrugged back into it. Leaving her tea on the table, she headed for the comfortable padded wicker chair on her porch. When she opened the box, a beautiful, calico cat peeked out.

"Oh, you sweet thing," she crooned and extended her hand, palm up, in a gesture of friendship.

The beautiful feline leaned gracefully toward Ronda's outstretched hand, sniffed and rubbed her face against her fingers.

Ronda had been on the porch, playing with the cat for about five minutes when Marci Jo opened the door a crack. "I'm off the phone now."

Ronda and the purring cat hurried in, shivering.

Marci Jo grinned and patted the soft, furry head. "So, do you like her?"

"I love her. Did you bring her here?"

"Sure did...prettiest kitty at the animal shelter. How could I leave her there? You'll need to name her."

"Name her? Is she for me?" Ronda giggled, delighted with the gift.

"Unless you want me to return her."

"Don't you dare!" She swiveled her torso, positioning the cat far out of Marci Jo's reach.

"Okay. So she needs a name."

"I think I'll call her Talon." Ronda scratched the purring feline under her chin. "She was sharpening her claws on my lap."

"Good name. By the way, your interview is Monday morning at nine. Basically, Tommy said you've got the job unless you come to your senses and decide against it."

"I don't know how to thank you, Marci Jo. You've been so good to me. I should have called, but I didn't want to drag you away from your business to sit around and watch me cry."

"Just be good to Talon, darlin'. I want visitation rights when I come up to see you."

"You know I will," she replied, nuzzling Talon's soft fur.

Not only did she love her new pet but also she realized that her sister's message, received an hour ago, had come true.

On Monday morning Ronda, wearing only her panties and bra, stood in front of her closet. She crossed her arms under her C-cups and wondered what to wear to meet her new boss. She would be late if she didn't make up her mind soon.

Her hair and makeup had been carefully done with the idea of wearing her navy blue dress and matching jacket, but now it seemed much too formal. Certainly the pearls she often wore with the outfit would scream, "I don't belong here."

She realized that she had probably spent too long on her morning routine: lather, rinse, repeat, condition, scented soap, unscented deodorant, blow dry the hair, flat-iron the shine in, apply the cosmetics made for dark-haired women —and now she was out of time.

"What the hell should I wear?" she wailed. Talon seemed to sense her need for comfort and rubbed up against her leg.

Almost eerily, a simple, cream-colored, cotton top fell off its hanger and onto the closet floor in front of her.

"Holy..." She looked around, almost expecting to see the ghost of her late mother but saw nothing.

"Thanks," she whispered and picked up the casual blouse. After the top half of her was dressed, she put on a pair of tan wool pants and high heeled boots. She rarely wore heels, but the slacks were too long and hadn't been hemmed yet. She grabbed a blue cardigan sweater, hand-knit by her late aunt and—Voila—at last, she was ready.

Driving along Route 1, Ronda allowed her mind to wander. Was she selling herself short? Would she earn enough in tips to make it worthwhile?

All doubts melted away when she drove into the truck-stop complex. It boasted eleven gas pumps, a video arcade, convenience store and "home cooking" in the restaurant. The parking lot was full. Tommy must be doing quite well.

Ronda straightened her posture and walked into the restaurant. When she asked the cashier to direct her to the proprietor, the young woman behind the register gave her a blank stare. Ronda stammered and coughed.

"Tommy, I mean. I'm looking for Tommy Kelley."

"Oh," the girl said, chuckling. "He's in the convenience store. The guy who works over there is out sick today."

Ronda called, "Thanks," over her shoulder as she headed in the direction of the maze that led to the convenience store.

As she walked past the counter, a good-looking man, tan, well built, with light ash blond, sun-streaked hair, whirled around on his stool and said, "Ronda? Good Lord, what are you doing here?"

Ronda didn't recognize him for a moment. Without the preppie look, it took a minute to place him, then it hit her and she gasped. She hadn't seen Nate Smith since their days in an upscale private high school.

Taller, tan and well-muscled, the instant attraction would have occurred even without knowing who he was. Her heart leapt and a subtle tingling feeling invaded her body. Once her first love, he was still a hunk, even twenty years later. His sun-streaked blond hair showed a few grays, but only in the temples, and without a receding hairline it only made him more handsome. She also realized that he might accidentally shatter her new humble image if she didn't act fast.

"Nate!" She charged toward him to deliver a huge hug.

Just before she reached him, the high-heeled boots with no tread skidded on the polished linoleum. Ronda gasped, lost her balance and felt herself going down. Nate caught her in his strong clutch. A safer more secure hold she had never felt, and warmth spread through her body and soul.

As soon as she knew she wasn't going to hit the floor, a schoolgirl giggle escaped her lips.

"Nate Smith. You look great, and wow, you still have those wrestling team muscles! What have you been doing, working out?"

———

Nate was thrilled to see her. Ronda had been one of his many girlfriends in their private boarding school days but she was more than that. If he had only realized it at the time, Ronda was one in a million. Unfortunately, like most adolescent males, he had behaved like an immature ass, didn't realize what he had, and broke up with her to sample the other sweets at the smorgasbord.

The mere fact that she ran to him and embraced him so enthusiastically made him think—hope—that perhaps she had forgiven him. Heat rushed to his face in response to her open hearted personality. The familiar tug of attraction pulled at his gut—and lower. He steadied her and stammered, "Uh, yeah. I go to a gym sometimes."

"No kidding."

Ronda was upright now but still holding onto him. His arms were locked around her waist and his body tingled as he remembered their passionate adolescent sexual exploration. They didn't quite make it "all the way" but he knew if he had only been patient...

"And where did you get a tan in March?" she asked.

"Bermuda." Nate straightened his posture and couldn't

resist the urge to flirt. "I just got back yesterday. Nice place. Can I take you there sometime?"

"Me?" Ronda laughed. "So what do you do when you're not vacationing in Bermuda?"

"I'm a private investigator. I work in Boston. Took some lucrative cases, made some decent investments, and now I'm buying a beach house up here."

"You're kidding. Where?"

"Biddeford Pool. That's a good area, isn't it?"

"Oh, yes. It's still very private and pretty." She straightened his lapel and glanced at her watch. "Nate, I hate to leave you. I'd really love to stay and chat some more, but I'm on my way to an interview."

"You're going to be working here?" Nate had to look for leads on his cases in various armpits of the world, but what was his angel doing here?

"If I don't mess up this interview." She flashed a bright smile and winked, taking his breath away.

Mesmerized, he watched her sashay out of view with the lithe grace he remembered so well. *She's even more beautiful now than when we were teenagers.*

One of the male patrons next to him was watching her too. "Man, that's the good stuff. I'd like to get me a piece of that."

Nate jerked his head toward the man. Bristling he said, "That, my friend, is a classy woman, and I'd treat her with more respect if I were you."

He wished he could follow that up with, 'and if I ever catch you looking at *my girl* again...' but it was unnecessary. The customer apparently decided not to mess with Nate and turned his eyes back to his coffee cup.

CHAPTER TWO

Ronda wondered if her interview would have to be postponed. Tommy couldn't interview her from behind the counter with customers swarming around.

"Mornin', miss," he said while bagging a leather-jacketed customer's purchase.

"Good morning. I'm Ronda Calhoun."

"Of course you are." He had a warm, disarming grin. "Pull up a stool."

Ronda glanced around and had to go behind the counter to sit on the only stool she saw. Soon the customer balanced his crinkling paper bag in one arm, dug out his keys and left.

Tommy had apparently decided that they would be able to speak where they were. "How do you know Marci Jo?"

"We lived in the same apartment building in New York, several years ago. We shared a laundry room and some front steps and just kept bumping into each other. When we realized we were both from Maine we became good friends."

"She filled me in on your background. We don't have to go into it here, but she offered you good advice already. I'd have to say the same thing."

"I'm sorry?"

Tommy looked around first. Seeing no one nearby, he continued in a whisper. "If I were you, I'd forget about sharing certain personal information—like the degree from NYU."

"Oh, that. See? I already forgot."

He grinned. "I like that. A sense of humor is helpful here. Truckers pull in from all over the country, and some of our most frequent customers are retired but think of this as their second home. Some of them get lonely and come as much for the good company as they do for Antoine's good cooking. Keep the conversation light and happy. They'll be happy, and if they're happy, I'm happy. They represent the majority of my business."

"Can do. In fact, I'm looking forward to that. I've been a bit isolated lately."

"I can imagine. Marci Jo told me about your family. I'm awfully sorry about your losses." Tommy pulled out a notebook. "Well, let's see if the hours work out. When are you available?"

"Anytime."

"Any shift? Even early mornings? What about weekends?"

"I can work any shift any day."

"Easter Sunday?" He sounded incredulous.

"Especially Easter Sunday. I have no family to spend holidays with. Give me a double shift and tell people it's because I'm the new kid."

Tommy shook his head and smiled. "Wow. You're too good to be true. I pay a little extra for holidays, but I don't pay overtime. You'll need your rest."

"I suppose I should ask about the pay, but I assumed I'd be working mostly for tips."

Tommy laughed in a good-natured way and put away the notebook. "You assumed right. I wish I could pay the wait-staff more than minimum wage. They earn it, believe me. But be nice to the customers and my regulars will take care of you."

At that moment the door opened and a burly man in the usual truckers' uniform, jeans and plaid jacket, stepped in.

"Roy!" Tommy beamed and shook the big man's hand. "What can I get for you?"

"Ooooo. One of these cuties to go, please," Roy said, smiling at Ronda.

Tommy laughed and said to her, "By the way, how do you handle sexual harassment?"

"With a lawyer," she quipped before she realized how that might sound.

"Uh, I'll just go pick up a few things," Roy said. He ambled off, down the store aisles.

Tommy studied her face. "Well, maybe I should ask what behavior you consider to be harassment?"

"Oh, you know, stalking, groping, raping."

Tommy breathed a sigh of relief. "Hell, if that ever happened, I'd hire you a lawyer myself. No, Ronda, I've never had any incidents like that, and I don't want any."

By this time, Roy clutched his packaged apple pies and chocolate milk, and returned to the register to plunk his items down on the counter.

"Not only that, miss, but if anybody tried anything like that with you, about ten of us would be waiting for him in the parking lot. Don't worry. We look out for the waitresses at our favorite greasy spoon."

Tommy smiled and didn't appear to take any offense. After he had rung up Roy's purchases, he locked the cash register drawer and suggested, "Let's go meet your co-workers."

Ronda followed her new boss past the ice-cream freezer case, past a closed door emitting the unmistakable swishing sound of a washing machine, past the flashing lights and bells of the arcade and into the hall leading to the restau-

ASHLYN CHASE

rant. He looked over his shoulder, presumably to be sure she
was still behind him.

"Do you have much of a turnover?" she asked.

"Can't say that we do," Tommy replied. "Most of my wait-
staff have been here a couple of years or more."

Tommy appeared to be an odd mix of country hick and
well-educated businessman. Nevertheless, he seemed
straightforward and honest. Ronda couldn't ask for more
than that. She also noticed his fit, six-foot frame and that he
looked younger than his more-salt-than-pepper-hair would
indicate. She guessed he was probably a well-maintained
fifty-something. He didn't grow this little empire overnight.

Tommy ushered her to the kitchen first, and its mixed
array of tempting aromas wafted out as he opened the door.
"Antoine, I'd like you to meet our new waitress, Ronda
Calhoun."

Antoine looked up and grinned at her. He seemed
friendly enough, though his dark eyes and five-o'clock
shadow gave him an ominous air. He waved, rather than
offering her a handshake. It was just as well since he was
wearing plastic gloves covered with ground meat.

"Welcome, Ronda. A lovely addition, Tommy. I approve."

Ronda smiled. "Pleased to meet you, Antoine."

"No need to be so formal, honey. By your third shift
you'll be calling me new, more interesting names under
your breath."

Tommy laughed. "Antoine here runs a tight ship. Don't
take it personally if he gets sarcastic from time to time. He's
like that with everyone."

There was a time clock to punch, and it was on the wall
next to the door. On their way out, Tommy showed it to her
but simply as an oddity.

"We haven't used that thing in years. I trust my staff to be
on time. They catch hell from the staff taking up their slack
if they're late. Don't say I didn't warn you."

24

"Plus they catch hell from *me,*" yelled Antoine as they left the kitchen.

Tommy grinned and whispered, "Antoine is very serious about his place on the seniority totem pole. He's been here twenty-five years, and we've been friends ever since discovering we both served in Vietnam. He takes a personal interest in anything that might affect the business."

"I understand," she said.

They finally walked out to the restaurant and stopped first at the counter. They didn't sit. It was busy and Tommy must have wanted these meetings to be brief. Nate, still perched on his stool, chatted with the truck driver next to him looking like a sleek thoroughbred next to a workhorse.

"Jenna, this is Ronda," Tommy said to the waitress behind the counter. "You two will be working the same shifts most of the time."

"Jenna..." Ronda offered her right hand.

Jenna took it looking a bit confused, and they shared an awkward handshake. "Is this Marie's replacement?"

"Yup," was all Tommy said.

"Ohhh..."

It looked as if Jenna wasn't the brightest tube in the neon sign, but she had a sweet face and the most burgundy hair never seen in nature.

"And over here..." Tommy said, escorting her to the cash register. Another waitress was cashing out one of the portly customers.

"Mornin', Dominick."

"Mornin', Tommy." The two men shook hands firmly.

"New talent?" Dominick asked.

"Yup."

"Oh, thank God," said the waitress behind the register. Her brown hair looked as if it had been brushed in a wind tunnel.

"Seems you're popular already, Ronda. This excited young lady is Nanette."

"You'd be excited too, if you were working both sides of the restaurant and the register without breaks for the last week and a half. I barely have the energy to play with my son when I get home."

"Hasn't Jenna been helping out in the dining room?"

"Miss Oblivious?"

"Okay, okay. That's enough of that. I think Ronda is what you may have been praying for."

Nanette grinned, looked up at the ceiling and said, "Not to be critical, but it's about goddamn time."

Ronda smirked. She could relate. With the introductions complete, Tommy began to lead her back toward his office. When Nate stood up to leave, he almost bumped into her.

"Oh! Pardon me," they both said at once.

Ronda let out a nervous laugh that she wasn't accustomed to hearing from her own mouth. Not only was Nate still handsome, but he was a few inches taller than she remembered. She seemed glued to the floor for a moment as she gazed up into his bright, shining, blue eyes. *God, he looks good.* She thought she noticed the tingle of mutual attraction between them.

She whirled around, realizing that she should introduce him to her new boss, who was waiting patiently. "Oh, I'm sorry, Tommy. This is an old high school friend of mine, Nate Smith."

"Nate." Tommy smiled and extended his hand for a firm handshake.

Ronda noticed that he greeted Nate exactly as he had greeted Roy and Dominick. No wonder business was booming. Everyone was made to feel like family at "Cousin Tommy's".

Looking to end the conversation before Nate said something incriminating about prep school around the regulars,

Ronda said, "Nate, will you excuse me? I have to finish up my interview."

He called after her, "Hey, I hope to see you again. I come in every time I'm in the area. I might even make a special trip."

Tommy placed his hand on the small of her back as he guided her to the adjacent hall and over to an unobtrusive-looking door that she hadn't noticed on the way to the kitchen.

"At the end of this hall are the restrooms, and this," he said, opening the door, "is my office where you can find me if I seem to have disappeared completely." The open door revealed a compact office with desk, old-fashioned adding machine, filing cabinets, and dust.

"No computer?" Ronda noticed the low-tech surroundings immediately.

"You sound like my son. He's been trying to hook me up with one of those damn things for years."

"They can be a great help in the business world," Ronda offered.

Tommy smiled. "Yeah, I know. I'm a bit of a dinosaur, but my system works so why fix it?"

"I suppose. But it seems that with the large business—actually, multiple businesses you have here—it would save you a few headaches."

"Truth be told, my son is in graduate school for business. I'll have him on board as soon as he finishes. He'll pry me out of the dark ages."

"Oh, good. I'm sorry, I didn't mean…"

Tommy laughed and walked around the desk to sit in his swivel chair, motioning to one of the mismatched wooden chairs on the opposite side for Ronda.

"Don't worry, kid. You can say what you think around here. In fact, I'm going to say something to you that you might not want to hear."

"Oh?"

"You're too polite. You want to fit in, don't you?"

"Yes, of course."

"You're obviously a well-bred, well-mannered, young lady. It does my heart good to see such a thing still exists, but knock it off. We're very casual around here."

Ronda was surprised, but she understood. "Okay, then. I'll pretend I'm back in New Yawk."

He leaned back in his chair and laughed. "No. I don't think that's a good idea either." Then he deftly changed the subject. "You'll meet my son soon. He's usually away at school—UCLA."

"California? That's so far away."

"I know, believe me. I wish he were closer. It's just the two of us now, but he graduates in May. I'll be going out for his graduation even if I have to close the place for a couple of days."

Her eyes widened. "Can you do that?"

"No. I sure can't." Tommy chuckled, shaking his head. "I'd have a regulars' revolt to deal with. I've left Antoine in charge before. As long as no one challenges his authority, all goes well." Leaning back, he folded his arms and rocked gently.

"Is that apt to happen? Someone challenging his authority?"

"Ha! That's guaranteed to happen, but I'm going to my son's graduation. If the place burns down while I'm gone, that's what insurance is for. Hell, it might even pay off his school loans."

Ronda smiled. She liked this guy's attitude. He seemed laid-back, even with the many responsibilities he carried.

"So, do you have an ID and social security number handy?"

"Of course." She dug her wallet out of her purse.

"Thank goodness. In that case I can hire you. So, are you sure you want the job?"

"When do I start?"

"I'd suggest you wear some comfy sneakers and come in tomorrow morning at six. You said you don't mind working weekends?"

"Don't mind a bit."

"What are you, about an eight?"

"Excuse me?"

"Your dress size—for your uniform."

"Oh, sorry. No, I'm a ten—you know...dress size. I didn't mean it to sound vain—calling myself a ten." *Yeah, I was an eight before my breasts and hips developed.*

Tommy laughed and found the size ten uniforms in a box behind him and gathered several of them in one hand. Then he reached for a box marked, "aprons."

"None of my business, but doesn't a pretty girl like you date on weekends?"

"Not at the moment. I fired someone a while ago and I'm not interviewing for replacements yet." *Unless my damn immortal shows up.*

"Ah, well, his loss is our gain." Tommy handed her four shocking pink dresses and four white aprons. "Come in tomorrow morning at six sharp. I'll have you on the schedule by then. You'll work some weekends, but you'll get some off for good behavior." He winked. "I'm glad you're coming on board."

Ronda shook his hand, accepted the fuchsia uniforms with a smile, even though she looked hideous in that color, and found her way out via the back door. Walking past the gas pumps, most of which were in use, she inhaled the smell of diesel gasoline fumes and exhaust. *Ugh.*

Around the back was ample parking and there she found her black Volvo. It was beginning to rust from the harsh New York winters even before she'd bought it.

Looking at it from an objective point of view, the once luxury sedan seemed like a much older, more utilitarian car.

As she slipped behind the wheel and turned the key, she recalled what she had told Tommy about the recent boyfriend. Regretfully, it seemed to be the most expedient justification. She hated lying, but the truth wouldn't be worth explaining. How do you tell someone that you can't find an equal to like you and that the other men around aren't very interesting?

A few years ago she had been planning her wedding to Michael and the breakup had devastated her. Despite wanting to move on, she ruined any attempts by comparing the exciting future they'd planned to the idea of dating the local fishermen and shopkeepers. So, she moved to New York, expecting that would take care of the situation.

She shook her head as if to erase the foolish thought and reminded herself that today was a good day. The sun was shining, the snow was melting and she'd found a job with no difficulty.

Compelled to fulfill her mission to come up with some comfortable shoes, she drove in the direction of the mall.

———

By the time she had found a cushy pair of white sneakers at half price and returned home, the mail had been delivered. When she walked through her front door, she stepped on a couple of envelopes. *Oh well, just bills and junk mail.*

Her letter carrier was kind enough to walk all the way up to her door and throw her letters into the mail slot with such force that mail actually littered her hardwood floor every day. Ronda spotted a hand-scribbled note that lay on top of the mess. It appeared to be unsigned.

"Look at this, Talon. It says, 'I was looking for Ronda

Calhoun. Call me when you receive this.' There's a phone number, but no name."

Odd. Was it from someone trying to sell her vinyl siding or a new roof? But who would know her name?

Curiosity got the better of her. She gathered up the rest of her mail, placed it on the table, and grabbed her phone.

The number rang four times before a female voice answered.

"Hello. This is Ronda Calhoun. To whom am I speaking, please?"

"Oh, Miss Calhoun, I'm glad you called. My name is Lorena. You don't know me, but we have a mutual friend."

"Oh, really?" Suspicious, she thought maybe it was a product-party saleswoman working by referral. But who'd refer her?

"Yes. Um, I have to talk to you about Michael."

Ronda's jaw dropped. She couldn't be talking about *her* Michael, could she? Unable to think or speak for several seconds, it must have sounded as if the phone had gone dead on the other end.

"Hello? Ronda? Are you there?"

She cleared her throat and croaked, "I'm here."

"I'm really sorry to bother you, and I don't know how to say this gently, so I'll just say it. Michael Lawson has disappeared. I thought he might have come to see you, or, I hoped you might know where he is."

Why the hell does she need to know about the former love of my life? "Who are you, and why are you looking for Michael?"

"I'm sorry. I know this might come as a shock, but I have to find him, and I can't overlook any possible lead. I'm his fiancée."

Ronda's whole body became numb. She heard a slight buzzing in her ears. The phone fell out of her hand, and she had to slide down the wall to sit without tumbling to the floor. That Michael was missing was no shock at all. The mere fact that he had done the same thing to someone else was astounding.

"And you want him back?" was all Ronda could say when she finally lifted the phone to her ear again.

"Well, yes. I need to know why," Lorena said softly.

"I can tell you why, Lorena. It has nothing to do with you or anything you did. The only thing you did wrong was to fall for a handsome, exciting man who cannot commit. Period. That's it."

She was just about to hang up when she heard the girl crying on the other end.

"Damn. I'm sorry. I can be an insensitive clod sometimes."

"No. You're absolutely right. I just can't believe I didn't see it sooner."

"Oh my God. He didn't leave you at the altar, did he?"

"No. Nothing like that. He just began acting strange. I didn't know what was going on, and then he said he had to see you."

"Me? Did he say why?" Ronda propped her hand against the wall and stood.

"Not really. I thought it must be something like closure. I know you two were close. That was two weeks ago. No one has seen or heard from him since."

Close. She winced. *Yeah. You could say that.* "Did you try him at work?"

"I called the office. They said he'd planned to be away for a few days, but they hadn't heard from him and were getting concerned too."

"Where are you right now?" Ronda pinched the bridge of her nose not sure what, if anything, she wanted to do about this.

"I'm at home, on Drake's Island," Lorena said, audibly sniffing and then she blew her nose.

"I really don't know if I can help or not, Lorena, but if I do hear anything, I'll call you. I promise."

"Thank you. I..." The shattered woman choked up and couldn't finish her thought.

"I know," Ronda said softly. "I know."

"Bye," she managed to say and hung up.

Ronda placed the phone on its charging pad and shouted, "Why do you do this? Bastard!" Talon jumped away from nibbling her tuna and scampered out of the room.

"Oh, sorry, sweetie." *And now I'm talking to a cat.*

That night as Ronda was dreaming she had an alarming experience. A familiar voice called, "Ronda? Honey?"

"Mom?" Ronda dreamed that she looked over toward the voice and saw her mother in her prime and radiant.

"Ronda, this is important. There is a master teacher coming into your life. Look for him. Follow his example, his leadership."

"A master teacher? What the heck is that?"

"Honey, there is much you have to learn. He can show you what you need to know. Wait and watch for him."

"Just wait and watch? How do I recognize him?" Her mother quietly disappeared, and there was nothing further.

"Mom?" No answer.

Ronda awoke with a start and then quietly closed her eyes again, hoping for a bit more sleep and perhaps a reconnection to the dream. A few minutes later she realized that even if she stayed there for another six hours, there would be no more information. The dream, or her mother's energy, had vanished.

Walking downstairs, she thought about how all of these months she had wanted some sort of direct communication with her mother's spirit. Now that she had something, it was confusing.

First of all, what's a master teacher and how am I going to meet one? Talon rubbed up against Ronda's legs and said her morning, "Meow."

"If this master teacher wants me, he can just find me wherever I happen to be," she said out loud to her cat. The only answer was another "meow" and the cry of a seagull outside her window.

Somehow she knew her mother had tried to communicate an important message and this teacher would be coming to her—sometime, somewhere...hopefully soon.

If the concept of putting one's fate into the hands of the unknown was normally frightening, then Ronda decided it was normal to be terrified.

CHAPTER THREE

This was Ronda's first day as a waitress. The other girls had no way of knowing about her inexperience and she hoped they'd assume she was a veteran. How hard could it be?

Taking the order pad she was given, she glanced at it briefly. It didn't seem too daunting, so she shoved it into her apron pocket and proceeded to wait on her first table.

"What can I get you?" she asked, sounding bright and a little too perky for her own taste.

"How's the corned beef?" asked the stiff woman in a business suit.

"I'm not sure what you mean."

The woman rolled her eyes. "You know, not too much fat or salt?"

"Oh. I'm sure it's delicious, but I'll ask Antoine."

She peeked into the kitchen and received her first set of rude instructions. "If anyone asks how 'the anything' is, say it's delicious—the best you've ever had."

She felt foolish after this but figured it had to happen so she would know how to behave in this particular job. In some jobs, it was better to side step the subjective question. In other jobs, it was best to tell people whatever they wanted to hear. She concluded that in this job you told people what *Antoine* wanted them to hear.

"The chef said it's the best ever."

The woman ordered turkey.

Ronda was getting the hang of it by the time the lunch crowd arrived. Her station had grown to half of the tables in the restaurant. Her smile and positive attitude made up for a host of mistakes. Even Antoine treated her more kindly.

Her afternoon was punctuated by another meeting with her old friend Nate. There she was, big as life, waiting on tables in her little corner of the world when Nate walked in and looked at her curiously.

She saw an empty table in Nanette's area and waved him over, smiling. "Here's an open table. Nanette usually takes this station, but I'm sure she'd let me have it if I asked her nicely."

Nanette called over to her. "Oh, I'll let you have it, all right."

"Was that a yes or a no?"

"N-O, no."

Nanette must need every tip she can get. Ronda realized that it might be better to have less contact with Nate anyway since she still hadn't asked him to keep her personal details to himself. She escorted him to the table and placed a menu in front of him, saying, "Nanette will be with you shortly, hon. Good to see you."

His eyes sparkled. She was surprised by the surge of desire that hit her as she glanced at the contrast of his bright blues eyes to his glowing golden tan. Something else took her by surprise. Mmm, Nate's aftershave. What was that, Drakkar Noir? Didn't he used to wear it in high school just because she loved it? As she walked away she remembered how she used to nuzzle his neck to get a better whiff of it. She couldn't help noticing the rise in her body temperature.

Later, during a lull, Nate caught Ronda's hand as she walked by and asked if he could meet her on her day off.

She wanted to say "No" but couldn't force the word to come out of her mouth. He had hurt her so badly twenty years before, and she needed that again like a hole in the head.

"Sure. Let me check my schedule."

She stepped into the kitchen and leaned against the wall near the time clock, letting out an enormous breath.

Antoine turned to look, shook his head and resumed stirring his gravy. "Does that sigh mean you can't take the pace, or did someone just give you a hard time?"

"Neither. An old friend from high school just came in, and I think he asked me out. I wanted to say 'No' but instead, the word 'Sure' popped out of my mouth." She shook her head. *It was almost involuntary like someone took over my brain for a moment.*

Antoine laughed and seemed to enjoy her discomfort. He finished stirring his gravy and wiped his hands on a dishcloth.

"Who knows," Ronda continued. "It might be fun. Maybe there was a reason 'sure' jumped out of my mouth today." Thinking about that for a minute, she remembered her dream and her mother's prediction. Ronda's idea of a master teacher was a Gandhi or a Buddha. Somehow, a Nate didn't seem like a master-teacher type, but what about her other prediction? Could he be one of the two men she was expecting?

Antoine smiled and shook his head. Ronda heaved another sigh, looked at the schedule on the wall next to the clock and said, "Thursday and Friday off this week. I guess I'll have to offer him Friday since I'll be busy losing five pounds on Thursday."

Antoine laughed again. "Hey, if you aren't good enough

for him just the way you are, then he don't deserve you. Besides, you look good. Don't lose an ounce."

Now it was Ronda's turn to smile. "Thanks, Antoine. I like you, I think."

With that, she breezed into the dining room and walked over to Nate.

"How's Thursday or Friday?"

"Friday would be better. I need to go back to Boston for a couple of days." He pulled a small notepad out of his jacket pocket.

"What time on Friday?" she asked.

"I can be up here around six or six-thirty. Can I get your number to confirm?"

"Um, sure." The hated word had popped out of her mouth twice in one day.

She heard an already familiar laugh coming from the kitchen.

The next day her feet hurt, but she put on her apron and a smile, beginning her second day as a waitress. Ronda was busy enough to forget about everything for a short while. Thinking about disembodied voices, old flames, foot rubs and whether or not Friday night was a date or just dinner with a friend had been mentally exhausting.

While she was wiping down tables, a strikingly handsome young man with straight, golden-brown hair walked in from the back. He sailed behind the counter, set down his newspaper, and poured himself a cup of coffee. Then he returned from wherever he had come. Ronda must have been mesmerized because she didn't hear Nanette come up behind her until she whispered in her ear.

"That's Ty, Tommy's son. Try not to drool."

Ronda whirled around. "That's Tommy's son? I thought he was at UCLA."

"He must be home on spring break," Nanette whispered. "Just in case you need to be told, Ronnie, he's way out of our league."

"No. I don't need to be told. I understand he's going to be our boss someday."

"Well, maybe. I think Tommy might be in for a rude shock, though."

"Why? What do you mean?"

"Oh, come on," Nanette said. "Can you imagine coming back to Maine after living in LA?"

"Well, what about his loyalty to his dad? Didn't his father pay for his education with the idea that his son would be back to help him run the business?"

"Yeah, I guess. A kid would have to be loyal to leave southern California on spring break and come to friggin' arctic Maine."

As the waitresses were nodding in agreement, a couple of truck drivers at the counter turned around on their stools.

"Do you think it would be too much trouble to get another cup of coffee—when you're done deciding the fate of the world?"

Nanette stormed off toward the back room. "Where the hell is Jenna?"

Ronda sprinted around the counter and grabbed the coffee pot.

"Sorry about that, guys. Can I get you anything else?"

"No, hon. Me an' Mark just wanted to bust your chops. You're new here, aren't you?"

"Yeah. I'm Ronda." She started to extend her hand for a handshake but caught herself and grabbed their empty plates instead. "Sure you don't want any more of Antoine's eggs?"

"No. We're good," the younger, wiry man said.

"Well, we're full anyway," the hefty one said, and then he laughed, his beer belly jiggling.

"Full of what, I don't need to know," Ronda added, and he laughed even harder.

"I'm Ed. I've been coming here for thirteen years, and I've never seen a waitress as pretty as you. And this here is Mark. Neither has he."

"It's a good thing Nanette and Jenna are out of the room at the moment."

"Why?" asked Mark. "He'd say the same thing to them if they were here."

Everyone was having a good laugh when Tommy and Ty walked in. Tommy clasped Ed's shoulder with one hand and Mark's with the other.

"That's the sound we like to hear," he said.

"Yeah, that and the cash register," replied Ed, and the regulars were laughing again.

When the mirth died down, Tommy looked around and his brow furrowed.

"Ronda, I was going to borrow you, but you seem to be all alone. Where are Jenna and Nanette?"

"Uh," was all she had a chance to say when Nanette called out from somewhere behind them.

"We'll be right back, Tommy."

He looked in the direction of the voice and returned to the matter at hand. "I need to make introductions. Ty, this is our new waitress, Ronda. Ronda, my son, Ty. Excuse me a minute. I'm going to see where Jenna and Nanette are," and with that he left.

Ronda didn't know whether to shake Ty's hand or not, so she just nodded. He nodded too, and as he turned to go Ronda reached out and caught his arm.

"Ah, wait. Did I see you with a newspaper before? Was that the Portland Herald?"

He frowned at her hand on his arm until she let go. "Yes. Do you want to look at it?"

"On my break, later—if you don't mind."

"Sure. I'll leave it in the office for you." Ty turned and walked out without so much as a smile.

Ronda's first impression of him was not good. He seemed like a stuck-up snob. However, her intuition told her it was something else, like he was just trying to be professional or maybe he was shy. Or both.

Almost as if he had read her mind, Ed said, "Don't you mind him. It's just the LA attitude. They're either ditzy or stuck up."

Mark added, "Yeah. I hate taking long-distance runs out to LA. Mostly because of the dammed freeway traffic but also because the kid at Starbucks acts like it's a big bother to pour me a cup of coffee. Of course, they all think they're just about to become the next Tom Cruise."

Ronda shrugged. "Well, I'm glad I turned down that big movie career, then. I hate snobbery."

Nanette and Jenna returned to the restaurant, and it looked as if Jenna had been crying. Her nose and eyes were red. Ronda wanted to ask if she was okay, but Nanette shook her head warning her not to.

Ronda's break came at last. She headed out back to the little office hoping Ty had remembered to leave the paper. He had. She sat down and looked at the obits. Michael wasn't there. He was just off being a heartless neurotic.

"Find what you were looking for?"

She caught her breath. For a moment she thought she recognized the tall, attractive man leaning against the door-jamb, but she couldn't place him. His dark lashes framed his light hazel eyes. She dismissed that thought as soon as she realized it was Ty and that the resemblance to someone famous must have triggered her reaction.

"You remind me of someone." Ronda folded the newspaper and handed it back to him.

He rolled his eyes. "Yeah, my friends think I should get a job as Josh Hartnett's stunt double."

She chuckled. "Like in the movies? You're okay with crashing a plane into China?"

Ty finally smiled. "Yeah, no. I don't think that's for me. I'm glad you came back here for your break. I wanted to ask you something."

"Me? Really?"

Ty closed the door and said, "Don't act so innocent."

"I'm not acting."

"Look, I know about your history. You don't have to play dumb around me."

"Oh. Your father told you?"

"Yes." He moved around the desk to his father's chair, sat and leaned back, looking as comfortable there as Tommy did.

Ronda stayed in the opposite chair while Ty continued.

"I need to ask you to help me with something slightly conspiratorial. My father will never go for the computer system I really want and need in here. I've picked it out. I just need to ship it back here to someone who can hide it until he's safely out of the way. Then that person would have to set it up where I want it and hire an electrician. I need another hook up on this wall." He pointed to a corner behind him where filing cabinets now stood. "Once that's done and his adding machine is in the trash, he won't dismantle it." Ty reached into his back pocket and withdrew his wallet.

"Hmmm..." Why did this sound like a bad idea? "I understand why you want this, Ty, but you have nothing to lose. Your dad won't fire you. I, on the other hand, could be fired if he's upset and knows I had something to do with it."

"Don't worry. I won't let anything happen to you."

"I'll think about it." She stood and prepared to leave.

"Don't think too long, Ronda. I go back Sunday night." Ty wrote something on a piece of scrap paper. "Here's my phone number. If my dad answers, disguise your voice and ask for Hugh. When he says it was someone asking for Hugh, I'll call you back. What's your number?"

Ronda wrote her number on a slip from her order pad wishing he wanted it for another reason. However, something didn't feel right about this. It might be for his own good, but Tommy had a right to know what was about to happen to his business. She had bought some time to think it over, anyway.

At last Friday arrived, and she was looking forward to her "meeting" with Nate. Something in her gut told her she might need to have Lorena's note with her tonight so she tucked it in her purse. Long ago Ronda had learned to go with her intuitive messages, or she'd wind up kicking herself later.

Ronda was glad Nate hadn't probed her about her request to meet at the restaurant. He called on Thursday to confirm, and agreed to meet her at a pub in the Old Port Historic District. The restaurant wasn't too expensive but trendy and hip, the perfect place for a—whatever.

Ronda had another dressing-room dilemma. She settled on a shortish black pencil skirt and a deep cranberry sweater that clung to her smooth t-shirt bra.

Nate showed up in black Dockers, a burgundy shirt and a manly brown leather jacket. They couldn't have coordinated better if they had consulted one another. Nate met her at the entrance and hugged her—holding her a little longer than expected. His warmth made her glad she had accepted the invitation.

Their table for two was situated near the fireplace and the atmosphere soon turned intimate. Asking Ronda first if she liked white wine, Nate ordered a bottle of Chardonnay, just happening upon her favorite white wine.

Their meeting, which could now be officially called a date, was going well when Nate confessed, "I'm worried about you, Ronnie."

"Worried about me? Why?"

"Well, because I know about what happened to your family, and suddenly you're working as a waitress in a truck stop."

"Cut it out, Nate. I'm fine. Lots of people take some time off to rethink their direction and priorities when a life-changing event happens."

"I know you're an independent woman, and I applaud that, but I still think you could use a little looking after."

Ronda rolled her eyes. "Oh, Nate, don't."

"Don't what? Care?"

"No. That's not it." Ronda looked into his deep blue eyes and wondered how he had known. "Thank you for your concern, really, but I'm not at the truck stop because I ran out of options. I'm there by choice."

"Oh. You really mean that?" He raised his eyebrows.

"Yes, I really mean it. Look, it's temporary. I don't know what I want to do with the rest of my life yet. It was an easy job to land and wouldn't demand much of me emotionally. The physical demand might be another story, but exercise is good for getting rid of stress. If it makes you feel any better, I'm saving for a trip to Ireland in a few months."

"Actually, that does sound a little better. But, what will happen if you never know what to do with your life?" He ran his finger down the condensation on his wine glass.

"I hadn't even thought about that," Ronda said. She just naturally assumed the right thing would present itself and she would know it when it did.

Suddenly Nate reached for her hand across the table. Just as suddenly she pulled back.

"How did you know about my family?"

"Are you forgetting what I do for a living?"

"You investigated me?" Ronda put her hand on her purse, prepared to walk out depending upon what he said next.

"The information is there for the merely curious, Ronda. I didn't need to do any kind of lengthy investigation. I simply wondered how you, who could have been anything you wanted to be, came to be working in a truck stop. The headlines popped up when I searched the local newspaper's database. The obituary said they were the parents of Ronda Calhoun, and also of the late Brady Calhoun and the late Sarah Calhoun. I'm so sorry, Ronnie."

This time he slowly reached for her hand, and she let him take it.

Tears were starting to heat her eyes. She looked away and held them back. "Thank you," she eventually said. They both grew quiet and she held onto his warm, comforting hand until the waiter interrupted with their dinner.

Ronda tried to eat some of her buffalo chicken and resume small talk.

"How's your family, Nate?"

"My dad's business took them to India. They're fine. We keep in touch by e-mail and texts, mostly."

"Wow. What a coincidence. I have two friends in India, working at an orphanage in a remote area. It's hard to get ahold of them." Before she let sadness overtake her, she changed the subject. "And how are *you?* I remember you had some kind of condition that required monthly tests."

"Oh, that. Yeah, I'm good now."

She had always been curious about his 'condition' as he called it and waited to see if he'd elaborate, but he remained quiet. *Oh well...I guess it doesn't matter now.* "So, why didn't you go into business after graduating from BU?"

"I found myself bored to tears."

"So you looked into the exciting world of private detection?"

"Something like that. Actually, there was this match-book..." he teased. He had the sweetest of smiles. As Ronda admired his bright white teeth, she noted that she was enjoying her date—very much.

The evening progressed to a walk after dinner, and whether because they had known each other years ago, or because he made her feel secure, Ronda comfortably settled into the crook of his arm and basked in the warmth of his manly body.

She glanced up at him. Confident, tall and handsome. He seemed to have matured both inside and out. If this new Nate stuck around, she'd give him no cause to find another "easy Denise," the girl in high school that lured him away with sexual innuendos. It's not that she didn't remember the hurt, but she had transcended it. It had been a learning experience. Understanding a man's needs better now, she wouldn't let that happen again...maybe. Probably. *I'll see how it goes.*

As they were strolling, Ronda worked up her courage to talk with him about the call from Lorena.

"I want to run something by you, Nate."

"Sure. What is it?"

"I got a call from my ex-fiancé's fiancée the other night," she began.

"You've got my attention," he said.

"He's missing."

"Missing as in missing persons?"

"I don't know. It could be nothing. He gets cold feet."

"Does he do this often?"

"He did it to me."

"Well, then, he's an idiot," Nate said. "Tell me more."

"She told me he was coming to see me."

"Has he?"

"No. I had no idea he was even thinking about me until she said he was."

"So he may have changed his mind, or lied to her, or met with foul play before he had a chance to show up at your door."

Alarmed, she tried not to show it. Of course, that he *could* have met with foul play had been in the back of her mind, but she had hoped it was a ridiculous idea. "What do you think?" she asked.

"I don't have an opinion yet. Can I ask you a few questions about his character and your relationship?"

"Oh, I'd rather not get into that. Not tonight, anyway."

"Sure," Nate said. He squeezed her in a side hug as they walked around a puddle from the melting snow. "Is it possible his fiancée could be inventing this story?"

"She has a real future in acting if she was. Why would she lie about that? Just to take a peek at the ex?"

Nate shrugged. "That and stranger things have been known to happen." *Careful, Nate. Don't scare her to death.*

"Do you think she could be up to something?"

"Don't know yet. Do you have any pictures of them?"

"Not her, but I kept one of him. I have it with me." She stopped walking, rummaged through her pocketbook and handed him the photo of Michael leaning against the rocks with wind-tousled, dark hair and deep-set eyes.

"You still carry it?"

Handing it to him, she gave him a sidelong glance. "No. I just dug it out of a box of mementos. Do you have any ex-significant others?"

He was quiet for a moment. How could he tell her that he still hadn't found anyone who measured up to her? "Not really. Can I keep the photo?"

"No. You can borrow it."

He raised an eyebrow. Looking at the picture, he said, "I'm glad you told me about this. Have you met the woman in person? How did you leave it?"

"It was just a phone call, and I said I'd call her if I learned anything helpful."

"That's fine. Now back away." Nate looked in her eyes with conviction.

"All right."

"Why don't you let me poke around a bit? I'd like to know that you're safe at least."

"Here." Ronda found the scrap of paper with Lorena's number on it. "Take her phone number so I won't be tempted to use it."

"Thanks. That may help me find something useful." He frowned at the paper. "What's her name?"

"Lorena. That's all I have, I'm afraid. No last name."

"That will have to be enough." Nate tucked the number and photo in his leather jacket's inner pocket.

He escorted her to her car and took both of her hands in his. Gazing into her eyes for a long moment, he wondered what kind of a goodbye she might expect. He hoped he was guessing correctly as he folded her into a close, warm hug. The self-restraint seemed a necessary evil at this stage with a woman who had been hurt so badly. Even so, he wanted to sweep her into a passionate embrace and kiss her with all the desire that rushed through him. Just holding her was causing his cock to stir. *Keep it in check, buddy. She's worth the wait.*

As he was stroking her back, Ronda sighed and said out loud, "Why do I meet the nicest men at the worst possible times?"

He smiled. *The nicest men.* Did he deserve that? Damn it, he would. He'd do whatever he had to do to prove to her that he cared—more than before—that he couldn't get her off of his mind and probably never would. "Don't worry about the timing, Ronnie. I'll be around for a while." *Except when the moon is full.*

CHAPTER FOUR

The next morning Ronda lugged herself into work and for the first time since she had started, she thought that maybe she was wasting her time there. She could be somewhere else, doing something more meaningful with her potential.

She was glad Antoine had weekends off. She didn't want to tell him all about last night even though remembering it made her sigh. He'd probably laugh at her. She had just grabbed her order pad and walked out to the counter area when the weekend cook, the regulars, and the other waitresses yelled, "How was your date last night, Ronda?"

She caught her breath, and then joined in the laughter. Even tourists whom she had never seen before were laughing.

Ronda whacked the counter with her order pad. "How did you know I had a date last night?"

Manny, the cook grinned. "Antoine gave us strict instructions. He wants all the dirt."

"Oh he does, does he?"

"Relax, Ronda," Nanette said. "We won't do it for the second date, or third or anything else."

"Well that's a relief. Otherwise there might not be a second or third."

Nanette lowered her voice and whispered, "Was it that hot-looking guy with the nice bod and tan? Are you seeing him again?"

"Did he spring for dinner, or did he make you pay half?" Roy asked.

"Never mind that," Ed interjected. "What base did he get to? Or was it a grand slam?"

Ronda's cheeks flushed. "Man, don't you people have any other form of entertainment?"

"No," Roy said, and then, "Look, she's blushing!"

Oh, no. Ronda had to do something. She retreated into the kitchen and leaned up against the useless time clock. Manny sauntered over, smiling.

"They're just having a little fun," he said.

"I know. I'd like to play along, but I'm just not in the mood this morning."

"Oh..." He nodded, like he knew something and went back to chopping celery. "Bad time, huh?"

"No. It wasn't bad at all. I don't know why I'm not dealing with this better than I am, but, honest to God, Manny, I'd almost rather start a fire to divert their attention from me right now. That's how little patience I have."

He snapped to attention and stared at her wide-eyed. "Jesus, woman, don't do that. I thought the red-head was the crazy emotional one."

"Well, what should I do to squash it then?"

"Here, I'll help," he said. He wiped his hands on a dish-towel and walked over to the serving window.

"Thank you." Ronda was just standing up straight, smoothing her uniform, and getting ready to go back out again when she heard Manny loudly announce, "Take it easy on Ronda, guys. She's having her period."

Ronda shot a look at Manny that said, "You bastard, how

could you?" Her complexion turned three shades pinker than before and she stumbled out of the kitchen. She saw the little office door open a crack and thought if she sat in there until the last customer left, it would serve them right. She closeted herself inside the little nine by nine room and locked the door, leaning against it as if she had to hold it closed against the wave of humiliation that threatened to engulf her.

The shape of a man hunched over behind the desk slowly emerged, and she gasped.

Ty stood up and smiled when he saw her. "Oh, I'm glad it's you. I was just configuring the layout and the connections I'm going to need in here."

"Huh? Oh yeah, that. Ty, I'm not having a very good morning, but I need to talk to you about your plan when I can."

Ty sat in the chair behind the desk looking very relaxed. "What's got you stressed out?"

Ronda closed her eyes and pinched the bridge of her nose.

"What's getting to you this morning, Ronda?" he asked again. "You don't seem like someone who's easily upset."

"No, I'm usually not." She sighed. "I'm glad you know about my history because I think that's part of it. This morning was the first time I was thinking that maybe I was wasting my potential here—that I'd made a mistake even taking this job."

One side of his lip curled up. "This morning was the first time you thought that?"

"Yeah. I'm fine if I can just do my job and go home at the end of the day. I'm not used to people at work intentionally getting under my skin. So, I'm already in this mood, thinking 'I don't belong here,' and then the staff and regulars razz me about my date last night.

Okay, I can stand that for a couple of seconds but all the

sordid details seemed to be in the six o'clock entertainment slot. I just stepped into the kitchen to interrupt the flow of conversation and made things worse instead."

Ty smiled and looked at the ceiling. "Did Manny tell everyone you had your period?"

Ronda almost choked. "How did you know?"

"He's famous for that. Things will change when I'm here full-time. Meanwhile, if you want to give him hell, I'd like to watch and do absolutely nothing to stop you."

It was Ronda's turn to smile. A moment later, there was a knock at the door, and she stepped back as the door opened.

Nanette popped her head in but didn't see her hidden behind the door. "I think we lost Ronda," she said, panic in her voice.

"I really don't want to lose a good waitress, Nanette."

"Neither do I. Do you know where she might be? Manny embarrassed her pretty bad, but I can't see her quitting because of that twit."

Ronda stepped around the door. "She didn't."

"Oh, thank God." Nanette grabbed and hugged her.

"I'll be right there, Nanette." She smiled at Ty as he stood up.

"Give 'em hell," he said.

All three of them walked out of the office and into the loaded restaurant. Ronda walked briskly around the counter and up to the serving window.

"I'd like to talk to you!" Ronda shouted to Manny over the background conversations. "I am not having my period. Moreover, I don't get periods..." The noise behind her ceased, and without realizing she had everyone's undivided attention, she roared, "...because I'm a MAN, and if I hear any more crap out of you, I'll deck you or drown you in your lousy lobster bisque." She whirled around to see a shocked breakfast crowd looking toward the serving window.

The truckers burst out laughing, some so hard their eyes

began to water. Ed pounded the counter. Ty and Nanette applauded. She turned the same bright pink as her uniform, stayed behind the counter, sighed, and calmly refilled coffee cups. Manny disappeared deep into the kitchen without a word.

On Ronda's next day off she hadn't planned anything exciting, except sleeping as late as possible and having lunch in her pajamas and bathrobe.

She was sitting on her porch in her "just rolled out of bed" condition, sipping her coffee when she saw someone heading for her front walk.

She intended to flee, yet something familiar about the person made her pause. He looked up and smiled. It was Nate. *Oh, damn.*

She had been thinking about a second date and was tentatively planning what she would wear, but she had never imagined herself wearing fluffy pink slippers and a white, terrycloth robe.

"I don't remember your phone call telling me that you were coming to see me," she called out as he strolled up the walk.

"Oh, that's because this is a panty-raid." He was carrying a newspaper under his arm, grinning broadly. He looked good enough to eat. Ronda chuckled, but she walked over and locked the screen door. "I also don't remember giving you my address."

Glancing around at the surrounding houses, he said, "Yeah, it was a very lucky guess on my part, wasn't it?"

"So, Mr. Smith, have you been investigating me again?"

"No, Ronda. I swear I haven't. But I do know how to find just about anybody's address, and sometimes I just can't wait to get it the old-fashioned way."

"I see." She smiled, wrapping her robe a little tighter. "And, why couldn't you wait?"

By this time he was at the door, waiting patiently to be asked in. "Well, I had to see if the rumors were true."

"What rumors?" she asked.

"That I'm dating a man." He smiled wickedly as he delivered his punch line.

Her mouth gaped open. She backed up and almost stumbled over the ottoman, but instead, she sat down on it, hard, and giggled uncontrollably.

Nate grinned at her. "Of course, one flash of your bathrobe could end the controversy right here and now."

Trying to stop, she took some deep breaths and said, "I'm going upstairs to get dressed now." She had walked a few feet away before turning around. "Wait here," she said.

"As you wish." He leaned against the railing and unfolded the newspaper as if perfectly content to stand there and read the sports pages.

She ran up to her bedroom, wriggled into her tightest, sexiest jeans and donned a feminine lavender shirt and then pulled a soft white sweater over it. Next she quickly brushed her teeth and ran a brush through her tangled hair before she bounded downstairs. There he was, right where she left him.

She unlocked the screen door. "So what shall we do, now that you know I'm a man? With a penis and everything..."

He stepped inside and smiled at her. "I don't know. I've never been so attracted to a man before."

"Hmmm. Such a problem. Maybe we should play it by ear."

She sat on the wicker love seat and he settled down beside her.

"Seriously, Nate. How did you hear about it? I'm dying to know."

"You're infamous, Ronnie—you're the talk of every truck stop in New England. I frequent those places because I overhear vital information. A trucker will pick up a hitchhiker, which turns out to be the run-away I'm looking for, or they see things that are out of place on the road and they talk. They usually give very accurate descriptions too. I almost swallowed my sandwich whole when I heard about the sexy, new waitress working at Cousin Tommy's who loudly announced that she was a man."

Ronda laughed again. "There were extenuating circumstances, Nate."

"I know. I got the whole story eventually. Even your boss was applauding you."

"Well, 'Boss Junior.' He'll be my boss if I don't get fired before he graduates in May."

"You'll last, if you don't quit. You have to commit murder before they fire you from jobs like that. Besides, your future boss thinks you're the greatest. I even admitted that I knew you."

She gave him a sidelong glance. "You didn't mention to anyone else that you knew me from a snooty private school, did you?"

"No. I just said I used to go to school with you back when we were teenagers, and to my knowledge, you had always been a girl."

"Okay, but I should have told you, I'm keeping my past very quiet. Tommy thought I should. The other girls can let petty jealousy influence how they treat people. I don't need that right now."

"So you wanted to be one of the boys instead?"

Ronda grabbed a throw pillow and started beating him with it. The newspaper fell to the floor, opened, and spilled out everywhere. Nate easily took her pillow away, disarming her. He pulled her close and nibbled her lower lip for a moment, and when she didn't pull away, he kissed her. She melted into his embrace returning the kiss. Heat traveled from her cheeks to deeper places. It had been much too long since she had been kissed by a man who knew how and when to make her toes curl.

An appreciative sound escaped from him, as if tasting something luscious. His lips were soft and he smelled like fresh soap. Holding her in his strong grasp, he deepened the kiss, and she slid her arms around his neck.

At first, she tingled with excitement and surprise, but the longer he kissed her the more Ronda relaxed into his warm body and let herself run with the sensations. Their tongues danced in a circle. Passion stirred within her, fluttering and clutching. She remembered that Nate was an excellent kisser. She hoped he was just as good in bed since she was already thinking about taking him there.

When they reluctantly released their lips, he watched her eyes flutter open and touched her cheek tenderly, smiling into her sparkling blue eyes.

She sighed. "You've done this before. I can tell."

"Yeah, with you. Don't you remember?"

"Mmm. I remember."

Her gaze shifted to the newspapers all over the floor. "What's this about?" She leaned down and picked up a page displaying Michael Lawson's picture.

"Actually, that's why I came," he confessed. "I figured it might come as a shock, so I thought I'd tell you in person."

Ronda was already reading the article. Her ex had made the front page—above the fold. The article stated that Michael Lawson, a writer for the Portland newspaper, had been reported missing for several days and that foul play could not be ruled out.

"What does that mean, exactly?" Ronda demanded.

"When they say that foul play can't be ruled out, what do they mean?"

"Nothing. It doesn't mean anything, Ronnie. Foul play is never ruled out until the person shows up and swears that they just went out for a pack of cigarettes. Trust me. They just don't know, that's all."

"Did you talk to Lorena?" Ronda shifted to look at his face.

He tried not to cringe. "I can't tell you that."

"She's your client, isn't she?"

"Don't go jumping to conclusions. I'm checking a few leads, that's all." He gazed at the floor, away from her probing stare.

"Is that what I am? Am I a lead?"

"No. Damn it, Ronnie, that's what I meant by not jumping to conclusions." He blew out a long breath. How could he explain why he had taken the job, other than confessing that he wanted to stay as close to her as possible?

"Why not? Why wouldn't I be a lead? If the last thing he said before he went out for his pack of cigarettes was that he was coming to see me..."

"Ronda, I know you." Nate swept her hair behind her ear and placed his thumb on her chin so he could stroke her cheek. "I know you better than you think I do."

"Of course you know me better than I think you do. You seem to know every friggin' thing about me." She leaned away from him. "The idea of having bumped into you again was beginning to appeal to me, but I'm so angry I can't even think about that right now. I like my life good and private. What the hell made you think it was a good idea to start an investigation I might be involved in, and a relationship with me at the same time?"

"Ronda, I'm not suspecting you of anything." He took a deep breath and closed his eyes. "You can help with the investigation if you want to. If I suspected you of anything, would I ask for your help?"

"Maybe."

"Okay. If I suspected you of bumping off your old boyfriend, would I do this?" He placed his hand behind her head and kissed her again, deeply and passionately, and he held her so close he could feel her breasts pushing against his chest and his own heart pounding. When he pulled back, it was just enough to catch her mouth between his parted lips and kiss her again and again with soft, gentle nipping, little kisses.

This time when he released her, she was breathing unevenly. She stroked the stubble on his chin and asked, "How can I help?"

"You can answer a couple of questions for me."

"Okay. Go ahead." She leaned against the back of the loveseat as if she were steeling herself for whatever he would ask.

"How did you meet Michael Lawson?"

"He sold my father some insurance when he worked briefly for Prudential, and I found him a house in South Portland when I worked briefly as a realtor. It was a beautiful restored colonial right near the water—gorgeous views, large porch, gardens." Her expression could only be called wistful.

"Sounds pretty."

"Yes. He loved it. *I* loved it. When we broke up he sold it. He had one of our biggest competitors handle the sale."

"That must have hurt. Did you spend much time in Michael's home?"

"Yeah. It was my home too for a few months."

She frowned at the painful memory. "As soon as I moved in, the relationship started going badly."

Nate took her hand and kissed her knuckles. "I'm sorry you had to go through that."

"Yeah. Me too," then added with resignation, "It busted me up for quite a while. Eventually I moved to New York, finished my business degree, and as soon as I was completely over him, I had the "joy" of serial dating some of the biggest pricks in the city."

Nate stopped asking questions while Ronda closed her eyes and took a couple of deep breaths.

He put an arm around her shoulder. "Are you okay?"

"Yeah, sure. I'm fine," she lied. His calm presence helped, but not enough to keep the familiar lump from forming in her throat. "Nate, is there any other way I can help besides visiting Memory Lane?"

"You can keep your ears open. The truckers may be talking about it. Listen carefully for any information they might have, but be careful not to look too interested. Act like you're just passing the time with conversation. Tell me everything you hear."

Nate cautioned against the two women getting together. That advice suited Ronda just fine. She didn't relish the idea of witnessing the other woman's heartbreak, especially since she'd experienced the exact same thing with the same person.

"Okay, Nate. I'll be discreet. Do we have some sort of code names?"

"Yeah. You can call me your boyfriend."

She was surprised by the sound of that, yet pleasantly. It had been a long time since finding a man who seemed to prefer her to young bimbos, and she smiled at the idea. Nate was someone she had once trusted only to regret it. Should she let him try to jumpstart her heart? Or would one more dating disaster encourage her to take a long walk off a short pier?

"I don't know, Nate. I've been through too much to risk another heartbreak right now. If I have one more blow to contend with, I'll have to become a stand-up comic."

"I won't break your heart again, Ronda. I've matured in the past twenty years. Unlike some people, I know what I want."

Back at work, truckers had tired of saying, "You da man, Ronda," which was good for about a month of affectionate teasing. The weather was becoming pleasant on more than just a freak occasion. Tommy was making final plans for his trip to LA for Ty's graduation, and there was no more talk of the newspaper reporter who had disappeared.

The general consensus of opinion was that Michael probably pissed somebody off and would be found in the marshes, stuffed into a burlap bag. For Ronda to hear this and not react to it took some self-control. It was not only plausible but probable. Michael had a penchant for saying whatever was on his mind, and she knew that tact wasn't one of his strong suits.

Ronda had decided to spend her coffee break in Tommy's office with her feet up on the desk. She pushed at her cuticles and thought about Lorena. The woman seemed to be the only one who cared about finding Michael anymore, and she had indeed hired Nate. Since he thought most of her leads were just wild guesses, Nate still needed Ronda's input regarding Michael's past haunts and habits.

Hoping something would come through from her intuitive thoughts, she wanted to spend her break in quiet isolation. No messages were filtering through from the beyond today. No master teacher had presented himself either. She was beginning to think her dream had been the result of her own wishful thinking. When her break was over, she retied her apron and with a mental shrug returned to finding the meaning of life while filling hungry stomachs.

Antoine was serving up an order of omelets and hitting his little bell when Ronda felt a prickly sensation on the back of her neck. She turned around, searching. Was she being watched? A female sitting in the back of the dining room stared at her. The woman quickly looked away, slipped on a pair of sunglasses and stared out the window.

"Damn," Ronda muttered. Nanette had the station. She would need an excuse to get close and have a look at her. What sort of excuse could she use to go over there?

"Hey, Nanette. Want to trade stations just for fun?"

Nanette looked at her as if she had suggested they get into a car accident. "I'm just fine with my station, hon, but if you ever want to trade boyfriends, you let me know."

Ronda chuckled and served the omelets to Roy and Dominick.

"Thanks, sugar." Roy sported a full smile despite a couple of missing teeth.

Sugar. She grabbed the sugar and artificial sweetener packets, prepared to fill the containers all around the restaurant. Before she reached the woman by the window, the lady in question stood up to a height of at least six feet and exited by way of the convenience store.

Disappointed, Ronda walked back to her station, wondering if she had just seen Lorena. She didn't know how she'd found her, but Ronda was fairly certain that Nate hadn't told her anything.

If it was Lorena, she must have followed her commuting from home. That disturbing thought sent a shiver up her spine. The woman, very tall and thin, seemed odd. Was it the strong chin and jaw, the scarf and sunglasses or something else? She was Caucasian, but it was hard to guess her hair color because it was wrapped in that embroidered scarf. She wore a sweater and a long skirt. Ronda didn't remember the shoes. They may have been boots.

She made a mental note to tell Nate about it. Even though it might be nothing to worry about, what if it was? She would be seeing him tomorrow. She smiled inside just thinking about him. Was it foolish to turn to mush inside this early in the game? Somehow their relationship didn't feel like a game and she didn't want it to. She wanted someone she could trust to stay with her—no matter what. The kind of relationship her friends from New York had found. She thought about Maura with her vampire, Haley and Barb with their shapeshifting tigers, and wondered again why the summoning hadn't seemed to work for her.

CHAPTER FIVE

Nate was turning out to be a nice addition to her life—mostly. She had to remind him a couple of times about his tendency to ask where she was going and what she was doing. He said he'd try to cool it—only it was easier said than done. He seemed to want to spend every spare minute with her.

Nate had just purchased his cottage in Biddeford Pool and they had made plans to get together and go shopping at the Saturday flea markets. He arrived early Saturday morning to take her out to breakfast.

She had suggested La Belle Cafe. It was worth going there just to inhale.

Sitting in the small café, which was known for its fresh bakery items and good coffee, they ordered a continental breakfast of croissants and espresso.

Nate buttered his croissant while Ronda ate hers with jam.

"What do I need to furnish an entire two bedroom cottage, Ronnie?"

"Don't you have some of what you need already?"

"Well, let's see. I have no silverware or dishes. I have no furniture or bedding and no curtains."

She paused with croissant in mid-air, shocked. "What the hell do you have?"

"I have a plant, but I'm afraid it might die if I don't water and talk to it often enough." He shrugged. "Of course that would give me an excuse to come up here and see you more often."

She looked out the window at the bright morning sky and muttered, "Typical man..."

"You would know, darlin'."

"Ooooo. We'd better leave for that flea market soon. But first, I should let you know that Lorena came to see me at work."

"She did?" He looked genuinely surprised.

"Well, I think it was her. A woman was staring at me, and when I walked toward her she got edgy and ran."

Nate sat back and finished his espresso. "What did she look like?"

"I'm not sure about hair and eye color. She was wearing a scarf around her whole head and sunglasses, but she was very tall and had a thin nose and wide, square face."

"That doesn't describe the woman I met."

"Oh. I have no idea who it could be then." Ronda finished her breakfast and dabbed at the corners of her mouth with a napkin.

Nate smiled and one side of his lip curled up. "Possibly, a cross-dressing truck driver who wanted to check out the transsexual waitress."

Ronda thought he was serious. "Oh, no. You think?"

Nate was having a good chuckle when the check arrived. Ronda grabbed it before he could protest.

"It's your *Welcome to Maine* breakfast," and she puckered her lips, blowing a kiss in his direction.

His eyes crinkled at the corners when he grinned.

"Thank you, darling. It sounds like I'm going to need all of my cash to furnish my new home anyway."

Ronda was about to slide into Nate's black BMW when she heard the voice of her intuition. *Don't ignore it.* She froze. She wondered why this information was delayed, but she didn't want to talk to Nate about it. Somehow she didn't think he'd understand her intuitive messages. When no more information came her way, she slowly slid down into the car.

"Are you okay?"

"I'm fine." Nuts, Nate doesn't miss a thing.

She tried to be her bright, bubbly self, but it was an effort that showed and his suspicious look let her know he wasn't buying it.

"Ronnie?"

They drove in silence for a while before Nate asked, "Is there something you don't want to tell me?"

"Nate, don't."

"What? I ask questions for a living. I can't help myself."

"Well, it's nothing."

"I don't think so. If there's one thing I'm good at, Ronda, it's non-verbal communication. I know when people are holding something back."

"I'm not ready to tell you everything I'm thinking. Maybe someday I'll be able to do that but not yet."

"Yeah, I know. Trust issues, right?" He sounded aggravated.

"No. Not even. It's just me ... the way I am." She shrugged. "No one has ever had a problem with it but you." Fidgeting in her seat, trying to get comfortable, she noticed Nate's frown as he drove on in silence.

"You don't tell me everything, do you?"

"I tell you what I can." He had turned away from her to make a left turn, and she couldn't read his expression.

"Then why haven't you told me about any of your ex-girlfriends, or anything from your personal past?"

"Because it's rude to talk about old flames with your love interest."

The words "love interest" struck her. Not the same way "boyfriend" did. Still, she didn't feel like getting into it yet.

"I told you about Michael. Was that rude?"

"No, I needed the information for a case. Why are you trying to pick a fight with me?"

Ronda heaved a huge sigh and slumped down in her seat, staring out the window. Silence settled over them until they arrived at the flea market.

"Do you still want to do this?" Nate asked.

"Yes. I'm sorry, Nate. I wasn't trying to start a fight."

"Yeah. I'm sorry too. I can be a little too inquisitive sometimes, but only because I care what's going on in your life." He leaned over, gave her a soft kiss and smiled. They hesitated a moment and gazed at one another. Nate took her chin in his hand and kissed her again, but this time he kissed her as if he intended to say something more—like what was in his heart.

She was fairly sure he was a sincere and a valuable friend—maybe more, but she didn't know if she should take it any further yet. It was a risk to trust someone who'd been a fickle player in the past. Maybe he had changed, but what if he hadn't? His tender kiss warmed her and she had to admit that she loved his lips on hers. Kissing him back, a truce was silently declared.

Nate took one look at the junky furniture and folding tables covered with dusty lamps, knickknacks, and broken mirrors and wrinkled his nose. "This place is depressing. The mall or the outlet stores are probably where I should be. To hell with the cost."

"Yeah, flea markets require some patience. You have to

be willing to sort through a lot of junk to find a few fabulous treasures."

"I don't have enough time or patience for that. Besides, I'm going for the less-fussy, minimalist look, so let's drive a mile down the road to the mall."

Spending the day shopping at Crate & Barrel, Macy's, and Pottery Barn, deliveries were arranged, but even so, plenty of shopping bags came home with him in the back seat and trunk of his sporty car.

On the way to his house, Ronda glanced at him. "You're still a spoiled rich kid, aren't you?"

"Am I?" he asked, surprised.

"I'm just kidding. You're no more spoiled than the next guy who can't stand the flea market."

"That's probably most of us." He chuckled. "Thank you for your help today, by the way. I couldn't have handled it without you."

"What? It was fun...exhausting and endless, but fun. I love shopping with a friend, and now I can't wait to see your new cottage."

When they arrived at Nate's house, Ronda gasped. What she had pictured was a tiny cottage for one. Maine had hundreds of them. This was an open-concept ranch home, complete with hardwood floors, a six-burner stove, double ovens, and a dishwasher in the huge, eat-in kitchen.

"There are two bedrooms down the hall."

"I had no idea it was so nice," she said.

Nate was delighted with her reaction. He wanted her to like it. He hoped to see her living in it someday but couldn't resist a tease. "I could dump it and buy an old beat-up one if you want."

"Stop it." She laughed and set her packages on the

counter. As she explored, she peeked into the rooms at the end of the hall. "What are you going to do with a second bedroom?"

"Don't know yet," he shrugged. "Maybe it'll become my branch office, or maybe I'll have wild parties and that can be the drunk tank."

Ronda chuckled. "I love your sense of humor—among other things." She looked at her feet but the smile remained.

He knew he was growing on her. Although he thought it was probably too soon to get her into the sack, part of him wanted to try. That part might make her nervous, and he didn't want her to run. His animal nature was straining his fly, but he'd have to squelch the heat, hoping not to scare her.

They had time to unpack most of the kitchen items before reheating the pizza they had brought with them. While sitting cross-legged on the floor, they finished a six-pack of microbrewery ale, then put away the rest of the purchases. Nate's bed wasn't scheduled to be delivered until the following Saturday, so they unrolled the area rug, spread the fluffy throw over it, then soft a cotton blanket over that. He threw some pillows on top, then finally a sheet over all of it and flopped down. It felt almost as soft as a mattress.

Nate pulled her close and kissed her like he had never kissed her before. The long, deep, tender kiss had her trembling in his arms.

When he released her lips, he looked deeply into her eyes and tested her. "Ronda, if only I had just a little energy left..."

She smiled and looked away. "I know what you mean."

Good answer. That meant there were pleasant possibilities. Nate gently stroked her hair and pulled her close, tucking her head under his chin. "Cuddling is good too." After a long pause, he shifted to find her lips and kissed her with all the pent-up passion he had felt for what seemed like a hundred years.

Her breathing slowed and deepened. She let her hand slip from his waist to the bulging area below.

"Ronda," he whispered. "I'm suddenly not as tired as I thought."

"Me neither."

Nate looked into her smoldering blue eyes and grinned. They both sat up and began stripping off their clothing. Nate was completely naked, but he stopped her as she was about to remove the last piece, red bikini panties. "Wait. Let me."

Ronda smiled and lowered herself to the floor. Nate, propped on one elbow, admired every inch of her. "I want to savor you." He ran his hand over her slowly, from her neck to her breasts. "So firm and heavy," he said cupping one. He bent to tenderly kiss her hard nipple. He sucked it into his mouth and swirled his tongue around it while she moaned.

"Oh, that feels so good. I want more."

He suckled her breast thoroughly before moving to the other side. He gave the same tender attention to the other breast while gliding his fingers down her stomach. He slipped under her panties as if they weren't there, and reached the tangle of bark brown curls between her legs. She arched and moaned louder when he stroked her clitoris.

"I want to watch you come," he whispered. Ronda murmured something so garbled he couldn't understand it, but she seemed content to let him do whatever he wanted. He stroked her clit faster and applied a little more pressure. She let out a gasp and her thighs began to tremble.

"Nate..." she whispered.

"Yes, love?"

"I—" She never finished her sentence. Her body bucked, spasmed and thrashed. Warmth and desire spread through

Nate's body as he watched her come. She sustained her orgasm longer than he had expected and it fascinated him. Her eyes opened and they locked gazes, yet still she shivered with waves of aftershocks.

He respectfully removed his fingers and asked, "What were you trying to say, before I rudely interrupted you with your orgasm?"

"I was going to say, I want you inside me." She rolled on her side and reached for his cock. His urges were way out of proportion to hers and burned inside him. Completion. He wanted to, at long last, thrust his swollen erection into her. He could sense the primal desire to mate with her. But it was more than that. He needed to claim her. To make her his.

It was all he could do to keep his lovemaking slow and tender. He had promised himself he'd give her a memorable first time. First time together, that is...and last time with anyone else. He eased her underwear down with his teeth. When the panties were separated from the beautiful woman before him, he stared at the full extent of her body's beauty. Ronda ... How long had he dreamed of this? He eased her legs apart with his knee and prepared to go down on her.

"I want you, now," Ronda said. Her face was flushed, and she lifted her pelvis off the floor as if aiming her opening toward his hard throbbing cock.

"Then I'll take you now," he said and almost growled. He grabbed a pillow and slid it under her hips as a last thoughtful gesture. He poised above her, gazed into her eyes, and pushed himself inside.

"Ohhh..." she moaned.

Thrilled by the sensation, he descended and rose, in and out, and the pressure built. His thoughts repeated over and over, *this is my mate. Mine.* He put all of his senses on hyper-alert. His nerve endings tingled. He wanted to remember this feeling. He glanced down at the place where their bodies joined to watch their mating dance. She was meeting his thrusts and pushing herself onto his shaft, moaning louder each time. They were sharing the greatest of carnalities, and he trembled as he felt the tension mounting.

Her whimpers and moans had turned to shouts of "Oh, oh, oh!" She shuddered and grabbed him around the shoulders. Her orgasm clenched his cock, and he quickly escalated to a dizzying peak realizing that she was experiencing orgasm without clitoral stimulation. In all his years of trying to make a woman come that way, no one ever had. She threw him over the edge, and he jolted in spasms of joy. At last they collapsed on the new sheet.

Incapable of speech, he nuzzled her neck.

Her breathing slowed and deepened. She let her hand slip from his waist, and they fell asleep still coupled.

The next morning, Ronda awakened from a dream about rearranging furniture, but the dream had taken place in her parents' home. She opened her eyes forgetting for a moment where she was, and then she saw Nate sleeping on his side.

His breathing was slow and rhythmic. She smiled at him, but soon her mood turned to sadness as her thoughts returned to her parents' home.

Another flash of intuition followed. She knew she couldn't wait another day. She had to start cleaning out her parents' house in Kennebunkport. It had been a few months now, and she hadn't been able to drag herself to her childhood home and start the painful process of clearing it out.

Sitting up, she fought back tears, and spoke silently to herself. *I'll go today. It's time to move on. Past time.*

As she was hugging her knees, Nate opened his eyes, rolled over and reached for her. "Good morning, beautiful."

Ronda was well aware that she hadn't brushed her teeth or washed up the night before.

"Ugh. I feel disgusting. I'm sorry, but I need to be hurrying home, Nate."

Nate looked disappointed but nodded, stood up, put on his pants and prepared to take her home.

Always the gentleman.

As soon as they reached her tiny house, she jumped out of his BMW, ran up the walk, and blew him a kiss before going inside. She could hear him calling after her, something about seeing her later. She knew she'd be busy in Kennebunkport all day, and assumed later would be later in the week.

Ronda showered, brushed her teeth, and felt like she had been reborn. Of course, a lot of that was due to Nate's skillful lovemaking. She couldn't help being glad it happened and hoped it would happen again.

Dressed in old beat-up jeans and a plaid shirt, she wondered how much dirt and dust she might find as she sorted through the hundred-year-old house. She drove south on the Maine Turnpike with time to plan her attack.

She would start on the second floor and work her way down. There were five bedrooms, but three of them were guest rooms and would be almost empty of *stuff*. Her parents' room would have their clothes. Those could be given away to homeless shelters or Goodwill. Once that much was done, she'd have to go through their jewelry boxes and shelves to be sure special heirlooms weren't overlooked.

The bedding, curtains and most of the furnishings would stay put since the house would show better that way.

The second floor would be just about finished by then. *Lord, I am so dreading this.*

When she drove up to the house, Ronda noticed a white van parked at the end of the driveway. She guessed that one of their neighbors must be using it. Pulling her Volvo up to the sidewalk's curb she gazed at the gray house with white trim. This seaside jewel must appear mighty impressive to a bystander. However, looking at it with trepidation, her uninhabited home appeared almost haunted.

Taking a deep breath, Ronda steeled herself to the task at hand. She walked tentatively up the steps, stood on the wrap-around porch facing the large oak door, tried her key and had to fiddle with it for a minute before the door clicked twice and let her in.

Stepping into the foyer, something told her to leave the door open a crack. Why should she do that? Fear of being trapped inside with her ghosts? As ridiculous as it seemed, she didn't shut the door completely. She advanced into the stale smell of her father's pipe and her mother's dried eucalyptus. A lump formed in her throat as she glanced around.

Catching sight of her mother's red, flowered scarf on the sofa in the living room, she did a double take. Walking to the scarf, foreboding prickled up her spine. She lifted it, fingered the fine embroidery and remembered seeing it somewhere else recently.

The scarf worn by the mystery man or woman, or whoever was watching her at the restaurant—it was the same one.

Ronda was astonished but not nearly as shocked as she was a moment later when she heard faint voices coming from upstairs. It sounded like two males talking, and then a female laughed. She couldn't be sure if it was real or her imagination.

Frozen for a moment, she forced her feet to cooperate

and ran outside, past her car and all the way to the corner, still clutching the red embroidered scarf.

She stood there, shivering, which had nothing to do with the cool breeze off the ocean. While wondering what to do next, a local cop drove down the short side street and was about to round the corner. He slowed down when he saw Ronda by the curb. Had she smiled or waved he might have kept driving, but the expression on her face must have made him stop.

Rolling down the window, he called out, "Are you all right, miss?"

"No, I guess I got kind of spooked. I'm Ronda Calhoun, and I came to start cleaning out my parents' place. They passed away."

"Oh, *those* Calhouns. I'm sorry about your parents, Miss Calhoun. I guess that's natural. To be spooked, I mean."

"Officer, have you seen anyone around there lately?"

The cop stepped out of his cruiser. "No, ma'am, I haven't. What made you ask?"

"Umm ... Forget it. It's probably nothing."

"Would you like me to go inside and have a look around? It might put your mind at ease."

"Oh, I don't want to bother you," Ronda said, even though part of her wished he would go in and sit with her while she packed the whole place. There was another part of her that wanted to stop and think this over logically...and she wanted to talk to Nate.

"I'm Officer Donnelly, by the way. It's not a problem. It's my job."

She looked at young Officer Donnelly and on a gut level recognized him as someone she could trust. Ronda held out the scarf.

"I don't think this scarf was on the sofa when I locked up after the memorial service," she said.

"Does anyone else have the key?"

"No. I'm the only surviving family member and I have the only keys."

"And you haven't been down here since the memorial service?" he asked.

"No," Ronda answered with her eyes downcast. "I know I should have come by sooner, but I just couldn't. I needed some time before I could face this task."

"Understandable," Donnelly said. "Does anything else look suspicious? Is anything missing?"

Ronda, turned, looked back up the hill at her house and knew that if anyone broke in, they'd most likely be looking for valuables. Why hadn't they taken the antiques and paintings? What if the voices were all in her head?

The more she thought about it, the more she realized how upsetting this whole task was. The voices could very well have been the result of stress and her imagination. *Oh, great, now I'm hearing things.* "I only got to the living room, but I don't think so."

"Shall we go in and have a look around?" the young officer asked again.

"No." Ronda shook her head. "I really don't want to do that just yet."

He raised his eyebrows.

"The guy I'm dating is a private detective. I'd like to talk with him first. Maybe I could change the locks right away— for peace of mind. I mean, nothing is missing, right?"

"I'd like to talk you out of waiting. Something could happen in the meantime."

"I doubt you can."

He shrugged. "Well, I can't force you. But don't go into that house alone until someone has had a chance to check it out and the locks have been changed."

"Yes, sir. I'll try to do that today. I have to work the rest of the week. Thank you for stopping." She finally managed to relax enough to present him with a convincing smile.

"Where do you work?"

"I'm a waitress at Cousin Tommy's."

The cop's eyes nearly fell out of his head. "The truck stop on the interstate?"

"Yeah. The very same." She pulled a few strands of hair away from her eyes where the ocean breeze had blown them.

"That's kind of a strange place for a girl like you, isn't it?"

"Why? You don't think NYU could prepare me for the career of a waitress? They claimed to be able to prepare me for any career at all."

"Oh, I know. I—I'm sure..." he stammered.

Taking pity on him, she steered the conversation back to the matter at hand. "So, do you know of any locksmiths open on a Sunday?"

"Not offhand. Would you like to come back to the station and check our resources? You can have a cup of coffee and fill out a report at the same time."

"Thanks, but..." She glanced back at the house. "I think I'll go grab a cup of coffee in town and call from there. I can look up local locksmiths online."

He smiled. "I don't blame you for turning down the coffee at the station. Come by later and fill out a report."

"Thanks for your help," she said.

Young Donnelly stepped back into his cruiser and waved before he drove off.

The idea of going to the local police station to fill out a report just didn't feel right and she didn't know why. Having a young officer possibly put himself in danger if he were outnumbered didn't feel right either. She was relying on her intuition again, but it hadn't steered her wrong so far.

In all the years she'd lived there, she had never entered the Kennebunkport Police Station. Maybe she wasn't the badass she thought she was.

Ronda drove to a nearby restaurant for coffee and left a

message for Nate to call her. While she perused the online yellow pages, Nate returned her call.

"What's up?"

"I was at my parents' house just now and found something out of place. A scarf that belonged to my mother was sitting on the sofa. I didn't see it the last time I was there."

"Could you have overlooked the scarf before?"

"I doubt it. I haven't been there since the day of the memorial service. I did a thorough once over before I locked up to be sure none of the guests had left anything behind." She played with the scarf in her hand. "It was a souvenir from the Czech Republic. My mother never wore it, but it stands out. It has a unique hand-embroidered design. Nate, I recognize the scarf as the same one worn by the—whoever that was, at the restaurant the other day. I didn't put it together until now. I just realized it was the same one when I saw it in the house."

"I'm really glad you called me. Listen, I want to be in on this. Cops don't like working with PI's, but if you insist, they'll have to put up with me. Will you do that for me?"

"Yeah, I guess I can."

"Thanks, hon. Um, Ronnie, I know you're not fond of Memory Lane, but can I ask you another question or two?"

She frowned. "What are you thinking?"

"Well, I have a theory, but theories don't result in convictions. Will you try?"

"Okay. So, Memory Lane. What did you want to know?"

"Did Michael spend any time at your parents' house when you two were together?"

She blew out a deep breath. "I brought him home for dinner once. The whole 'spending time with the parents' thing wasn't his favorite pastime. He insured the house and its contents before that, so he was there at least twice."

"Did he see any valuables either time?"

"Yes, he had a tour of the house." She whirled around to

make sure that she still had plenty of privacy. She lowered her voice, regardless of only one other person present. "He must have had a good idea of the value of the paintings and antiques even before we dated."

"Can you honestly say he was seriously involved in the relationship? As serious as you were?"

Her brow furrowed as she thought it over. "I guess so. We were telling people about our wedding plans and then we moved in together. Things were fine between us then." Ronda's mind drifted to the Michael she used to know. A happy, carefree soul, romping on the beach with her. *Ugh. Stop it, Ronda.*

Nate said something but she wasn't listening. At least his voice sounded sympathetic. She had to yank herself back to the present.

"Okay. I was just about to change the locks like any normal person would do. I feel stupid for asking, but should I do that?"

"No. We don't want them to suspect we're on to them. I'll enlist the cooperation of the local officer in charge. Don't do anything out of the ordinary to cause suspicion. I want to catch them in the act. Go back to work tomorrow. I'll let you know when you can help."

Ronda sighed and finally said something that she had been thinking for some time. "Why me?"

"I'm sorry. You don't deserve this, Ronnie. Don't talk to anyone else about it, okay? The more people who know, the more potential leaks exist."

"I'm glad I declined their invitation to fill out a police report then."

"So am I. Put that off as long as you can. Those things wind up in the weekly newspaper. I'll do all I can to help, hon. Meanwhile, don't go back there. Don't take anything. Just go home. I'll call the captain and ask him to have the local patrolmen keep an eye on the place. How about if I do my best to take your mind off of it? Dinner in the Old Port tonight? Sound good?"

"You're being overprotective, aren't you?"

"No. I'm trying to comfort you."

Ronda agreed to the dinner invitation before hanging up. Biting her lip, she couldn't help wondering about why Nate wanted to know about Michael. Did he suspect him?

CHAPTER SIX

If there were people in the house, she couldn't be sure the intruders wouldn't notice the missing scarf, not to mention the open door. She was sure she could restore the crime scene without disturbing it further.

Ronda drove to a nearby side street. She left her car there and snuck up to her house.

The door was still partway open, so she tip-toed into the foyer. Once her feet were off the hardwood and on the living room carpet, she walked normally to the sofa and replaced the scarf as she had found it. Hearing nothing, she decided that she was being ridiculous and she should just go upstairs and take a peek.

Halfway up, she froze in mid-step, pulse quickening, well aware of real voices coming from her parents' bedroom.

Good God. Did they hear me? She looked under her feet and realized that the thick, padded carpeting had probably muffled the sound of her footsteps.

A family portrait fell off of the wall over the fireplace, and landed with a thud on the brick hearth. She had to hide or run, and she had to decide which to do quickly. The master bedroom door squeaked slightly, warning her that it was opening. Ronda dashed back down the stairs, and thought about heading for the coat closet. No. Some of the closet doors squeaked too. She dove behind a large leather reclining chair in the living room just in time to avoid being discovered.

"Are you sure you heard something?" a male voice asked.

"Yeah. I thought so," said a deeper voice.

Heavy muffled footsteps tromped down the stairway, and then one of them said, "Look. A picture fell off the wall. That's what the noise was."

A moment later the female voice called them back upstairs. "Hey guys, come here. Look at this."

Oh, shit, Ronda thought. *I should have cleaned out the place sooner, before someone decided to move in.* A third low voice spoke with the female in the hall as two sets of footsteps bounded upstairs again to join the others. It sounded as if they were excitedly returning to the master bedroom at the end of the hall.

Ronda strained to hear what they were saying. She had heard the female say something about a spike of energy.

She wasn't sure, but the low male voice may have said, "Could it be them?"

Ronda didn't know how long before a more thorough search could expose her. Panicking, she wanted to get the hell out of there.

She inched her way out from behind the chair, tiptoed through the foyer and out the front door, closing it as quietly as she could. Once out, she wasn't as concerned with making noise and ran like hell across the lawn and down the street to her Volvo. She yanked open the car door, leapt in and drove. Ronda didn't want to talk to the police. She wasn't even sure that she wanted to talk to Nate yet.

On the way home she wrestled with herself. Part of her knew Nate might be upset with her for going back there after she was told not to. She figured he'd have some high-tech approach to record the identity of the intruders, and didn't want Officer Donnelly charging in there without backup.

Ronda's nerves pushed the aging car to eighty miles per hour and it began to shake. She slowed only enough to smooth the ride and made it home. *Got to get that looked at.* She'd add it to her mental to do list, which was growing steadily.

After arriving at her little rented home, she grabbed the bottle of champagne she had been saving for a special occasion. Glancing at the vintage year on the label, she quickly tucked it back in its place on the shelf. At seventy-five bucks a bottle, this didn't qualify as an occasion special enough. She grabbed a cheap bottle of beer out of the fridge and dialed Nate. She had to leave a voice mail, but he called back immediately.

"Hi, Ronnie. How're you doing?'

"Not so great. Please don't be upset."

"Upset about what?"

"I went back to the house, even though you told me not to." She sat on the couch, kicked her shoes off and drew her feet up underneath her. "Nate, I heard people there, real people. I doubted it was anything but my imagination until I was back inside."

"How many people?"

"Four, I think. Three men and one woman. Those were the different voices I heard, anyway."

"Did anyone see you?"

"No, I don't think so. I hid and I got out as soon as I could."

"Thank God."

"I'm sorry if I compromised the crime scene."

"Ronda, I wouldn't give a damn about the crime scene if anything happened to you, but don't go back there without me, okay?"

"Okay, I think I'll listen to you this time. Nate? I'm not sure what it means, but one of them said something about a spike in energy and another person asked, 'Is it them?'"

"Is it *them?*"

"Yes. That's what I heard."

"I think it's about time to surprise these uninvited guests."

"You don't mean tonight, do you?"

"No, I want talk to the police first. I'd also like to record them with surveillance equipment. Maybe we can get a better idea of what they're up to and bring in enough cops to arrest the whole group. They're already keeping an eye on the place, but I'll see if we can set something up quickly."

"Good, I mean, I want them out, but I don't want you to go in there alone or with just one cop."

She pictured a group of hardened criminals overpowering them, squeezed her eyes shut and edited the resulting visual from her mind. "It's so weird having strangers camping out in my parents' house without knowing why they're there or what they want. The paintings are still on the walls and the people are in a bedroom. The only scenarios I'm imagining are disgusting."

"I'll bet."

"Can I cancel dinner tonight? I just don't feel up to it, but I promise I won't set foot in Kennebunkport again until you give the go ahead."

"Are you sure?"

"Yeah. I really think it would be better. I'm more than a little frazzled. Should I still go to work tomorrow?"

"By all means. If we need you, I'll call. I'll miss your company tonight. If you reconsider, you can always call me."

Ronda thought about how nice it would be to slip into his arms and let him hold her, kiss her—and maybe more. She would be heavily distracted, though and it wouldn't be fair to either of them.

She wanted to jaunt over to her favorite place—her beloved beach—let the cool breeze blow the jitters right out of her, but exhaustion had set in. She'd just lay her head down on the couch for a brief nap.

After that she could take a sunset walk, grab a bottle of wine and some cheese and crackers for dinner, then tuck herself into bed and hopefully fall asleep with a book on her face. She'd try not to dream about Michael or her parents' home, or who the other guy vying for her love might be. Well...maybe she'd dream about Nate. Why had she turned him down for tonight? His strong arms were exactly what she needed.

———

Ronda heard a rapping sound as if in the distance. It became louder and more insistent until her eyes flickered open. Struggling to sit up, she squinted at the dusk outside her windows and heard Nate's voice calling her name. *How long have I been asleep?*

She pulled herself to her feet, tried to finger comb her hair and glanced at the mirror. *Oh, lovely.* She had one of those crease marks across her face from the pillow fabric.

"Coming," she called as she shuffled to the door. When she opened it Nate flashed his sexy grin and held up a paper bag, stapled at the top.

"Dinner from Chow's," he announced. "I knew you didn't want to go out, but I figured you'd still have to eat."

"Thanks, Nate." She leaned over and gave him a peck on the cheek. "Come in."

"Did I wake you?"

"I'd say I was just resting my eyes, but you'd never believe me with the tell-tale groove my pillow just chiseled into my face."

Nate followed her, chuckling, and set the bag on the

kitchen table. "You don't have to make excuses, Ronnie. Besides, I kind of like the look. Put on an eye patch and we can go up to your bedroom and role play *pirates*."

That got her to smile. As much as she hated drop-in company, the idea of romping with Nate in her bedroom sounded so much more appealing than the pity party she had planned.

She opened the paper bag and unloaded the white square cartons decorated with red, Chinese characters. "What did you get?"

"Beef Wellington and crumpets."

She shook her head, smiling. "I'll get the good china." She went to a cabinet and returned with two paper plates.

Over their teriyaki chicken, fried rice, and vegetables, Nate discussed what he and the police had decided. He'd take a back seat role and the cops would provide the muscle. Ronda listened, but before the meal was over she felt a dip in her mood.

"Nate, I was hoping you'd take my mind off of this craziness. There doesn't seem to be a damn thing I can do about it right now, and every time I think about it I get depressed."

"Sorry. I guess I got wrapped up in my work. I had every intention of distracting you tonight." He winked and put his fork down.

"Before we go anywhere or do anything, I want my fortune cookie."

He leaned back and draped his arm over the back of his chair. "By all means. You know how you're supposed to read those fortunes, don't you?"

She broke open a cookie. "How?"

"Regardless of what it says, you're supposed to add the words 'in bed'. That's your real fortune."

She smirked as she straightened the bowed paper message. At last she read it and burst out laughing.

"What does it say?"

"Your dearest wish will come true."

"In bed," he added.

She didn't even need to look up to see the ear to ear grin he was wearing.

"Okay, smartass, what does yours say?"

Nate leaned forward, grabbed the remaining cookie and tore it open. The fortune fluttered to the floor. Ronda scooped it up, read it, and giggled.

"What does it say?"

"I'm not telling." She jumped up from the table and ran.

"Oh, no, you're not getting away with that," he called and took off after her, closing in before she reached the stairs. He grabbed her around the waist and tried to rip the paper from her hand as she waved it wildly about. At last, he managed to take it away from her. Unfolding it, he read aloud, "You need understanding friends."

"In bed." She strained against his arm and her giggle turned into loud laughter.

"You think that's funny, do you? Well, we'll see about that."

Ronda began shaking her head 'no' but changed it to a vigorous nod. Nate lifted her a few inches off the floor and walked her over to the sofa as she laughed. When he had set her down, he crushed her lips with a long, passionate, silencing kiss.

Her muffled giggles ceased and turned to audible deep breaths and a sigh when they eventually pulled apart.

"I think I'd better sit down," she said.

Nate's blue gaze darkened. "I think you'd better *lie* down."

Ronda raised her eyebrows but obliged.

Nate sat on the edge of the sofa and slowly unbuttoned her shirt. He glanced up at her a few times. His eyes were smoldering. She thought she might as well help and unzipped her jeans. The expression on his face indicated that she had just made him a happy man.

She wriggled out of the old work shirt. He took it from her and dropped it on the floor. After scooting down, he grabbed her jeans at the top while she lifted her hips. He removed them and tossed them on top of the shirt.

"Now it's your turn," she said. He moved back up the sofa and leaned over so she could reach his buttons. At the same time he used the opportunity to reach around her and unsnap her bra. She let him slip it over her arms before she went back to unfastening his buttons. As she was finishing the job, he gave her a soft breast massage. "Mmm. You'd better help me whip those jeans off. Pleasure shouldn't be one way."

Nate grinned and stood long enough to peel off his shirt, jeans, and boxer-briefs, flinging them halfway across the room. Just looking at him in clothing aroused her, but gazing at his strong, naked body and impressive erection made her swallow hard.

She closed her hand around his hard cock and stroked. He closed his eyes and leaned down to suckle her breasts. His wandering hand found her clit and teased it. She moaned in ecstasy. The stimulation and fiery heat escalated until she could feel the shuddering vibrations that usually meant her orgasm was near. She forced herself to stop him.

"Nate, I want to give you a blow job."

He raised his head only slightly, but she could see his delighted expression.

"I'd love that, but I can make you come this way first."

"No. I want to save it. Let me drive you crazy for a while like you're doing to me, then we can both satisfy each other at the same time."

"Nothing would please me more, Ronnie."

He reclined against the opposite end of the couch, while

she positioned herself between his knees. Wrapping her lips around his cock, she slid her tongue down the sensitive underside of his shaft and then back up again. She could tell by his moan that he enjoyed that particular motion. Wanting nothing more than to torture him with pleasure, she did it repeatedly. He moaned louder and cupped the back of her head.

As much as she loved his reaction, she let up when it sounded like he might be getting close and flicked her tongue across the shaft instead. He gasped. She let him catch his breath, then she dipped her head lower and lapped at his balls. His moans escalated louder than before. His pleasure turned her on like no one's ever had. She loved sucking his hard cock, squeezing the rubbery tip between her lips, and flicking her tongue along his shaft. She could keep it up as long as he could stand it.

"Wait, sweetheart," he begged. "If you want to come together, we'd better do it soon. Why don't you climb on top?"

"I like giving you oral almost as much as you going down on me."

Nate laughed and reached for her. "I doubt that. Now come here and let me give you a ride."

She grinned and positioned herself above his swollen, dark red cock and sunk down over it. She was plenty wet and engulfed him like a soft glove.

This time they moaned in unison. As she raised and lowered herself on his erection he stroked her clit. She reared back and groaned with increasing sexual bliss.

He cupped and squeezed her breast and rubbed her nipple with his thumb. She moaned louder and leaned into his hand to encourage him. After giving the other side the same full attention, he pulled her forward and sucked her breast into his mouth and teased her nipple with his tongue. Soon her vaginal walls clenched and her legs vibrated wildly. Inadvertently breaking his suction, her breast popped out of his mouth.

Nate held onto her waist with his free hand, and encouraged her to climax, still rubbing her clit. "Go ahead, baby. I'm right there with you."

She felt the breakthrough begin and knew that all manner of delight was rushing in to follow it. Then, like a dam that burst, her orgasm swept her away. She rode the wave of joy all the way to complete sexual satiation. Nate was right on her heels. He jerked several times and let out a grunt each time he spasmed.

She waited until every aftershock had passed, then leaned over to snuggle his neck. "I'm so glad we ran into each other again," she whispered.

"I'll be true blue this time. I never meant to hurt you, Ronda. I was just too young and stupid to know what I had. Forgive me?"

She chuckled. "Obviously."

Ronda arrived at Cousin Tommy's feeling like she was a little off her game. She assumed it had to do with worrying about Nate and the police at her parents' home.

As she walked in through the convenience store and passed the little office, she suddenly knew that something important had slipped her mind. *Ty.* She had forgotten to call Ty by Sunday. He must be gone. *Oh hell, how could I forget that?*

She might have continued to berate herself, but Tommy sailed around the corner and stopped in front of her.

"Hey, Ronda. How was your weekend?"

"Oh, pretty good." She yawned. "Kind of boring, actually."

"Well things may get more interesting for you soon.

There's a reporter at table thirteen who wants to talk to you."

"A reporter? You're joking."

"Nope. She says she wants to ask you a few questions. All I can say is, make us look good."

"Uh, I'll do what I can," Ronda said, walking tentatively toward the dining room. Tommy reached out and grabbed her by the hand before she got very far.

"By the way, I just found out what Ty was trying to pull behind my back. Thank you for not going along."

"Well, it didn't seem right to change your work habits without your permission."

"Damn straight. I appreciate your loyalty, Ronnie." He gently clasped her shoulder and smiled.

Ronda nodded and walked into the dining room feeling like she had dodged a huge bullet, and then she looked over at table thirteen and saw it was deserted.

Roy was sitting at the counter and turned his stool to face her.

"Ronda, where were you? I thought you were out sick today or somethin'. We just had some of the best fun at your expense."

"Oh no. Tell me everything."

"This reporter woman was here asking about you. She sure was a strange chick."

"Wait a minute. Was she really tall and did she have her hair up in a scarf?" Ronda held her hand level about five inches above her head. "Did she have a long, thin nose and square jaw?"

"Yeah, kind of. She was tall but skinny," Roy said.

"And wore a blue scarf," Mark added. "Did you already talk to her?"

"No. You shouldn't talk to her either. What did you tell her?" she demanded.

"Nothin'. You know us. We just goofed around and made

stuff up. Besides, no one really knows much about you anyways."

Roy smiled wickedly. "We told her you were a man. That's the one thing we *do* know."

She burst out laughing, suddenly very glad she had protected her privacy.

"Guys, I'll be right back. I have to make a phone call." Ronda couldn't care less who was making fun of her. She needed to know what this reporter wanted. She thought that maybe the break-in had been solved and it was unusual enough to write about. Maybe Michael had been found. Whatever it was, she had to talk to Nate since he might know something via the police.

Settling into the chair behind the desk, she dialed Nate's number. The answering service took her message. Why on earth didn't Nate use a cell phone? She mentally shrugged and proceeded to answer her own question. Probably not secure enough for a private detective.

Ronda wanted to return to the counter and refill a few coffee cups while she waited for Nate to call back. Preoccupied on her way out, she almost crashed into Tommy and jumped about a foot in the air.

He took one look at her and said, "Geez you're pale. Are you all right, Ronda?"

"Yeah. I guess."

"C'mon inside. Tell Cousin Tommy what's on your mind."

Ronda thought it might be better to wait in the office for Nate's call, so she willingly followed him in and sat down.

"That reporter. Did you see him? I mean, her?"

"Not really. I've been busy. Nanette told me where she was sitting, and I glanced at her."

"I'm not sure there's anything to worry about really," Ronda said. "It's just that a lot of strange stuff has been happening lately."

"Such as?"

She wasn't sure if she should start telling the whole tale. Work was her escape. This place should not be tainted by unsolved craziness.

"You know, I just don't think I should get into all of it. This isn't the time. It's busy and I need to get out there. I'll be fine. I will. I promise."

The office phone had been turned up to the loudest volume so it could be heard through the closed door. When it rang Ronda jumped and Tommy stared at her. Neither one reacted like they were going to pick it up.

"I'm expecting a call," Ronda confessed.

"Go ahead and answer it. I'll step out if it's for you."

She picked up the phone. It was Nate. She grabbed Tommy's arm as he stood up to leave. "Do you mind if my boss listens in?"

It was one of those impulsive moves she would occasionally make, not knowing why at the time, yet it would all make sense to her later.

Tommy tried to protest and pull away, but Ronda kept a firm grip on his arm.

"Yes. I think it would be good for someone here to know what's going on. Nate, I'm putting you on speaker." She pushed the small button on the phone and Nate's voice came through clearly.

"I'm putting you on speaker too. I'm in Kennebunkport with the police captain. What's the matter?"

Tommy sat, his curiosity piqued.

"A woman claiming to be a reporter came by the restaurant this morning. I think it might have been the same person I've seen staring at me before. Possibly Michael."

Tommy's eyebrows shot up.

"What did he or she want?" Nate asked.

"Apparently she wanted to talk to me. I was just a few minutes late this morning, but she didn't wait. She talked to other people about me. They didn't tell her anything useful."

"What are you thinking?"

"I don't know. If she's legit, and you made some sort of breakthrough maybe she wanted to talk to me about Michael's disappearance or the break-in. If she's not legit, well, I'm not sure what to do."

Tommy's eyes narrowed and he looked puzzled, but kept quiet.

Nate sounded cool under the circumstances. "If she comes back, don't talk to her."

"No problem."

"Ronnie, no arrest has been made and Michael hasn't turned up yet. The police and I checked out the house last night, but there was nobody there. The lock on the basement door had been forced, but nothing seemed to be disturbed inside. We're going to search your parents' house thoroughly this morning for any evidence, and they'll be setting a trap for the people who broke in. Stay away from there until I call you. Understood?"

"Yes."

"And it might be better if you stay away from your own house too, in case someone has followed you and knows where you live. You can stay at my house in the meantime."

"With no furniture? That sounds like an adventure."

"She can stay with me," Tommy offered.

Ronda was speechless.

Nate was quiet for a moment, but finally spoke. "That's good of you, Tommy. Do you have someplace private, so Ronda won't be discovered?"

"Yes. I have a house pretty much by itself on a marsh."

"Oh, I couldn't," Ronda protested.

"You certainly can," Tommy said.

"It seems like a good idea to me, Ronnie, I wouldn't be

home anyway, and now that I think about it you shouldn't be alone."

"You're both being ludicrous."

"This is Captain Millman, Miss Calhoun. It seems like a wise precaution."

Ronda had to relent. "Okay, then. I'll do that."

"Thanks, Tommy," Nate added. "Is there anything else you called to tell me, Ronda?"

"No. The reporter wouldn't have upset me so badly except the truckers described her, and it sounded like the same person that creeped me out before."

Tommy looked very confused. "Is there anything I should know? Like what's going on?"

"Ronda will have to fill you in as she sees fit, Tommy," Nate said. "I have to go, Ronda. The police are getting ready to move."

"Be careful, Nate, okay?"

She could almost hear the smile in Nate's voice. "I will, hon. You too. Take care of her for me, Tommy."

After finishing the rest of her shift, Ronda returned home. A gloomy sky had changed from drizzle to downpour. Feeling glum, she found her old suitcase and packed a few things to take to the slumber party at her boss's house. "Isn't this all too bizarre?" she said out loud to Talon. *Talon. What will I do with her?* She hoped Mr. Carroll next door would be willing to take her.

First she packed toiletries. She'd need a book, not that she could concentrate on it. She threw the latest bestseller into her suitcase. She'd need some underwear. Forget the lace and satin. She packed three sets of white cotton essentials, and then she packed two plaid flannel nightshirts and moved on to her closet.

Oh, the age-old dilemma again. What to wear? She grabbed faded jeans and knit tops, sweats and her uniforms. She hoped Nate would come by and take her out of isolation, so she tossed a dress in too.

Ronda, suddenly overwhelmed by self-pity, threw the dress onto the floor. Realizing just how much she had been through and how odd her life had become, tears started to fall. The more she tried to hold her fingers in the dam, the hotter and faster they flowed.

A month ago she didn't even know Tommy. Now she was going to be working and living with him. A month ago she had forgotten Nate was alive. Now he was running her life. What happened to the strong, city woman who could run her own life? She desperately wanted to talk to Maura or Haley—heck, even Barb! But Haley and Barb were in a tiny village in India and who knows where Maura was at any point in time. She was probably rolling around in the grapes with her vampire lover at his vineyard in France.

Marci Jo. Grabbing her phone book, she threw it into the suitcase before closing it, dried her eyes, and headed for the door.

She told herself to be grateful for a supportive boss and a boyfriend looking out for her, dammit. Running through the rain on her way to the car, she became even harder on herself. *What's happened to me? I used to be strong and independent.* She threw her suitcase in the passenger's bucket seat and slammed the door.

Mr. Carroll greeted her at his front door and agreed to watch Talon for a few days. He said he would be delighted. As she was taking Talon's food and litter box out of the house, Talon followed. Ronda was so preoccupied she didn't even notice. Luckily, Talon followed her next door. "Damn. Maybe they're right. I shouldn't be alone. I'm a space-shot."

She kissed her precious cat on her fluffy head, and the

dear old man on his rough cheek, then she drove away into the pattering rain.

Exasperated with the whole business, she thought that talking to a higher power was in order.

"Lord, I know I don't talk to you regularly, but I figure you're pretty busy. Anyway, I could use your help now. I wish you could give me an answer to all of this. I'd take a flash of intuition, a dream ... something ... anything."

All remained quiet except for the rain and the windshield wipers. Why should she feel so alone? How long had it been since seeing Janice? What did she say, 'wait six months'? *To hell with that, it's an emergency.* She abruptly turned the wheel and headed south.

The woman lived in Saco. She didn't advertise and she didn't have a sign out front, but her turn-of-the-century, yellow Victorian was easy to find, glowing like a buttercup on the main road leading into town.

Ronda hoped she would be available on a spur-of-the moment basis, but knew she might be with someone else or not at home. She was rewarded immediately when Janice opened the door and gave her a wide, welcoming smile.

"I knew you'd be back, Ronda."

"Did you know I'd be back today?" Ronda took in a deep breath preparing to be impressed. In actuality, she was already impressed that Janice remembered her. She must have seen hundreds, perhaps thousands of people.

Janice chuckled. "No. I didn't know you were coming today. But I knew I'd see you again before the six months were up." Janice turned and proceeded to her alcove.

Following her, Ronda asked, "Is it okay? I mean, will you see me even though it hasn't been six months yet?"

"With that look on your face? Heavens, yes!"

Ronda hadn't been expecting that answer and waited until they were in the little room before she asked any more questions. Janice lit the candles and sat down opposite her.

"Have the spirits been trying to contact you about me?"

"They weren't before, but they sure are noisy now that you're here. Let's see if we can get them to calm down."

Janice closed her eyes and held up one finger in a gesture to be quiet and wait. She breathed deeply a couple of times, then opened her eyes and spoke. "A female energy. Your mother, I believe. She has the name that begins with E."

"My mother's name was Ellen," Ronda reminded her. She had hoped to hear from her mother again.

"Yes, I'm afraid I can't always remember details from session to session," Janice said. "She's here and she's waving a yellow caution sign."

"I'm paying attention."

"She insists that someone is deceiving you. Someone you know isn't what they seem to be."

"Is there more specific information about this person?"

"She's showing me a window looking out toward the ocean. There's a man you know who isn't supposed to be there. He doesn't belong in that house."

"Is he there now?"

"It's hard to pinpoint what time they're showing me, but it seems to be the present, yes. She's fading and a young male is coming through."

Ronda held her breath. She hoped it was her brother. It had been almost five years since his heart attack, but she still missed him so much it hurt.

"I'm getting the initial B ... Bruce, maybe Bradley?"

"Brady? My brother's name was Brady."

"Yes, his energy is beside you, and it's family—so, yes, your brother."

Ronda hoped he would have some wisdom for her in

death as he often did in life. She just wished she had listened to him more often. He'd been able to express his concern and opinions in a direct, no-nonsense way without moralizing.

"He's looking for something. Something is lost," Janice said.

"Something important to him?" Ronda asked.

"He's showing me his wrist and pointing to you. Is there a watch or a bracelet he could be looking for? Wait. He's extending his hands, like he's giving you a gift. He says it's something he gave to you when you were young."

"Um, I can't remember anything like that." Ronda looked at her empty wrist. "Oh, yeah. He gave me one of those MIA bracelets when I was little. I don't think I've lost it. It might just be home in the bottom of my jewelry box."

"Well you might want to find it. He seems rather insistent about this," Janice said. "Now a sister is joining us. She's beside you."

"Sarah." Ronda nodded.

Janice closed her eyes again. "Your sister is looking in a book. No, several books. She looks like she's studying or doing research."

"Hmm. I don't know. Sarah was young when she disappeared—too young to be doing research or even studying. Is my sister telling me to do research?"

"Yes, I'd say so, and she's stressing it so it's important," Janice said. "It's something to do with your departed family. She's making a link to you and to them and to something else. A group of some kind."

"What?" She had a flashback to the day she crouched behind the chair in her parents' living room. Now she was nervous. She remembered the male voice saying something about feeling or sensing energy.

"This is going to sound weird, but you've probably heard weird things before."

Janice smiled and nodded. "Go ahead. I'm not here to judge—unless you're talking about vampires and shapeshifters again."

"Could they be talking about an Edgar Cayce psychic or research group or something like that?" she asked.

Janice sat back and let out a deep breath. "It sounds plausible, but I'm afraid I'm not getting any more information. They're pulling back."

"No, they can't go now," she wailed. Oh God. The familiar emptiness settled in the pit of her stomach. Desertion. Abandonment.

"I'm sorry. For what it's worth, dear, they usually leave when you know all they have to tell you," Janice said. "If it's any consolation, many people don't get as much detail as you just did. They had some important things to tell you, and they did that."

"Okay." Ronda's breath hitched as she sat up straight and squared her shoulders. "I guess I've got plenty to think about." She paid the reasonable fee with a check and followed Janice to the front door. She was just going down the steps when she looked up at Janice again, hoping for another crumb of information.

"See you in about six months," Janice said.

Ronda nodded. The tears were starting to burn her eyes. She strolled to her car and drove straight to her cottage.

CHAPTER SEVEN

She glanced at her suitcase. She had spent an hour on her diversion and probably should have been driving herself to Scarborough, pronto—or—she could just as easily unpack and call with an apology. Ronda drove up to her cottage and jumped out of her car, leaving the suitcase where it was.

As she attempted to unlock her front door she discovered that she had never locked it. *Damn. It's a good thing I came back for the bracelet.* After running inside, up the stairs, and straight to her jewelry box in the bedroom, she heard a soft thud at the foot of the stairs and froze.

Moving to the window she saw a man, dressed in brown, darting down her street. It looked like Nate from the back. She told herself she needed to be calm and rational. Why would he be in her house? Even if he came over and found it unlocked, why would he run? Cold sweat broke out on the back of her neck. She grabbed the bracelet from the bottom of the costume jewelry heap and, trembling, set the box back on its shelf. As cautiously as she could, she tiptoed downstairs. Looking around and seeing no one present, she darted out of the house.

She deliberately locked the front door and then tried to

jiggle it open. The door held fast. She walked around to check the back. All was secure.

Did Brady want me to come back for the bracelet or to foil a robbery? Ronda glanced down at the bracelet in her hand. It was scratched and discolored. She rubbed it between her thumb and finger as she returned to her car. The engine revved, and she glanced at the name on the bracelet. She hadn't seen it for years. It read: "Captain Thomas Kelley." Suddenly shock registered on her face. Could her boss, Tommy Kelley, a Desert Storm veteran, be Captain Thomas Kelley, an MIA soldier?

She glanced up at the house Tommy lived in and thought it suited him. The place had beachy charm written all over it, from natural shingles and full front porch to a hip roof with two chimneys on either side. Ronda recognized hand labor and custom touches and fell in love with the house immediately. She could see the nearest homes visible across the marsh, but they weren't close enough to shout to.

Tommy saw her struggling up the steps with her suitcase and came outside to meet her.

"Here, let me help you with that." He took her suitcase from her.

She followed him into the house and marveled at the lodge-like feel of the place. She turned around to view the cathedral ceiling and stone fireplace. Having worked in a real estate office to help pay for college, she had a realtor's appreciation for wonderful homes.

"What a beautiful place, Tommy."

"Thanks. I designed and helped build it."

"Seriously? You're full of surprises."

Tommy smiled and said, "Yup," then started toward the staircase. "Let me show you to your room."

"Wait. Before you do that, I want to show you something." She handed him the MIA bracelet.

Tommy looked at it and raised his eyebrows. "Huh. Same name. I was in the army, but I was a private and I'm not missing." He let out what sounded like a nervous laugh.

"So it's a coincidence?" Ronda asked.

"Very much so." He handed her the bracelet. "Would you like to see the guest room now?"

"Yes. Thank you," Ronda said. She believed in signs. Maybe her brother just wanted to direct her to the man she knew with that name, for her safety or peace of mind. Janice said her family would try to send help from the Other Side whenever they could.

"Here we are," Tommy said, as they walked into a pretty yellow room filled with light. Bright lemony yellow color added cheer and the illusion of sunshine.

"This is really sweet," she said.

"Yeah. It doesn't get much use unless Ty brings a friend home."

"If I forgot to say so before, I really appreciate your taking me in like this."

"Oh, think nothing of it, Ronda. I have to take care of my best waitress, don't I?"

"I'm your best?"

"Don't tell anyone I said that. I'll have to deny it."

"Don't worry. I wouldn't want to deal with the jealousy."

Tommy cocked his head and folded his arms. "Speaking of jealousy ... is Nate the jealous type?"

"I hope not, but I can't say for sure. It hasn't come up."

Tommy walked into the hallway. "Well, if he wants to come and see you or stay with you anytime, he's welcome too."

"We're not ready to shack up yet, but thanks. Hopefully he'll have this investigation finished soon. If so he'll probably go back to Boston where he lives during the week, and I'll be able to go home."

Tommy smiled and turned to leave. "Make yourself comfortable. I'll be downstairs."

Ronda unpacked her suitcase and noticed the feminine touches in the room. There were white Priscilla curtains, a white wrought-iron headboard, and a yellow dust ruffle to go with the yellow comforter. A woman definitely decorated the room—maybe a few years ago, but the mark of femininity was unmistakable. As soon as she was finished, she bounded downstairs.

Ronda was curled up in a comfortable deck chair on the front porch, reading, when Nate's BMW roared up the gravel drive. At first she was happy to see him, and then she became annoyed when she realized she hadn't given Nate the address. Obviously he was still up to his tricks. Perhaps he had investigated Tommy too.

Nate stopped in the middle of a dust cloud and waited for it to dissipate before he got out. Ronda didn't get out of her chair to greet him. Instead, she waited for him to come to her.

"Hi, babe," Nate called when he finally stepped out of the car.

"Nathaniel," she said, with an icicle hanging from it.

"We've had a breakthrough," he announced.

She put her book down. "Tell me all about it."

Nate jogged up the steps, pulled a wooden chair around and sat on it backwards as if he visited this porch all the time. "You're not going to believe this, Ronnie. The people at your parents' house were a group of paranormal investigators for one of those TV shows on ghosts."

"Really?" Her eyes widened. "Do they always break in like that?"

"Fair question. According to the group, they were let in and given written permission to use the place by a Miss Ronda Calhoun."

Shocked, she sat up ramrod straight. "Good God! I never gave anyone permission..."

"I know. They produced the contract and the signature didn't match yours. Not even close."

"How did you get my signature?"

"Ve have vays..." Nate said with a glint in his eye.

"Look. Just so you know, I'm getting sick of feeling like I have no privacy. There's nothing you don't know about me and nowhere I can go without you turning up. You're pushing my buttons big-time."

Nate's expression fell. He looked like he might whimper if she hit him on the nose with a newspaper.

"I'm trying to help you. Trying to keep you safe."

"I know. I'm just—tired. I've had one crazy-ass day."

Nate reached for her hand, but she didn't offer hers in response. He cleared his throat and carried on as if he hadn't noticed her mood.

"Ronda, according to caller ID, the person who called the researcher, claiming to be you, was calling from your parents' phone number. They had the contract faxed to a public fax machine at an office supply store. Somebody signed it and faxed it back. She told them she was only there part of the time and that she'd leave the front door unlocked on the days they came for filming."

"I don't understand. Why would someone want to do that?"

"Compensation. In this case, cash, wired to Western Union. She insisted on it."

"You keep saying 'she'. Are you certain it's a woman?"

"The producer who spoke to the person claiming to be you said it sounded like a female with a low voice."

"I'm not a low-voiced female."

"I know you're not. No one suspects you of anything, Ronnie. Why are you being so defensive?"

"I'm sorry. Let me tell you about my day. That might explain my ugliness."

"You couldn't be ugly if you tried."

Ronda sighed. "Well, I feel like a branch ready to snap. I need a glass of wine or a mug of foam or something."

"Can I—take you someplace?"

"Yes, please," Ronda stood and threw her book on the chair.

"I passed what looked like an Irish pub on the way, complete with shamrocks on the shutters."

"O'Brien's." Ronda smiled for the first time in hours. "Yes, I know it well. I don't even have to change. It's so casual I could probably get service in a bathing suit and bare feet."

"I'll resist the urge to tell you how quickly you'd get service in a bathing suit and bare feet."

Ronda rolled her eyes, then stuck her head in the door and called to Tommy. "Tommy, Nate is here and we're going out for a quick brew. We'll be back before you know it."

"Enjoy," he called back to her.

"I'll make dinner when I get back, if you like."

"Ha, you don't have to worry about that," Tommy said as he came into view, wiping his hands on a dishtowel. "The fridge is full of leftovers from the restaurant. Two bachelors could do much worse than Antoine's cooking, even microwaved."

"Sounds terrific. See you later, then."

Ronda and Nate were quiet on the way to the bar. He let her lead the way to her choice of table.

After they sat and had a chance to look over the wine and beer list, Nate spoke first. "I'm sorry if I've been a little overanxious to find you at times. I'm suddenly realizing how my behavior may have affected you, especially things that might be interpreted as overprotective. I didn't mean to be a pain in the ass."

"I know that," Ronda said. "Don't get me wrong. I don't mean to be bitchy, I'd just really like it if you could call me, make plans, and get directions if necessary, like a normal guy."

Nate stared at the table. The words stung. He had been trying to prove that he was much better than an average guy, and trying to impress her with his PI skills—hopefully to make up for his other 'condition.' Someday he'd have to tell her, but not today. "I'm sorry I'm not normal."

"Nate, I— I didn't mean you aren't normal. It's just ... what you do for a living isn't exactly nine to five."

Nate nodded and reached slowly for her hand. "Ronda, I haven't been with too many women that I could see myself spending a lot of time with, and that's mostly because of what I do for a living. And I do it because I am who and what I am."

She let him take her hand in his, and he was encouraged, so he went on. "You're worth much more to me than any of them. Don't get me wrong. All women have their bright and colorful moments, but to me, you're the Aurora Borealis in comparison. For you, I'll make the necessary adjustments."

Ronda smiled, and curled her fingers around his hand. "Thanks, Nate. Coming from a quality guy like you, that's the nicest compliment I've ever had."

Relief washed over him. At that moment the waitress arrived to take their orders. She rattled off what they had on tap. They had Bass ale, so Ronda ordered a black and tan. Nate ordered the same. When the waitress left, Ronda told him about her unexpected trip back home just before heading to Tommy's.

"Jesus, Ronnie. I wish you had called me. Did you get a good look at the guy?"

"No, not really. He was fairly tall with a good build and sandy blond hair. Do you know anyone fitting that description?" She tossed a sardonic smile in his direction.

She noticed Nate didn't seem blown away by the whole intruder thing. Of course, he's used to this.

"I can see why you were so upset, Ronnie, but you did the right things. You got out of the house, locked the doors, and drove to a safe place."

"What do you think about the bracelet?" she asked, drawing doodles in the condensation on her mug.

"It's a weird coincidence, but maybe that's all it is. Just a coincidence."

"I used to wear it all the time," she recalled, looking up into his steady blue gaze. "I said a prayer for Captain Kelley every night. If some deity was listening, they would have had to bring him home—if they could have."

"Do you really believe that?" Nate asked.

"Sort of. I know it may be naïve, but I just feel better to think someone listens to my prayers and gives a crap."

"Well, I give a crap, if that helps." Nate smiled in his sweet way.

"Yeah. It does, kind of." She sighed. "You're not omnipotent, but you'll do."

Finally enjoying each other's company again, they drank another round of black and tans and were soon laughing easily, teasing one another—and kissing.

About an hour later Nate said he had to get back to Boston and he'd be gone a couple of days. Ronda was returned to Tommy's safe-house where dinner was ready.

She set the table, but she wasn't sure where to sit. Tommy would most likely be on the end. It was a large table, and she imagined they'd be passing bowls and dishes family-style.

She placed herself in the traditional spot set aside for the guest of honor, on the host's right. She was, after all, the only guest.

How silly to be thinking of etiquette at a time like this. It's not like she was invited to a stiff, formal dinner with the boss. Being in his home and feeling so comfortable around him, it occurred to her that she felt like family.

When dinner was ready and on the table, he smiled and sat next to her.

"Help yourself," Tommy said, as he pushed the steaming bowls and platter toward her. "I keep loads of Antoine's meatloaf and mashed potatoes on hand."

"I'm not very hungry to tell you the truth. I got a bit full on Bass ale."

"I keep Sam Adams in the fridge. Would you like one?"

"God no, but thank you. I'm a little buzzed as it is." Ronda missed her plate with a few of the green beans and they landed in her lap.

Tommy chuckled as she looked down in surprise at the napkin that caught them.

"Let me know if there's anything you need while you're here, okay?"

"Other than a bib, I don't need a thing, honest. I'm just hoping I can get out of your hair and back home soon."

"I don't mind you being here a bit. Has Nate come up with anything yet?"

"I'm not supposed to talk about it, but there has been some progress. Did Ty get back to LA okay?"

"He did." Tommy helped himself to a large piece of meatloaf. "He doesn't come home very often anymore. I miss him."

I know the feeling. "I hope he isn't upset about my not getting back to him," she said.

"No. He was disappointed at first, but when he fessed-up to what he wanted to do, we reached a compromise. I'm sure he's over it by now."

"Really? A compromise?" Ronda tried the meatloaf. *Yum.* Antoine's food tasted good even after reheating.

"Yeah. I think it will work just fine. Since Ty's going to handle the books, he'll have his computer with all that accounting stuff on it, plus a printer. No Internet though. I don't want my office used for everything from e-mail to shopping. I won't be expected to operate any of it at first, but I'll learn gradually like the old dog that I am."

"Well that sounds tremendous," Ronda said. "I think you'll be surprised."

"Yeah. I hope I don't regret it. I have visions of a mechanical nightmare if the thing breaks down while Ty's on vacation. I can fix almost anything, but I wouldn't have the faintest idea how to fix an electronic magic box."

"I don't think you'll regret it, speaking from experience. Most of the people who use computers don't know anything about what goes on behind the screen."

"Do you know how to use ... well, of course you do. You're young and smart."

"Ha! Thanks for calling me young. But you don't have to be young or even especially smart. Don't worry. You'll pick it up and run with it, probably faster than you think. Besides, I'll be there to help you if Ty's not around."

"God bless you, Ronnie." Pointing to her with his beer, he said, "I understand you're saving for a trip abroad?"

"Yeah. Marci Jo is putting together a trip for the end of the summer. I hope to go to Ireland and check out the motherland."

"Ah, you'll love it. I've heard a lot about the Emerald Isle, although I've never been. My ex-wife is from Dublin."

"Is she the one who decorated the guest room?"

Tommy said, "Weel now. Whot if she wosn't an' oi said oi did thaht?"

"Nice Irish brogue, and I'd say you were probably an interior designer in a former life."

Tommy laughed. "You were right the first time. I used to share this house with her and there were lots of feminine touches. I butched it up a bit, but I never got around to that room."

"Don't. It's perfect. Where is she now?"

"Actually, she's a set designer in New York City. She remarried. To some snooty cello player."

"And Ty grew up with you?"

"Yeah. He hated the cello," Tommy smiled. The meaning wasn't lost on Ronda. She guessed that he must have hated the cellist too.

"What a choice for a mother to have to make. It must have been awful."

"I don't know. I haven't talked to her since I signed the divorce papers."

"Oh." She thought she noticed a flash of sadness cross his face. Maybe she should change the subject. "So, how did you come up with the idea for 'Cousin Tommy's'?"

Sitting up a little straighter, he beamed. "I started with a couple of gas pumps and a coffee pot. I inherited the land and the gas station. The coffee pot was mine. A truck driver gave me the idea. I don't see him anymore, but I still think about where I'd be without him." Tommy had finished his meal and was leaning back in his chair, enjoying the rest of his beer.

"Some people seem to walk into our lives at just the right time for a reason. So what was his idea, exactly?" she asked. Having finished most of her own meal, she relaxed and let it digest.

"He wanted a place that didn't feel like a fast-food joint,

where he could stretch his legs, have some easy conversation, a decent home-cooked meal, and be on his way."

"Sounds like you gave him and a lot of other guys exactly what they wanted."

"Yeah. The convenience store, video arcade and laundry were my ideas, though," he added. "Now we're a recommended stop in *The Next Exit*."

"What's that?" Ronda finished her last sip of ice water.

"A book for travelers and truck drivers."

"Oh. Good to know. So how long did it take you to build this empire?"

"I guess it started to grow when Ty was about two years old," he said. "Twenty-three years ago." Tommy sighed as if recalling fond memories.

"Was your wife with you then?"

"She left during the building phase. She hated the whole idea. Thought I was nuts for catering to a bunch of 'low-lifes'."

Ronda just shook her head. She pictured this woman in New York, rubbing elbows with the artsy-fartsy snobs at cocktail parties, and she felt sorry for her. Tommy was a successful, intelligent man with a heart of gold, and Ty was the kind of son any mother would be proud of.

"Her loss," she sighed. Hungrier than she realized, Ronda helped herself to more meatloaf.

Tommy adjusted in his seat. "So tell me about Nate."

"Ah, putting the shoe on the other foot?" Then she thought a moment and said, "I honestly don't know how to tell you about Nate. I feel like I barely know him anymore. We attended the same high school and dated. It didn't last long because he wanted to play the field. A month ago when I started working at your place, I saw him for the first time in twenty years. I wasn't even sure we were dating at first." She smiled at her lap and started twisting her napkin. "Sometimes he's really sweet and it makes me want a deeper relationship, but there's something...internal that holds me back."

"Hmmm. Well, it's kind of handy you know. As soon as you needed a private detective, he showed up."

"I know. Maybe it's one of those things like your truck driver showing up with the idea you needed, right when you needed it."

She stabbed a forkful of green beans. "Whatever it is, I shouldn't let him do all this work for me without pay. My involvement needs to be stepped up, so I was thinking I'd pop in on the Kennebunkport police during my day off and see what Captain Millman has to say."

"Sounds like a good idea. A thought just occurred to me." He appeared to be hesitating, but shrugged and proceeded. "Now, I may be out in left field, but did you ever consider that Nate may have had inside information? He knew exactly when to show up, knowing you'd need his PI services. I'm probably more suspicious than necessary, but I know the power a beautiful girl can hold over a man, and you said he's someone from your past..."

Ronda remembered the figure running from her house. Tall. Broad shoulders. Blond hair. *Holy mother of ... Maybe that's what the nagging reluctance has been about.*

"I—I don't know, Tommy. I guess it's possible but, then again, anything's possible." She pushed her plate away.

"I'm sorry. I know I should mind my own business, but sometimes I feel a little more like a father than a boss to some of my staff. You, Nanette, and Jenna, particularly."

CHAPTER EIGHT

Ronda had slept soundly and awakened refreshed for the first time in days. Over toaster waffles she and Tommy discussed the possibility of commuting. They were going to the same place at the same time, and Ronda was considering it because her Volvo was dangerously low on gas.

Playing with the MIA bracelet while they were talking, Ronda asked, "What do we say if anyone notices the two of us getting out of your Jeep?"

Tommy grinned. "Tell 'em you're sleeping with the boss."

She rolled her eyes. "That would be good for another month of gossip."

"It's really nobody's business who I drive to work, and hey, they're gonna talk. People do that," he said, matter-of-factly.

"I know. But I'd rather they talk about someone else for a change." Ronda stabbed a piece of toaster waffle with her fork.

"But you're fresh and new. They've worn out the old stories and jokes, and they're bored. You've injected new life into the place."

"You think so?"

"I know so. I can't tell you how many regulars have thanked me for hiring you." Tommy became more serious. "Ronnie, can I ask you a favor?"

"Sure."

He nodded at her wrist. "Can you keep that thing out of sight while you're working?"

"This?" She looked at the bracelet, then up at her boss. His forehead was creased. "Oh, sure, but why? Do you think people are going to think it refers to you?"

"I don't know what people are going to think, and I guess I do care what they might come up with. Of course I don't care if they think I'm fooling around with a good-looking young waitress, but that's my big Irish pride for you. I sure don't want them to think I spent years in the desert, eating scorpions, and hiding from the enemy long after the war ended."

"Gotcha. Consider it our secret."

A dark look passed over his eyes, but he quickly brightened and said, "Thanks."

She decided that she'd ride with Tommy that morning. Later she could get gas at the cheap station she preferred, drive to Old Orchard Beach to pick up her mail and check the locks.

As they were getting up from the table, she asked, "Why do people call you Tommy instead of Tom?"

"That goes back to my days in the Army," he said. "One of the guys drew a Dick Tracy-like cartoon of our outfit. We all got cute names. I was good with weapons so he called me Tommy Gunn. I guess it stuck."

They walked to the kitchen and placed the dirty dishes in the sink. Ronda rinsed them and put them into the dishwasher before Tommy could protest.

"Okay, so why 'Cousin'?"

"My cousin and I inherited the gas station together. He

had no interest in it. Bigwig in Hollywood now. I bought him out and that's when it became Cousin Tommy's."

"Clever," Ronda nodded. "I guess we'd better get going. I don't want to get in trouble with Antoine." Ronda swept her pocketbook up over her shoulder, and the MIA bracelet flew off the table. It fell to the floor making no noise as it hit the rug.

———

No one saw Ronda get out of Tommy's Jeep Grand Cherokee, so she didn't have to worry about more rumors taking on a life of their own. Antoine was his usual gruff, demanding self, and the only unusual situation was the number of tourists passing through.

"What gives?" Ronda asked Nanette. "That's the fourth busload of people today." Both waitresses hurried to accommodate the large brunch crowd.

"Canadians going home," Nanette called over her shoulder.

"Going home from where?"

Nanette shrugged and disappeared. Ronda hurried to a couple that had been waiting a little longer than they should have.

She pulled the order pad out of her apron pocket and asked, "What can I get you?"

"Well, you can get us a little service to begin with," grumbled the scowling man with a thick French accent.

"I'm sorry. We got really busy all of a sudden. But here I am. Do you know what you'd like to order?"

"Yes," said the woman without looking up. She spoke with the same accent and curtness. "Coffee, scrambled eggs, and white toast."

The gentleman ordered the same. Ronda was rushing to relay orders, pick them up, bus tables, get coffee, and ring up the register. She had no time for nonsense today. Tommy was in the convenience store. Today of all days, the young kid who worked there had called in sick.

Antoine was banging on his bell when Ronda ran over to pick up the scrambled egg orders. She turned and was ready to run to the table, thus proving to the couple how much she wanted to atone for the wait, and just as Nanette who had been bussing a large table with several plates covered in half-eaten food turned into her path. The eggs flew out of Ronda's hands, the plates crashed to the floor, food splattered all over Nanette's and Ronda's cute uniforms, and already frazzled nerves were now officially shot.

While Ronda stood there, her hands over her mouth in horror, Nanette picked off a hunk of scrambled egg and threw it at her. It was a direct hit in the chest.

Stunned, she didn't respond for a moment. "I'm so sorry. I'll clean up the mess, Nanette."

She let out a deep sigh. "No, I'll help." Before they were finished picking off pieces of egg and scooping up half-eaten pieces of toast and jelly, several customers were walking out, the charge led by the couple Ronda had been trying to serve.

"Oh my God. I think we just blew a great business day for Tommy."

"Well, there's not much we can do about it, is there? We still have to get the broken dishes off the floor." Nanette eyed Jenna shivering in the corner.

"You can help too, Jenna!"

Jenna had huddled there from the moment of the crash. She climbed over the counter and ran out back to alert Tommy.

Tommy walked in and his jaw dropped. When he looked around, all that could be seen were unhappy patrons filing out the front door. Peering over the counter he saw Nanette and Ronda picking up shards of plates with their bare fingers as fast as they could.

Tommy jumped over the counter and called to the girls, "Whoa. Don't touch another thing."

Ronda thought he was going to be furious.

"Let me get it with the dustpan. Antoine, bring that dustpan and brush around."

"Already there, boss." Antoine appeared a second later and handed the requested items to Tommy over the counter. Antoine's dark eyes flashed an angry look at the girls before he returned to the kitchen.

Ronda watched for a few seconds as Tommy grabbed the dustpan and brush and swept up the shards himself.

Finally he looked up at the girls and said, "Be careful back here, okay?" As soon as he finished cleaning, he rushed back to the convenience store.

The girls had to clean the worst of it off of their uniforms, and finish waiting on tables wearing grease stains. Roy tipped Ronda with a twenty either because he knew how badly she felt or because everyone but the regulars walked out and no amount of reassurance consoled her.

She suspected that Antoine's reaction was part of his territorial reflexes, but his glare stayed fresh in her mind. The only good thing to come of it, besides twenty bucks, was some female bonding while she and Nanette did a quick wash and dry of their uniforms during a lull.

There's something about sitting around on cases of canned peaches in your underwear that breaks down barriers, Ronda thought.

With nothing else to do but wait, Nanette had told her about life as a single parent, how the man she thought she could count on had disappeared without a trace, and they suddenly had something in common. Processing what had happened, they agreed it was a catastrophe that neither had to take full responsibility for. The topic ended there.

"I think we'll need lockers to keep a change of clothes in." Ronda chuckled. "I'll ask Tommy."

"I don't know if I'd ask Tommy for much of anything right now, Ronnie. After all, he's out there waiting tables with Jenna, and she's pretty useless most of the time, but especially after any kind of incident. She just shakes and looks like a deer in the headlights. After that, she goes into slow motion."

Ronda immediately thought of the incident when Nanette had refused to let her talk to Jenna about why she had been crying. Now that they were buddies, maybe Nanette would tell her something. "Why is she such a mouse?"

"Haven't you ever noticed the bruises?"

"Bruises? No!"

"I guess he's been behaving himself recently. She and the guy she lives with go through a bad patch once in a while."

"You mean he hits her?" The dryer buzzed and they both hopped up to get dressed.

"He likes to drag her to the stairs and give her a push."

"Jesus!" Ronda gasped. "She could break her neck that way."

"I think he's hoping she will."

"Good God."

By the end of their shift, the uniforms were clean, the counter was clean, the floor was clean, and Ronda was obsessing about how to help Jenna.

As she was leaving, she heard Antoine telling Dan, the evening cook, "You ain't gonna believe what happened here today..."

Time to go. Once in the parking lot, she looked around

for the black Volvo and had a moment of panic when she didn't see it. Then she remembered that she rode in with Tommy and groaned. He hadn't seemed upset, but she was not looking forward to the lecture she figured was coming on the way back to his house. A twenty-minute ride can seem like twenty hours if someone is upset. Ronda waited by the Cherokee until Tommy came out with a bounce in his step. He smiled, unlocked and opened her door for her, and then jogged around to the other side and hopped in.

Ronda slid in, cautiously. "You don't seem angry."

"Angry? Why should I be?"

She didn't know if he was being sincere or sarcastic.

"How'd you do in tips today, Ronnie?"

"I made a decent amount. Of course, twenty dollars of that was from Roy."

"What did I tell you? If you're good to the regulars, they'll take care of you."

"I don't feel like I was good to any of the customers today, or you. It could have been avoided if I just looked before I turned and ran head-on into Nanette."

"Are you kidding? Accidents happen. Besides, you gave them the best you had to give under the circumstances. There are those days when you've given a hundred and ten percent. You can't get upset about one incident when you look at the big picture."

Ronda raised her eyebrows. "So you're not upset?"

"Hell no." He pulled out of the parking lot. "You and Nanette cleaned up after yourselves, no one got hurt, and life will go on." He glanced over at her and one side of his mouth curled up. "Everyone who works for me does the best they can. Even Jenna. Thank you for being patient with her, Ronda. She may only have sixty percent to give some days, but if she gives her sixty percent, well then, she's doing the best she can."

Ronda could hardly believe her ears. *How wonderful is*

this man? She was a little surprised as a thought occurred to her. *Could he be the master teacher?*

"Tommy, can I ask you about something without starting a big panic?"

"Probably," he said. "I don't panic easily."

"I know, but it's about Jenna. I heard that her boyfriend is abusing her."

"Again?" Tommy's eyes widened and he gaped at her.

"No. I don't think it's recent. But from what Nanette told me, it sounds like she's been in real danger."

"I don't want you to think I'm cold or unsympathetic, but it's just unwise to get in the middle of these things. She knows she can crash with me anytime she needs to. My guest room is available to all of my employees in an emergency."

"And has she?"

"No. I doubt she ever will."

"Jesus. I wish there was more that could be done." Ronda sighed and shook her head. "This sort of thing just makes me furious."

"That's because you're healthy."

"I don't know. I've been in bad circumstances too at times. I seem to attract more than my share of non-commit-tals and control freaks."

"Not the same. Jenna still can't see the sickness, and until she wants help advice will be unwelcome, not to mention embarrassing," he said. "She'd probably deny it. It's best to help her when she wants to be helped."

Ronda was quiet during the rest of the drive to Tommy's house. Still, the situation remained unsettling. She frowned and fidgeted.

"Are you okay, Ronnie?

"Huh? Yeah." She retreated into her thoughts. Not knowing if Tommy would understand, she thought it was better not to mention the odd sensitivity she sometimes had that she called her "intuition". It was poking her in the ribs, yet she didn't know why.

On her way to the gas station, Ronda passed a car dealership. By the time she had filled up, she knew she was going back to have a look at the red Jeep Renegade she saw out front. It was used, that much she knew, but it looked to be in good shape and the price in the window seemed reasonable.

A couple of hours later, she was filling out the paperwork and saying 'Goodbye' to the car that screamed 'practical old lady' to her. The sales manager had even discounted the Jeep an extra fifty dollars when he found out that Ronda worked for Tommy.

"Could that be the Tommy Kelley I knew in 'Iraq" he said.

"Yeah, I guess it could be. He was over there."

"Tommy, well, well. Last I heard he was listed as missing. I owe that man my life. The least I can do is give his employee a good price on reliable transportation."

Remembering that Tommy denied the MIA status, she asked, "But what if it isn't him?"

"No matter. Just in case it might be, let me give you a little discount."

I bet you say that to all the waitresses.

She figured that in Maine, a four-wheel drive was the only way to get where you were going when winter didn't want anyone to get anywhere. Even near the beach, snowdrifts over her head were not unheard of.

Ordinarily, without the inertia of grief, she would have enjoyed the camaraderie of neighbor helping neighbor to free their cars from their snow-encased prisons last winter. But, she was a depressed couch potato. She let her car sit in the driveway until ice storms on top of snowstorms rendered her immobile. She'd stocked up with the belief that getting snowbound beat having to talk to people.

She reflected on how much better she was feeling now that June had arrived and the weather was warm and blissful. She would take care of the car's registration and inspection tomorrow. She swung by her house to literally pick up her mail. Mr. Carroll was out on his front porch reading his newspaper, which he held up to his nose. Ronda waved as she strolled to her door.

"Nice day, eh, Ronda?" he said.

"Yeah. You like?"

"Uh huh. Almost makes me want to cut the grass." They both laughed as they looked at the small garden of rocks and sparse ground cover that substituted for a lawn.

"How's Talon?" Ronda asked. "I hope she's not too much trouble."

"Oh, no. She's behaving nicely. How're you?"

"I'm behaving nicely too. Thanks again for watching her. I'll probably be coming home real soon."

"I'm not sure that's a good idea, Ronda. I saw a young man coming out of your house again."

She had unlocked her door as he was talking and caught her breath. Not only had he said that he saw another intruder, but there was evidence. The mail had landed on her floor in a neat pile. That never happened. She relocked the front door and left the house right away instead of checking messages or picking up extra clothes.

Strolling over to Mr. Carroll, she asked, "What exactly did you see?"

"I didn't think anything of it the first time because it was your boyfriend and you were there. He was running like a bat outta hell though, so I figured maybe you used the "M" word and scared him half to death."

"No, nothing like that." She would have laughed if not for her anxiety. "You're sure it was Nate?"

"Pretty sure. Looked real sharp in a brown sweater and tan pants. I thought he was all dressed up to take you out. But then he came by later, after you left."

Ronda's emotions were a jumble—mostly anger. She waved goodbye to her neighbor and hit the road back to Scarborough.

This is the last straw. Nate has to go. She didn't care if he was a fabulous sex partner in the middle of a free-of-charge investigation. She'd get a restraining order if she had to. What gave him the right to poke around inside her house? It felt downright stalker-ish.

As she was entering Scarborough, her wrath had simmered down enough for her to think about the name of the town, now her sanctuary—Scarborough. It must be a healing place—just the word 'scar' meant there was once a wound, but it was healing or healed. Some wounds, even once fully healed, left a scar. Ronda knew she was changed forever. Her scars would always be part of her.

When Ronda reached Tommy's house just before six o'clock, she had calmed down enough to think clearly. He was setting the table and flashed a big bright smile when she came through the door.

"You're right on time!"

"I didn't mean to cut it so close, but I bought a car today. From a friend of yours, maybe."

"Really? Who?"

"Willie Guest."

"Who?"

"You don't know a Willie Guest?" she asked.

Tommy seemed to consider the possibility before shaking his head, dismissing it. "Willie Guest; Billy Guest; Bill Guest. Nope. I don't know any of 'em."

"Huh. I suppose he might have been handing me a line."

"Probably," Tommy said. "Salesmen do that all the time hoping you'll buy from them instead of the guy down the street."

"I guess so." She remembered having made the decision to buy long before the dealer offered a discount.

"Well, I hope you're hungry," Tommy said, "Because we have delicious leftovers heating up."

While he was in the kitchen, Ronda looked around for her MIA bracelet and realized it wasn't where she had left it. She searched the area, including down on the floor and under the table, but didn't see it.

Coming to the table with steaming dishes, Tommy asked, "So what kind of car did you buy?"

"A red Jeep Renegade," she said smiling.

"Nice sporty vehicle."

"Yeah. Low miles too. By the way, have you seen my MIA bracelet anywhere?"

"No. The housekeeper came today. Maybe she found it and stuck it somewhere. I'll call her and ask tomorrow."

"No. Don't bother. Either it will turn up or it won't. Sometimes when things disappear, it means they've served their purpose. It's some sort of Eastern philosophy, I think."

He smiled. "You sound like Ty. Oh, I almost forgot. Nate called you."

"How did he get your num..." Ronda stopped because she knew the answer to her question and was instantly annoyed. "Talk about things that have served their purpose," she mumbled to herself. "Yeah. I need to speak to him. Did he leave a number where I could call him?"

"No. He said you knew the number."

"Well, I know the number of his answering service, that's all."

"You sound a little upset. Is everything okay with Nate?"

"Yeah. Everything's peachy."

"Well, if you want some privacy, there's a phone in the study."

"Thank you. I'm not sure I want to call him tonight. I think I'll wait until tomorrow."

"Whatever you want to do, Ronnie."

"Can I ride in with you again tomorrow? I'm not supposed to let anything happen to the Volvo until the trade-in."

"Of course," Tommy said. "Feeling like veering off into a bridge abutment?"

"If only it were that easy."

CHAPTER NINE

The next day was fairly uneventful except that Antoine saw her stepping out of the boss's car first thing in the morning.

"Don't worry about the teasing," Tommy said. "It'll die down when we tell them the story about your car suddenly dying. I've been known to carpool employees rather than work short-staffed."

"The beauty of the story is that I'll be driving my new car the next time they see me. So our credibility will remain intact."

"Not to mention our stellar reputations." He elbowed her gently in the ribs as they walked to the back door.

The day crawled by and she couldn't wait until the evening shift arrived. Ronda was restocking the items behind the counter and checking the clock every few minutes. Hearing an unfamiliar female voice saying her name, she whirled around. A tall woman, wearing a blue scarf tied around her head had come up to the counter.

"Excuse me. I didn't mean to startle you," she said sweetly.

"Oh, no, that's all right. Just daydreaming."

"My name is Monica Pierce, and I'd like to ask you a few questions."

Ronda stared at her for a moment, remembering the reporter's description. "I'm sorry," she stated without being sorry at all. "I don't talk to reporters."

"I'm not a reporter. I work for a research and paranormal investigation foundation, and I need to talk with you about your family."

Ronda stepped back, unable to speak for a moment. Her sister's spirit and Nate's report mentioned researchers. "Do you have any credentials?"

"I do." The woman produced a card and contract from her pocketbook.

"Monica Pierce. Paranormal Investigator." Ronda turned her attention to the contract and pocketed the card. Ronda's name was signed at the bottom, but in someone else's hand-writing.

"Nanette," she yelled toward the opening that led to the hall.

Nanette's voice called back, "I'm on my break, but, yeah?"

"Could you be a sweetheart and take the counter for me, please?"

After a pause, Nanette popped her head around the corner, glanced at the woman in the scarf standing opposite Ronda, and must have realized it was important. "Yeah, I guess so."

"Thanks. You can have my tips."

Nanette tied on her apron, pocketed the three dollars on the counter, and let them sit down at a booth.

Ronda picked up the contract again and pointed to the signature. "This isn't mine."

"I know. As soon as we found out that the signature was forged we suspended what we were doing and tried to get in touch with you."

"What was this for, exactly?" she asked.

"Ronda, I'm a member of a group that researches paranormal activity. I've seen and heard many unexplainable things in this line of work. Right now I'm interested in gathering concrete evidence of life after death. We need grant money to continue our work."

Ronda cocked her head. "Okay, but what does that have to do with me?"

"We've found that parents who are suddenly separated from their children in an unexpected death, often come through."

"Are you a psychic?"

"We prefer the term 'sensitive', so as not to be confused with 1-900 number so-called psychics. Yes, I'm a sensitive, but not all of us are. We take scientific readings of energy fluctuations in homes when possible because spirit entities may return to familiar places and familiar people."

What a strange profession. "Why do you do this?"

"Because I believe in it. I'd like to provide some scientific proof to those who seem to need it, and..." Monica removed the scarf to reveal a badly balding head. "I may be going to the other side sooner than I thought."

Ronda let out an unintentional gasp.

"Our work at your childhood home was proving very fruitful," Monica said, retying the scarf. "If we could get your permission to continue..."

"Um, I'll have to think about it."

She believed her. She knew she could be somewhat gullible, yet everyone in this drama remained sincere and in character. She hadn't yet discovered a misstep or so much as a divulging facial expression. *Someone has to be lying.*

"Monica," Ronda began hesitantly, "I would like to help you, but I need to think about it. Can you give me some time?"

"Of course. We were hoping to get back into your

parents' home as soon as possible, but we can wait a day or two. Oh, there's one other thing."

"What's that?"

"We hope you'll be able to spend some time with us there. Were you in the house on Sunday?"

Ronda nodded.

"On Sunday our readings of spirit energy shot off the charts for a while. I can only assume that your presence made the difference."

"I won't appear on TV or anything?" Ronda asked.

"No. You can be doing whatever you like elsewhere in the house."

Ronda thought about how she had wished Officer Donnelly would sit there while she packed the contents, simply so she wouldn't be alone. Maybe she could do some packing with the researchers there.

"I'll definitely consider it," Ronda said. "Oh, also, when did you arrive?"

"Sunday morning. We spoke to the police on Monday and discovered things were probably set up, not by you, but by someone claiming to be you. We got right out. By the way," Monica continued, "who hired the private detective?"

"That would be nobody," Ronda said. "He's my too controlling, soon-to-be, ex-boyfriend."

"Oh. I'm glad to hear that," Monica said. "He was a bit unorthodox."

"What did he do?"

"Well, someone—I'm not saying for sure that it was him —but a man cost us some very important equipment and evidence when he kicked over our recording devices as he ran out the back door. I don't know where he had been hiding or why."

Ronda's mouth was open but no words came out.

She was quiet all the way back to Scarborough, ruminating over everything that had happened. Tommy drove silently, but she was aware of him looking over at her periodically.

The vandalism didn't sound like Nate. He was Mr. Law-abiding-citizen, or so she thought. Maybe she didn't know him at all. She wished she could tell Tommy but she didn't want to drag him into it. He hesitated to get involved with his employees' boyfriend troubles, and Nate was her problem. Once he dropped her at her car, Tommy wished her luck with the new one.

Driving toward Old Orchard, she thought of her father and, with eyes watering, wondered why he was the only one who didn't show up in her readings with Janice. Instead of going straight to the dealership with red, teary eyes, she drove to her cottage.

Ronda wandered inside to check her mail and messages and felt a little better when she noticed that the mail was thrown all over the floor, as usual. Checking the answering machine there were three messages. One was Monica from Monday. She had already talked to her. The next was Marci Jo, keeping in touch, and the other was Janice. She didn't say why she had called, she simply asked Ronda to get back to her when she could. She called her right away.

"I don't usually do this," she heard Janice say, "but I received a message that I believe was for you."

Ronda's eyes grew wide. "What can you tell me?"

"I believe it was your father who came through."

"Really?" Ronda was stunned but grateful. She had just been thinking of him, and it looked as if he hadn't forgotten her after all.

"He showed me something that makes no sense to me. I hope it makes sense to you. Do you know of any fruit in their house? He showed me fruit. It wasn't symbolic. There's something of importance about some kind of fruit. Apples, grapes, pears."

"Well, I already cleaned out the fridge. The only fruit I know of is a still-life painting on the wall."

"That's probably it then," Janice said. "Look behind it. It could be hiding a safe or maybe there's a key taped to it. If not, have it appraised. I get the sense that something about it is very valuable. They don't often contact me after the client has left."

Ronda thanked Janice, impressed that she would go to the trouble of calling her with more information, free of charge. She knew she'd have to look at that painting more closely, but she had two more calls to make and a car to buy, first.

She'd call Marci Jo next and save the hard one for last—Nate. Meanwhile, she called his answering service to leave the message to call her.

To her surprise, she didn't get the answering service. The receptionist put her right through.

"Ronnie. I've left messages. Didn't Tommy tell you to call me?"

"Yes. I just wasn't ready to talk to you until now."

"Are you okay?"

"I'm fine, Nate, but I'm wondering, what the hell is the matter with you?"

"Pardon me? I have no idea what you're talking about."

"Oh, of course not. I suppose you thought no one saw you running out of my cottage that day, but somebody did."

"Wait a minute. You think that I was in your cottage? Ronda, I haven't been to your home except for the two times you let me in."

"Why should I believe you?"

"I don't know why you shouldn't believe me. I have to lie occasionally, but I don't make a habit of it, and I certainly don't want to lie to you. I hear that relationships are built on trust." He emphasized the last word.

"Okay. Well, what do you have to say about the equipment you knocked over belonging to the psychic research team?"

"What? Ronda, someone's messing with us. I didn't touch any equipment belonging to the research group. Why would I?"

"I don't know. I was told that you came out of hiding and kicked something over as you ran from my parents' house."

"I was with the captain and lieutenant all that morning. Check if you don't believe me."

Ronda was more confused than ever. "Who could be messing with us and why? Nate, I don't know what to think anymore."

"Neither do I. I'm kind of surprised you thought I could do those things, Ronnie. First of all, I have no need to break into your house. If I asked nicely, you'd let me in. Secondly, I would never get in the way of research. I respect that process, and third—I told you I'd never hurt you. More now than ever. I think I'm falling in love with you."

She couldn't speak. The long silence was stretching out.

"Ronda ... Ronnie?"

"I'll call you back," she said, curtly, and hung up.

"Oh my God," she groaned, pinching the bridge of her nose. She wandered into the kitchen and made a cup of tea while dialing Marci Jo.

"Hey, Ronda, how are you?"

"Put it this way. Do you have about an hour?"

"For you? Of course. Just let me run to the bathroom, first."

Ronda was able to organize her thoughts while Marci Jo was off the phone. When they talked, she told her everything.

"Damn. You've had it rough, Ronnie."

"My head is spinning. I don't know what to think or who to trust."

"Well, you can trust me."

"That much I know. Thank God I have one good friend around who has nothing to do with this."

"I wish I knew what to tell you as far as who to trust, but other than Tommy, I can't. I think you might not want to give up on Nate just yet. It could be someone trying to get you to push him out of the picture."

"I know, but I was kinda getting angry at Nate before these incidents happened."

"What didn't you like about him?"

"Specifically, he shows up everywhere I am without calling. I feel like he's watching me."

"That's fixable. Tell him he's driving you crazy and to stop that. Be assertive."

"I'm not usually wishy-washy, am I?"

"No. But, if he's worth a second try, be definite and serious about what you want. If he really cares about you, he'll listen. If not, he's a controlling jackass who knows how you feel and doesn't give a damn."

"Yeah." Thinking about his kisses and smile and the way he looked at her, she melted inside. "I guess he is worth it."

"Well, good. I'd like to meet him sometime."

"That would be great actually, especially since I could use a second opinion."

The next day, Captain Millman was busy when Ronda arrived, and she realized that she should have made an appointment. The one thing she really had to do to ease her mind about Nate was to double-check his story about entering her parents' house with the cops and being with them afterwards. Still, if the story proved to be true, then who kicked over the researchers' equipment and why did he want to ruin their evidence? She elected to wait for the captain, however long it took.

Just as she was beginning to check for split ends, a habit she slid into when extremely bored, Captain Millman sauntered around the partition and invited her into his office.

"There's only so much I can tell you about an ongoing investigation, Ronda, but you may be able to help us if you have any additional or conflicting information."

"Of course. I'd like to help any way I can."

"The group had a contract, but your signature was forged and they seemed genuinely upset about it," Millman began.

"Was Nate with you?"

"Yeah. He was pretty quiet. Of course, we told him we'd do all the talking. He just hung back until it came time to examine the contract. That's when he said the signature wasn't yours, and that's how we knew right away that something was up."

"Did he say how he knew it wasn't mine?"

"He said he had a copy of something you signed for him."

That's weird.

She told the captain about the possibility a customer in her restaurant was spying on her. She talked about her nearsighted neighbor who saw someone, possibly Nate, running from her house. She told him that the researchers blamed "the private detective" for ruining their equipment. She said that she confronted Nate and he seemed sincerely surprised by the accusation—and she confessed that she wanted to check out that story for herself because she wasn't sure whether or not she should trust her boyfriend. She even relayed to him how Nate could find her anywhere, and she wondered if he was following her.

"Ronda, thanks for coming in. This was very helpful. I

just want to put your mind at ease about a couple of things. First of all, as you suspected, Nate was here with us at the time of the incident. That gives him a pretty solid alibi for the vandalism."

"Then who did it and why?"

"Good question. Do you know anyone of similar description who might want Nate out of the way?"

Ronda racked her brain until it rattled. "I honestly can't think of anyone. My old boyfriend, Michael, is similar in height, but not build. He's thin and has dark brown hair."

"Heads can be shaved, hair can be dyed and bulk can be added or subtracted. Have you seen him lately?" Millman asked.

"No. No one has. He disappeared recently. Apparently he got cold feet on his way to the altar."

"Is that the case Nate was originally investigating?"

"Yes. I guess our little corner of Maine is giving him plenty of business."

"To your knowledge, has Michael ever met Nate?"

"No. I don't think so. He sat down with Lorena, Michael's fiancée, but Michael was already missing. I showed Nate a picture of him. He didn't act like he knew him."

"What does this Michael do for a living?"

"He's a freelance writer. In the past, he has sold insurance, been a white-water rafting guide, substitute teacher, lifeguard, and a few other temporary things—but what he really wanted to do was to buy his own plane and become a bush pilot."

"Does he have his pilot's license?"

"Yes. He rented a Cessna and took me up once. Once was enough for me."

"You like good, ol' terra firma, do you?"

"I did then, and I do now—especially after what happened to my parents." Her eyes became misty.

"Of course. I'm sorry. Well, I won't keep you any longer,

Ronda. Thank you for coming in." He escorted her down the hall to the front door.

"And thank you for looking into all of this."

The captain held the door for her. "I'll let you know if anything else comes up."

On the way back to Scarborough she ruminated over the clues she had. Nate seemed to be on the up and up. She realized that perhaps what Mr. Carroll saw without his glasses was a well-dressed man with light hair, and what his mind envisioned was Nate—someone he knew who fit the description.

And if someone might be trying to impersonate him, to get her angry enough to push him out of her life that made sense. Nate's presence on her side might be very inconvenient. Now where had Nate seen her signature?

As soon as she returned to Tommy's she called Nate. Leaving a message, she waited for him to call her back. At ten o'clock she was still waiting.

CHAPTER TEN

Ugh. I blew it. What's the matter with me, anyhow? She thought about how she ended their last phone call. Nate Smith was probably the best thing to happen to her in two years. She was beginning to think that she probably deserved this when the phone rang. Startled, she picked it up after only one ring and said an anxious "Hello?"

There was a long pause. Finally an unexpected voice said, "Is my father there?"

"Ty?" Ronda asked.

"Yes. Who's this?"

"Ronda ... Ronda Calhoun."

"Really?" Ty's voice betrayed his amazement.

"Oh, it's not what you might be thinking. I had to stay in your guest room for a couple of nights because someone broke into my house."

"Oh. Geez, I'm sorry. Are you okay? Is your place all right?"

"Yes and yes. I don't think I'll be here much longer. In fact I thought you were Nate calling me back. I was going to ask permission to go home."

"You have to ask his permission?"

Ronda chuckled, more at herself than at Ty. "I guess when someone violates your space you can turn into a little girl in nothing flat."

"I understand. I'm not sure *I* wouldn't turn into a little girl. Listen, not to cut you short, but I have to talk to my dad about his flight plans so that I know when to pick him up at the airport."

"Oh, of course. Let me get him." Ronda pressed the hold button, leaned over the railing outside the guest room, and called, "TOMMY, it's TY."

Ronda, giving up on Nate, turned out the light, put her head on the pillow, and tried to sleep. About five minutes after her light was out, the phone rang again.

This time Tommy answered and yelled upstairs. "RONDA, it's NATE."

She sat up, flicked on the light and picked up the phone. "Nate?"

"Yes. You called me?" His voice sounded flat and matter of fact.

"Yeah, I did. First of all, I want to apologize for hanging up on you earlier. Are you mad at me?"

"Well my ego was bruised, but I'm okay. No, I'm not mad."

"Good. Um ... that was really sweet what you said before."

"I'm sorry, Ronnie. It was premature, and you have other things on your mind."

"Yeah, but I didn't have to be terrified. I'm really sorry. Honest."

"Forget it. Listen, when can I see you?"

"Tomorrow night at my cottage? I think it's safe to go back there, don't you?"

"Sure. Whatever you want. It's up to you."

"Seriously?"

Nate chuckled. "Yeah."

"What's so funny?"

"I'll tell you tomorrow. What time?"

"I don't know ... around six?"

"I should be able to get up there by six. Can I take you out to dinner?"

"How about if I cook?"

"Can you?" He sounded surprised, and she didn't know if he was serious or not.

"Of course I can. Or, at least I can learn by tomorrow night."

They both chuckled and she hung up happy. Ronda flopped backward onto the bed, relieved. He was cute and good to her and awfully smart. Thank God he was forgiving too. Falling asleep after that was no trouble at all.

The next day Ronda and Jenna were working without Nanette, since she was scheduled to work over the weekend. Ronda was a pro by now, able to relax and have fun while being the ever-efficient one, but she and Jenna were having many of the same problems that Nanette and Jenna were having. The difference was that Ronda vowed not to get upset about it. If she had to work a bit harder to take up the slack, then she'd do it without grumbling. Jenna had enough problems, and she didn't want to add to them.

Shortly before Ronda's shift was over, as she was refilling Ed's coffee cup for the third time and dreaming of a foot massage, someone breezed up to the counter and took a seat. Ronda's back was turned since she was returning the coffee pot to its warmer.

She heard a nasal female voice. "Excuse me, Miss. Can you tell me what's in the mystery meat sandwich?"

Ronda whirled around, recognizing the wise-ass attitude. "Marci Jo. I knew you'd decide to come slumming sometime."

They hugged over the counter and the regulars made crude comments as if they were all turned on.

"Oh, quit your acting," Ronda scolded.

"We're not acting," Ed said, gleefully.

Ronda rolled her eyes and spoke to Marci Jo. "I don't know how to tell you this, but it's really busy today, and I'm going to be waiting on the counter, the first row of tables, and taking care of the register. I don't think I'll have much time to visit."

"Jesus. I don't know how much Tommy's paying you, but I'm recommending he give you a raise."

"Ha. Go ahead, for all the good it'll do. The first raise is in six months. I've been here less than six weeks."

"Honestly, if I had any idea you'd be working this hard, I would never have recommended you for this job."

Ed interjected, "You recommended her for the job?"

"Yeah, what of it?"

The eight regulars sitting at the counter said in one breath, "Thanks, Marci Jo."

Marci Jo glanced at Ronda with mischief in her eyes. "Isn't it wonderful? If you have a nice face and an even nicer body, you can make people wait hours for their fish and chips, and everybody still loves you."

"Thanks, Marci Jo," Ronda echoed with her most sarcastic intonation. "Oops, I'm needed over at the register."

Bouncing back and forth between the counter, register and dining room, waiting on customers, ringing up the register and filling the salt, pepper, sugar and catsup for the next shift wasn't Ronda's idea of quality visiting time. After getting Marci Jo her coffee and pie, she had to ignore her friend until the end of the shift. Marci Jo didn't seem to mind. She and Ed were sparring with their sword-sharp humor. Finally the dinner shift came in, and Ronda was never so happy to see them. She grabbed Marci Jo's hand and dragged her out of the restaurant.

"Hey, you were on fire in there," Marci Jo said.

"Yeah, where's a cute firefighter when you need one?" Ronda groaned. "Oh my God, Marci Jo, my feet *are* on fire. I'm supposed to cook dinner for Nate tonight and I haven't even shopped yet. Oh, I can't do this."

"Look, I'm here for the weekend. Why don't I shop on the way to your house, cook dinner, meet Nate briefly, and then get lost?"

"You would do all that for me?"

"Sure. I have to do something to make up for getting you into this crummy job."

Ronda laughed out loud. "Marci Jo, I'd be so grateful for whatever help you can give me, but don't worry about getting me into anything. I actually love this crummy job."

Ronda made it home, changed into a short, fitted denim skirt and a white eyelet top with thin straps. The effect was a mix of sexy and innocent. Once on the porch she soaked her sore feet in a plastic dishpan of warm water. Marci Jo finally pulled up in front and stepped out with two bags of groceries.

"Wow, you probably spent too much."

"Yeah, and took too long. Did you know there's only one grocery store in town? I had to go clear to Saco to get shallots and a decent red wine."

"Oh? What's a shallot? Never mind. Hey, what are we making?"

"Oysters and Spanish fly."

"Cut it out. What are we really making?"

"Roast Beef with a shallot and pepper rub, rice pilaf and

asparagus, a couple of bottles of Bordeaux, and for dessert, chocolate mousse."

"You're joking."

"What's wrong with it?"

"Nothing's wrong with it. It's perfect, except that I have no idea how to make it happen."

"Which is why I'm making it."

"I can't let you do all of that by yourself."

"Sure you can. Now sit there and soak your feet before I tell you to soak your head."

Ronda sighed and sunk her feet into the warm water and her back into the chair cushions. As Marci Jo took everything into the kitchen, Ronda called after her.

"Are you sure you don't want to move here?"

"Why? So I can do all your cooking full time?"

"No, only dinners. I can grab breakfast and lunch at the restaurant."

The sounds of chuckling, crumpling paper and chopping emanated from the kitchen. Soon the sound of sizzling was followed by the most delicious aroma.

Ronda was so grateful for a friendship like this. She had missed her New York friends, and now that they had all found their immortal mates it didn't look like they'd be coming back anytime soon—if at all.

"So Calhoun," Marci Jo yelled from the other room. "Have you slept with him yet?"

Ronda burst out laughing. "You realize that all the neighbors on the street can hear us, right?"

Mr. Carroll from next door yelled in his loudest trembling old man voice, "Tell us, Ronda. We all want to know."

Marci Jo stumbled out to the porch and hugged Ronda, and both of them collapsed in laughter. When one of them started to recover, the other would start laughing again and so the cycle continued. It was the first time Ronda had laughed like that since her parents died.

The two girls were rolling on the floor, giggling out of control when someone cleared his throat.

Marci Jo saw him first. She punched Ronda's shoulder. "Hey, Ronnie. There's a handsome stranger at your door."

Ronda looked up and saw Nate standing there and wondered how much he had heard. She blushed and began laughing all over again, but managed to tell him to come in.

Nate was smiling but looked confused at the same time as he stepped tentatively through the porch door. "What's so funny, ladies?"

Ronda was still composing herself. Marci Jo answered him. "I don't think it can be repeated. It would lose something in translation. Hi, I'm Marci Jo." She jumped up and shook Nate's hand.

"Hi, Marci Jo. Nate Smith."

Ronda cleared her throat, and could speak again. "I'm sorry. I should have made introductions."

"Relax, Ronnie. It's just us. The Etiquette Police will not be called," Marci Jo quipped.

"These are for you, beautiful," Nate said, and he handed Ronda the roses. "I'm sorry I didn't bring two dozen. Had I known you were here, Marci Jo, I would have."

Ronda planted a firm kiss on his lips and thanked him. Before proceeding to the kitchen to place the flowers in water, she offered him a glass of wine while dinner was cooking.

"Traffic north was horrendous, and wine would be much appreciated. Thank you." He sat on the loveseat and scratched Talon under her chin.

Marci Jo followed Ronda into the kitchen to finish making dinner and whispered, "He's wonderful. What's to second-guess? I'll leave you two alone as soon as the roast is ready."

Ronda poured three glasses of wine, insisting that Marci Jo stay for dinner. Marci Jo had made enough for a family of six, so there was no need to worry about including one more. Nevertheless, Marci Jo said she knew when to leave and would depart right after dessert and coffee.

"This is delicious," Nate said after swallowing one bite of the roast.

Marci Jo smiled inwardly. "Yes, Ronnie, it's really good."

"Oh, stop pretending. Marci Jo made it, Nate. Work was very busy, and I was so tired I probably would have given you hot dogs."

Nate chuckled. "I would have understood. If you're ever too tired to cook I can bring take out with me. This was awfully nice of you, Marci Jo."

"Oh, don't worry about it. She'd do the same for me."

"Yeah, if you wanted hot dogs, I would."

Nate smiled, shook his head, and tried some asparagus. "So, where are you staying this weekend, Marci Jo?"

"I pulled some travel agent strings and booked a room with an ocean view in Ogunquit."

"Nice. Are you planning to stay all weekend?"

"I might. Are you?"

"Probably. I have a case I'm working on up here, and there are some loose ends to tie up."

Pausing with her fork in midair, Ronda asked, "Are you getting that close?"

Nate hesitated, then said, "I'll tell you all about it, but later, okay?" He glanced at Marci Jo and she jumped up.

"I'll go check on dessert."

"Ronnie, there is something to tell, but not in front of anyone else."

"Sure." She trusted Marci Jo, but Nate had just met her. She was so tired that she'd be better able to concentrate tomorrow, anyway.

Once Marci Jo was thanked profusely, and the dishes were cleared, Nate and Ronda were alone, at last. Nate wanted very much to showcase his talents as a remarkable lover.

The chill coming off the ocean cooled the house noticeably, so Ronda closed the front door. Meanwhile Nate found some music to play on the sound system. He selected a piano instrumental which proved to be soft, sexy and perfect.

Ronda lit some candles and curled up with Nate on the couch, covering both of them with a soft plaid blanket. He breathed in her perfume and was ready to make his move.

Ronda must have sensed it, because she pulled back slightly and looked at him. "Nate?"

"Yes, beautiful?" he said in a sexy whisper.

"Where have you seen my signature before?"

That wasn't a question he had been anticipating, and he cocked his head to side.

"The police and the researchers said that you knew it wasn't my signature because I had signed something for you, and I don't remember signing anything."

"Oh." He took her hand and began drawing circles on her palm. "In high school you passed me a note. I kept it."

"You're kidding. You remember what it looked like from that?"

"Well, I read it a few times. You said some very nice things about me." He smiled and kissed her knuckles. "And you signed my yearbook." He gathered Ronda into his arms and she leaned into him. He kissed her tenderly as she slid her arms around his neck.

He opened his mouth, deepening the kiss, and she responded. Their tongues explored. As they kissed, he gently ran his fingers over her ear and neck until she shivered.

He slowly lowered her to the couch and let his hands move over her beautiful body. Her nipples were hard nubs and he gave each of them a gentle pinch. He bent over her and kissed her more fervently, running his hand down her leg and up under her skirt. The fire ignited between them. Their breathing grew deeper and Ronda's chest rose to meet his.

He let go of her lips, and looking deeply into her shining eyes he slowly unbuttoned her white cotton top. She smiled up at him and stroked his arms. He touched, cupped and squeezed her breasts. As he fondled, she reached down and unhooked his belt, then slid his zipper down. His arousal swelled.

Ronda actually became limp in his embrace—or maybe it was the wine. His need was growing hotter and more insistent. She stroked his erection and Nate seized the opportune moment. "Time for bed, beautiful."

Picking her up in his arms, he carried her upstairs to her queen sized bed.

"Nate?"

"Yes, love?"

"I'm unprotected and it's a dangerous time in my cycle." Before he could comment, she added, "There are a couple of condoms in the medicine cabinet for emergencies."

Nate smiled, leaned over, kissed her hard and said he'd be back in a minute. While he was in the bathroom he took the time to brush his teeth with his finger, urinate, wash up a bit, and find the condoms.

He hesitated after he picked up only one rubber. What the hell, better to have both if they were needed, so he snatched the other one too. When Nate returned to their love nest, Ronda was sound asleep in it.

———

The next morning when Ronda awoke, she was groggy and out of it. Quickly she discovered Nate in bed next to her. The sheet covered most of him, but his naked torso rose and fell with the steady rhythm of sleep.

All she could remember was tossing her skirt and blouse onto the floor while Nate was in the bathroom—nothing after that. She'd had more than her share of wine the night before and that may have contributed, but she had a sneaking suspicion that maybe it was sleep that cut off her memory.

She lifted the blanket and saw that she and Nate were still in their Calvin Klein's. Then she spotted the two unopened condoms on the nightstand.

This was the first time she'd ever woken up with regret because she *didn't* have sex with someone.

Slipping out of bed, she gently tiptoed to the bathroom. She washed up, removed yesterday's panties and slipped into her satin robe. Then she walked softly down the creaky wooden stairs. She hoped a good breakfast would atone for falling asleep, leaving them both unfulfilled. At least she knew how to whip up scrambled eggs and pancakes. She decided to get everything prepared and wait for Nate to wake up naturally.

She didn't have to wait long. As the pancake batter was blending in the mixer on low, she felt his arms glide around her waist from behind. She was about to make coffee but had to set the glass carafe on the counter because he was kissing her neck and her knees were weakening. She was aware of his large, hard cock rubbing between the cheeks of her ass.

She turned and saw that he had tucked a condom in his waistband. She didn't protest the time or the place. He lowered her to the floor and kissed her tenderly. Slipping his hand under the loose robe he pulled the tie open, and the robe slid off of her shoulders. She wriggled out of the sleeves as he removed his briefs.

They fell together, at last, with nothing getting in the way, and nothing stopping them—as if anything could have.

Nate seemed to want to satisfy her completely, paying special attention to her most sensitive places. Her neck, her breasts, her lips, her knees but mostly her clitoris. She let out a long moan, arched and quivered when he touched her there. God, he made her feel primitive as she suppressed the urge to beg him to fuck her—right fucking now.

Taking his time, he demonstrated a smooth and graceful style of lovemaking. To Ronda it seemed as if they had been lovers for a long time. She was delighted that she didn't have to say a word. He knew exactly what she loved.

He had already admitted to her that he was falling in love. She was about ready to admit the same, at least to herself. She would tell him later, when the time was right—when he wouldn't think it was just the heat of the moment. For now, it was enough that she knew.

He was rock hard and obviously very aroused as was she. Nate breathed heavily and Ronda caught her breath more than once as they licked, nipped and petted. To Ronda's delight, foreplay was something Nate didn't skimp on. She needed this deep, visceral pleasure more than she had realized. As he massaged her clit and suckled her nipples, she felt her pleasure build to ever-increasing peaks, and her initial orgasm left her limp and breathless.

As soon as she caught her breath, he moved between her legs and took her sensitized clit into his mouth. She arched and gasped while he sucked her there. God help her, he wasn't letting up and she was quivering all over. The familiar sensation of a building volcanic blast soon followed. He stopped sucking and licked her into another shaking, shattering, blissful release.

Despite feeling weak all over, she wanted to satisfy him

as much as he was satisfying her. She pushed him onto his back and scooted down next to his cock.

"You don't have to, sweetheart."

"I want to," she said. "I mean that." She took his cock in her mouth and slid down on it slowly. He was so big that she couldn't fit all of him in her mouth, but she'd try to take him as deep as she could. He moaned in pleasure as she sucked hard and withdrew all the way to the reddened tip. She licked and kissed the shaft and devoured him again, sucking even harder as she was pulling back slowly. He groaned and tangled his hands in her hair. She knew this was the best way to make up for last night. The way to a man's heart is a little lower than his stomach, so she kept up her sensuous, hard suction and increased the speed. She was going down on him hard and fast and he was responding with moans of encouragement.

"Oh, honey. You're so good at that. Ohhh..." After a few more seconds he pulled back. "You've got to stop."

"I don't want to. I want you to come in my mouth."

"No, darling. I want to *fuck*."

She smiled and rose to her hands and knees. "Don't hold back. Tell me what you want."

"Stay right where you are. I want to take you from behind. I'll slide my cock into your sweet pussy and we can fuck our brains out."

Ronda was unbelievably turned on. She extended her ass toward him. His great erect cock wasn't sheathed yet. He touched and probed her with his finger. She knew she was more than wet and ready.

He found the condom that had fallen out of his underwear when he yanked them off. She heard the package rip open and pictured him unrolling it over his arousal. At last she could feel his cock at her opening.

She murmured his name, clutched the rug and leaned into him as they finally coupled. Swept away, she couldn't have been happier in a king-size bed than she was at that moment on a braided rug, rocking her body onto his cock, listening to him groaning and matching his sounds of pleasure with her own involuntary moans.

He felt so good inside her. So natural. He gave her a reach-around, fingering her clit, and she jerked in delight. The fire in her mons grew white hot. She picked up the speed and he matched it. He was thrusting into her at the same time that she was pounding herself onto him. Her breasts bounced until he rested his head on her back and with his free hand he held and squeezed them. She moaned and shuddered. Her legs vibrated uncontrollably.

She didn't even care if the neighbors heard her. She needed this so badly—a man penetrating her so deep—one who could make love so joyously and with such splendid skill. Oh, how she loved and missed this—making love, having sex, screwing, fucking, banging. She didn't care what it was called as long as it promised her the orgasmic release she knew was coming.

Her mind went blank. She heard her own breathless gasps and moans as if they belonged to someone else. His stroking and fondling brought her closer and closer to the point of no return. She was quivering and trembling, going almost numb with the buildup that was ready to erupt.

She hoped she wouldn't alert the neighbors with shattering screams. She gritted her teeth, gurgled, and came hard. Her body bucked, but he held on. He didn't lose contact with any of her ultra-sensitive parts, and she kept coming. Finally, she stifled a shriek and had to yank his hand away from her clit.

She had never experienced a sexual release this powerful. He grabbed her hips and pushed his cock deep within her vagina, holding there. When Nate bucked and shuddered, his tortured grunting sounded like a mixture of pain and pleasure. He spasmed and shook and sounded like he had to strangle his own groans. At last he stilled, panting.

"Are you all right?" she asked.

"Sorry about the animalistic noises. Believe me, it was pure pleasure."

CHAPTER ELEVEN

Nate had to take off after breakfast. He apologized and Ronda really did understand. All of his furniture was coming to his beach house, and he had paid extra for a Saturday delivery. He promised the bed would be "ready to go" by evening. They kissed a few more times and shared that satisfied, knowing, morning-after smile as Nate tore himself away.

Ronda had things to do too. She needed to pick up her clothes at Tommy's, and on the way to his house, buy some sort of gift to thank him. She had no idea what to buy though, and hoped she'd see something that would capture her attention. Good fortune was with her. She happened to see a sign for an annual art show in Gorham. It was a bit further north, but something told her that this was where she should go.

She found the show about forty minutes later. There were numerous tents set up, and she couldn't help noticing the number of talented people in this part of the world. Walking around on a warm, sunny Saturday, looking at beautiful things, still relaxed from the heavenly lovemaking, she was beyond content. Ronda was admiring a potter's work when someone came right up next to her and stood a little too close.

"I'm not sure which is prettier, the vase or you."

"What a line." Irked, Ronda turned toward the voice.

It was Tommy, laughing out loud at her reaction to his silly joke.

"Good Lord, what are you doing here?"

"I like art. Is that so surprising?"

"No. It's just that I came here to shop for you. I wanted to get you a thank you gift." Ronda still couldn't believe her eyes.

"Well, I saw something I wanted over on the other side," he said, and he gently guided her past the throng.

"You know, it's really lucky I ran into you here," Ronda said.

"Why is that?"

"Well because my next stop was going to be your house, and you aren't there."

"Hey, you're right." He led her over to the edge of the grounds to a hot dog stand.

"Here. This is what I want for my thank you gift."

"A hot dog?" she asked in disbelief.

"With mustard and relish, please."

"Stop it. I want to get you something nice," she protested.

"Instead of what I want?"

Ronda heaved a fake sigh. "Okay. Two hot dogs, please," she said to the vendor.

"I can afford something a little nicer you know."

"No you can't. I happen to know that your boss is a cheap bastard."

They chuckled and were walking with their hot dogs when she commented. "You know, I've never seen you eat healthy food. Your arteries must be full of crap."

"Why should my arteries be any different from the rest of me?"

As odd as it was, she loved his self-deprecating humor, but she wondered about it. "Why do you do that?"

"Do what? Eat badly?"

"No. Why do you make fun of yourself?"

"Well, because I'm an easy target. Besides, it distracted you from lecturing me about my cholesterol."

"Oh, so you've heard it before."

"Yup."

The two of them walked around the art show and Ronda presumed he would admire something. When he wasn't looking, she'd buy it for him. The problem was he was always looking.

"Ronda, you were going to come over to the house after this, right?" Tommy asked.

"Yeah, but I don't have to, if you were planning to go somewhere else."

"Oh, it's fine. I'd like to give you the itinerary for my trip to California. It's at the house."

"Are you sure? Shouldn't Antoine have it?"

"Oh, I'll give him a copy, but he'll never call me even if the place burns down. That would mean he didn't know how to run it. I'd like your good judgment on those decisions, but preferably without his knowledge."

"I guess I can handle that. Is that all I need to do?"

"That's it. I'll give you a key to my house too, if you need a place to crash in a hurry, feel free."

"Wow. What makes you think I won't empty the place while you're gone?"

Tommy grinned. "There's nothing worth stealing. My ex-wife took all the good stuff."

"Well, thanks for the offer, but you don't need to do that. Nate is getting his furniture delivered today. I could always crash at his place if I needed to."

"Oh." Tommy said.

Ronda thought she might have heard a touch of disappointment in his voice.

"So you're going to see Ty graduate?"

"Finally." He breathed a dramatic sigh of relief. "That boy's been in college for six years. I hope he really wants to come back to Maine and isn't just doing it for my sake."

They split up at the parking lot and arrived at their SUVs parked on opposite sides. Tommy called out that he'd see her back at the house. She acted like she was going to hop into her Jeep, but fiddled with her purse, waved her keys and watched as Tommy drove away. As soon as he was safely out of range, she dashed back to the potter and bought the vase that she and Tommy had both admired.

She didn't have time to wrap it but figured she didn't need to. He'd already seen it. She'd pick some wildflowers and put them in the vase before giving it to him.

Ronda arrived at the bottom of his front steps and heard Tommy yelling inside. Startled, she placed the vase down on the steps and listened for a moment. All she heard clearly was, "So, I have a Goddamn common name. I'm not who you think I am. Leave me the fuck alone!" Tentatively, she stood there wondering what to do. She ran back to her SUV quickly and quietly. Instead of intruding, she backed down the driveway as fast as she could.

Hearing him yell like that really bothered her. It was hard to believe he even had the capacity to become that angry.

She wanted to talk to Nate.

They still hadn't talked about the case yet. She had too many questions and not enough answers at this point. Her palms were sweating and she needed to talk to someone who could put her at ease. She figured Nate would still be at his place in Biddeford Pool, waiting for his furniture. She didn't like dropping in on people, but she knew he'd probably welcome her with open arms.

When she arrived, furniture crowded the entrance, and he was deep into "some assembly required".

"Good thing I dropped in. You need someone to help you move all of this stuff."

"Move it? You mean I can't leave it all right in the middle of the living room like this?" Nate smiled and stopped what he was doing long enough to lean over the pieces on the floor and give her a quick kiss.

"I really came over to ask your opinion on some things related to the case," she said.

Nate returned to tightening screws in the butcher-block kitchen table. "Oh, sure. If you want my opinion I'll gladly give it, but only if you really want it. I wouldn't want to control the conversation or situation."

"What's this? The new Nate?"

He smiled and affirmed in a Maine accent, "Ayuh."

Ronda looked puzzled, but decided to play along.

"And what brought on this change?"

"Well, you did. You and a wise old philosopher in my office building, actually."

"What did the wise old philosopher have to do with it?" Ronda asked.

"He said there was a time when the three little words were magic and melted a woman's heart. But, the three little words had lost their power, so they had to be replaced by three new little words."

"Uh huh. I'm probably going to regret this, but what are those three new little words?" she asked.

"Anything—you—want," Nate said wickedly.

Ronda grabbed a couch pillow and flung it at him. Then she grabbed another and another and hurled them too while he laughed.

When she had run out of ammunition, he stepped over the pillows and around the couch. With one hand around her waist and the other hand cradling her head, he gave her a deep smoldering kiss, and then murmured into her ear, "I was thinking about us all morning."

"Mmm—me too, until the spell was broken by my boss."

"What did Tommy do?"

"I don't really know, maybe nothing. I'd like to tell you about that and a few other things bothering me."

Nate told her to keep talking while he returned to assembling.

"Okay, well, there's the matter of the paranormal researchers. I have to give them an answer. I told them I'd get back to them."

"What are you worried about? You and your house being on TV or are you afraid they're not legit?"

"No. I've seen the show and they said I wouldn't be on TV, but they want me there. They think my presence attracts the spirit energies."

"So, you're ghost-bait?"

"You have a way of putting things succinctly."

"What do you want to do, Ronnie?"

"Part of me wants to cooperate. There's a whole piece I haven't told you about yet."

Nate put down his tools looking more interested. "What haven't you told me?"

"I've been to a psychic. She's a clairvoyant, actually. She sees things and gets messages from the dead."

"Okay. Seems like something you'd do. Don't be afraid to tell me anything. I won't think you're a nut case. What did she say?"

Ronda shook her head at the "nut case" reference but let

it go. "My sister came through with something that I never expected. Her message was something about some research and she pointed to my involvement."

"Wait a minute. The psychic implied that your sister wants you to cooperate with the paranormal researchers?"

"I suppose so."

"Is there any relationship between this psychic and the research team?"

"I don't think so. She gave me more information that proved to be true, such as, knowing I was going to have a cat. She couldn't know I would be getting a cat from Marci Jo about an hour later, and there was something else that had nothing to do with the researchers that proved to be true."

"What else?"

"Well, my brother pointed to his wrist, saying I owned a bracelet he gave to me. I had all but forgotten it, but when I was younger he gave me an MIA bracelet. I drove home and looked in my jewelry box, and I found it. The name on it was a Captain Thomas Kelley. That's also when I saw the guy running from my house."

"Which you thought was me."

"Yes, but I know it wasn't now. And that bracelet. Why would my brother lead me to it? And there's more that I want to tell you."

He put the Allen wrench down, sat on the floor and gave her his full attention. "Okay. What else?"

"Well, when I bought my new vehicle, the sales manager said he knew a Tommy Kelley in Iraq and asked if it could be the same one. I told him that I didn't know. He seemed excited to think it might be. He said he owed Kelley his life."

"Okay. Do you know how old Tommy is? He seems a little older than most Desert Storm vets."

"I don't know. He did say he was in Iraq. I left the thank you gift I bought for Tommy on his porch and came right here because he was yelling at someone. I heard him say something about having a 'God damned common name' and to leave him 'the fuck alone.' I've never known him to be angry with anyone. It was weird and I ran. I thought later I could say I remembered an appointment and couldn't stay or..."

"Or, you could say you overheard an argument and wanted to give him his privacy," Nate suggested. "Maybe he'll let you know what it was about."

"I never thought of that. A little, white truth. What a brave new idea."

"Is that everything Ronda? Sometimes a small detail can make a difference."

"Yeah. That's what the Kennebunkport police were saying."

"You talked to them? When?"

"On my day off, last week."

"Have they contacted you since?" Nate asked.

"No, why?"

"Because they found Michael Lawson."

Ronda froze. She almost didn't dare ask, but she had to.

"Is he dead or alive?"

"He was in pretty bad shape, Ronnie. His arm, ribs and jaw were broken. He can't talk yet."

"I'll be damned." She mulled that over, then she remembered for whom Nate was really working. "How's Lorena?"

"I don't know. Now, *she's* missing. I followed Lorena shortly before she disappeared. I had one of my gut feelings. It probably had something to do with the false leads she was feeding me. I'm betting that she was trying to keep me occupied elsewhere once Michael reappeared in her life—after she hired me to find him. I saw her meet up with Michael, or someone who looked like him, so he may have cut her in on it."

"In on what?"

"Probably the burglary of your home, although they

may have hired a third party, who impersonated me, so you'd fire my ass. I'll bet my presence has been mighty annoying for them."

"A third party? Any idea what they were trying to do or may have been looking for?"

"I suspect they were in your home trying to find a picture ID and social security card. Lorena may have been able to impersonate you with a brunette wig or some hair dye. Of course there's the possibility that they weren't trying to take anything at all. Maybe they were trying to plant something, like a microphone. I'd like to take a look around soon, before I piss you off again."

She gave in to the smirk she could feel forming at the corner of her mouth.

Suddenly, her eyes popped open, and her hand flew to cover her mouth. "I just realized...someone might have overheard our—encounter in the kitchen this morning. What makes you think there's a microphone planted in my house?"

"All the better to keep track of you, my dear."

"What about Michael? Who roughed him up?"

"It was probably the third party. Maybe there was another accomplice too. If anyone saw three different males and one female entering and exiting your parents' house, it could still look like the researchers. Anyway, someone must have become greedy. They probably took off as soon as they dumped Michael. Don't worry. No one can hide from me for long."

"How did you find him?"

"Kennebunkport police did a home check after I asked them to keep an eye on the place. He was unconscious at your parents' back door. Someone had been trying to break the new lock. When he came to, he signed a confession and promised to cooperate in exchange for leniency."

Ronda sat quietly digesting it all while watching Nate continue to work on his furniture.

"How can you be so calm?" she demanded.

"I didn't know them personally, Ronnie. If you were missing, I'd be slightly more upset about it."

"Only slightly?"

"Kidding. A lot. But honestly, if I got caught up in all of the screwed-up lives I investigate, I couldn't do this."

"I understand." It was hard for her to imagine staying calm and stable in his circumstances. However, in her former career it had been hard to deal with some clients unless she remained detached. *Everyone's an ad wizard.*

He raised his eyebrows. "You know, the bedroom's all set. I just need to arrange the stuff in there. Wanna help?"

She could see the glint in his eye, but sex wasn't on her mind at the moment.

"I'm not really able to do anything in there, *but* arrange furniture right now, Nate. I need a little more time to recover from a shock like this."

"Oh. I didn't know you were..." He stopped and his brow knit. "Are you still emotionally attached to Michael?"

"Not in the same way, but I spent a long time with him. I grew to know and love his family. I'd be upset if I heard that any old friend of mine who meant so much to me at one time or another was hurt."

Nate seemed to be pondering that for a while. "What about Marci Jo?"

"I'd be devastated if Marci Jo was hurt," Ronda gasped.

"Sorry. I switched gears. I meant, aren't you two going to spend the weekend together?"

"Not all of it. She has other people to see and places to go. She'll pop in when she's free."

"What if you're not free? What if you're here with me?"

"Well then, she'll pop out. What are you worried about, Nate?"

"Nothing. Just that she came up to see you and I seem to have done the same thing. If you feel like you're spreading yourself too thin, I just want you to know that I'll understand if you'd like to spend some time with her. Or you can invite her along with us. I'm okay with that too."

"Thanks, Nate. That's thoughtful."

Ronda decided to postpone seeing Tommy or Marci Jo. She watched Nate while he continued to work and thought about how quickly her life had progressed from empty to busy and full. It didn't seem like much had changed, but as she added it up she realized there had been plenty. A full-time job, a sex life, a few new friends, and a couple of psychics bringing back the whole dear, departed family.

She also puzzled over her mother's prediction that there would be two men vying for her affection. So far, Nate was it. She thought maybe Ty, but, no. He was a nice guy, but in no way as interesting as Nate.

Wait a minute. She never said that one of them couldn't be a memory. Ronda thought about how she had chosen the memory of Michael over anything real. She gazed at Nate's well-muscled, tanned arms with their blond hairs sparkling in the sun that streamed through the window. She could never have hurt Michael like he hurt her by trying to steal not only her valuables, but also her memories. Ronda knew Nate meant it when he said he'd never hurt her again. She marveled at his strength as he lifted the table and turned it upright on its legs in one swift, smooth motion.

"Nate?"

"Yes, love?"

"I think I could manage to forget all about Michael with your help." The corner of her mouth turned up in a sly smile. "Let's go move that bedroom furniture."

Nate stood up straight and grinned at her. "Are you sure?"

"Anything-you-want," she chuckled.

"I want you," he said softly.

"I want you too."

"Is it okay to say 'I love you' now?"

"Only if you let me say it first."

They moved toward the bedroom with no intention of arranging furniture. Kissing, fondling and groping every step of the way, they began working on the zippers and buttons of their jeans and shirts. By the time they made it to Nate's bed, all of their clothes had been strewn across two rooms.

Nate took a step back and cast his dark blue gaze over her body, admiring her naked beauty. "You're gorgeous."

"You're not bad yourself," she said, able to get a good look below her lover's six-pack abs when he was aroused. His broad chest and well-defined pectoral muscles led her gaze back up to his eyes, and *Oh my*. The intensity of his smoldering stare unnerved her.

She had to look away and found herself staring at his long, thick erection. Had she stepped back and seen him like this before, she may have run for her life.

"Relax, love" he said. "We fit perfectly."

Ronda glanced at the bare mattress and box spring set on the simple, Scandinavian frame. "Hey, we have a real bed this time, but no sheets on it yet."

"Give me one second." He grabbed a sealed plastic package and ripped it open freeing a blue top sheet. He shook it apart and tossed it on the bed, then grabbed Ronda and pulled her down onto the barely-sheeted mattress as she giggled.

This time they were even more eager, though he was still considerate. Ronda noted and appreciated his restraint. He seemed more concerned with her pleasure than his own. He moved his lips over her body and she shivered as his hot breath moved down. Kissing her neck, moving down, kissing her cleavage, moving over... Taking her nipple in his mouth, he cupped her breast and suckled.

Ronda felt a contraction somewhere deep within and moaned in pleasure. He took his time, gently yet thoroughly fanning the flame of her desire. It was as if he knew just how much she loved the feel of his suction, and he didn't stop while his hand moved over to cup and squeeze her other breast, and then to wander down further. He licked his way to the other breast and delivered glorious sensations by teasing her mons while sucking the other nipple.

Ronda arched and moaned louder when his fingers slid through her wet labia and found their way over her aching clitoris. Her legs trembled involuntarily as electricity shot through her. She moaned and clutched at his shoulders while he massaged her senseless. She was glad his place was private, because she couldn't have stifled her screams as her orgasm overtook her.

She opened her eyes and saw him watching her. He made sure he had satisfied her completely, that every possible aftershock had jolted her body before he finally guided his erection to her opening. He paused over her until she took his shaft in her hand and guided him in.

Arching into his thrust, she craved his masculine body to completely fill her, and she moaned, loving every deep penetrating minute of it.

Lost in the moment, her mind drifted aimlessly. She was only aware of how wonderful she felt in Nate's warm embrace, how he made her heart flutter, how she trembled when he kissed her ear and neck, and how he took her to some uninhibited place where she experienced lovemaking with relish and abandon like never before.

Building to another peak, it was as if she rode the waves on a stormy day with each one more thrilling than the last. They crashed into her body and emotions as if crashing against a crop of rocks. Finally, when Nate couldn't hold back any longer he rode his own wave home. They shook and spasmed and cried out together.

When finally exhausted, they panted and melted into one another, coupled for what seemed like an hour.

Finally Nate pulled out and lay beside her. "So, my darling, what shall we do now?"

She laughed and said, "Well if breakfast and lunch are any indication, I think I ought to go home and rest up for dinner—if you're still up for it."

"I sure will do my best to show you a good time. Wear something a little dressy. We've only had casual dates and tonight I want to treat you like the special woman you are."

She ran her hand over his damp hair and kissed him tenderly before she washed up and dressed. Afterward, she drove off to her cottage—a satisfied smile plastered on her face.

CHAPTER TWELVE

Ronda spotted a note on her screen door as she pulled into her driveway. The Audi was already there, parked on the street. She knew before she reached her porch that the note in flamboyant handwriting was from Marci Jo. Having gone for a walk, Marci Jo said she'd check back in a while. So Ronda floated inside and hummed as she began cleaning up her kitchen.

Up to her elbows in dirty dishwater, her phone rang. She grabbed a towel and the phone at the same time. "Hello?"

"Ronda? It's Tommy."

"Oh. Tommy, I'm glad you called. I was about to call you."

"You were? I was just calling to thank you for the thoughtful gift."

"Oh, you're welcome." She wiped her hands on the dish-towel. "I—I would have given it to you personally, instead of leaving it on your porch, but I heard you yelling at someone and I thought you'd want to do that privately."

"You heard that?"

"Yeah, but not much. I left right away."

"Well, I'm sorry you had to hear it. It was stupid. I don't

know why I got so upset. It was just someone looking for a different Tommy Kelley. I guess because he was so insistent, and I had other more important things on my mind, it got to me. When I got back from the art show I had a message on my machine that Jenna didn't show up for work this morning."

"Oh. Do you need me? I could go in..." Ronda squeezed her eyes shut, crossed her fingers and hoped he wouldn't take her up on that.

"No, Antoine called the list of wait staff until he roped someone into it. Wendy, our weekender came in for a double shift. She needs the money, so she was happy to do it."

"Whew, that's good. I was exhausted yesterday. I appreciate the chance to recover."

"Enjoy your day off and rest up. I may need you for more important things. When you stop by to pick up your clothes, I'll give you the keys to the restaurant and a few guidelines. Antoine will need your help whether he knows it or not."

"I thought he'd never ask for anyone's help."

"I'll tell him to let you do some of the office work. He doesn't like that part anyway. There's ordering, entering deposits, things like that. Believe me, he'll let you do it."

"I thought you were only going to be gone for a couple of days."

"Yeah, that's right. Still, it might not hurt to have a backup just in case the plane to LA crashes."

"Cut it out, Tommy. Don't even think like that."

"Hey, things happen, Ronnie. So what do you say? Will you let me teach you the fast-assed version of restaurant management?"

"Sure, however I can help...but first, please tell me Jenna's okay."

"I don't know. I worry about that girl when she doesn't

call and doesn't come in. She usually calls, even if it's at the last minute."

"You don't think..."

"No. I try not to think about it. I don't want to assume she's unconscious somewhere."

"No, of course not." Ronda propped the phone between her ear and her shoulder and finished the dishes as she talked. "I was thinking of getting my clothes and things as soon as Marci Jo gets here. I'm expecting her any minute. Will you be home?"

"All afternoon, darlin'. Stop by whenever you like. You and Marci Jo could stay for dinner."

"Well, I have plans for dinner with Nate, but Marci Jo might take you up on it."

"Sure, I'd like that. Tell her she's invited."

Ronda hung up and heard her screen door open. She met Marci Jo on the front porch.

"So, Ronda, how was your date?" She was whispering, presumably, so the neighbors wouldn't overhear.

"It was wonderful." Ronda teased her by whispering too. "Thank you for making dinner. That was so sweet of you."

"Oh, sure. My pleasure. However, that's not what I'm talking about and you know it. You're positively glowing. Did anything special happen after I left?"

"I know what you're getting at. Yes, it was great. We talked and kissed and he carried me upstairs."

"You're kidding! He carried you?" she shrieked.

Ronda rolled her eyes and waved her indiscreet friend inside, closing the door behind them.

"Yes, and then I promptly fell asleep."

"Get out." She collapsed with laughter.

"C'mon. Don't laugh. I felt really bad."

Marci Jo tried to straighten up but couldn't. Her laughter continued with no signs of stopping. Ronda could tell her that she atoned for it that morning and afternoon, but the heck with it. She'd want details.

When Marci Jo could finally sit up and talk again, she berated Ronda for not appreciating the great catch she had found.

Grabbing her Jeep keys, Ronda hoped to distract her friend into changing the subject. "I have to go to Tommy's for a few minutes, wanna come? We were both invited to dinner, and I can't make it since I'm going out with Nate. Tommy said he'd like to have you join him, though."

"I'd love to." Marci Jo's eyes sparkled.

Just before she drove away, Ronda climbed out of her SUV. Thinking a tiny bit of retribution was in order she called over to Marci Jo about to jump into her Audi. "Hey, how do you know Tommy, anyway?"

"I met him at the restaurant when he looked at my dead car battery and got it running again. Then he treated me to lunch." She had to yell to be heard over the sound of the engine. "It was pretty much a case of bad timing but the attraction was fierce. We didn't want to lose each other totally, so we kept the friendship. I'm still hopeful, though. He's really special isn't he?"

Ronda smiled at the obvious affection in her friend's excited voice. "Maybe it's time for second chances and happy endings."

"Let me know how that goes," Mr. Carroll called over.

Marci Jo laughed and yelled, "I will if you'll tell me how my friend and her man are doing."

"He didn't leave 'til after breakfast!"

Ronda considered the retribution idea a major backfire.

Her bag packed, Ronda took possession of the key to the restaurant, listened to a few simple instructions and hugged

Tommy goodbye after a cup of coffee and some conversation on his porch. She knew her friend probably hoped to be alone with him. Somehow she just knew that their relationship would begin if she weren't in the way.

Upon returning home she noticed Mr. Carroll sitting on his front steps.

"I wondered when you were going to come home," he said.

"Why? Have I been out too much?"

"Probably. A fellow was back in your house this morning and this time it wasn't your boyfriend."

She set her suitcase down and walked over to him. "Mr. Carroll, are you sure you saw this? Did you have your glasses on?"

"Yup. I found them and put them on my face before he came out. When he walked down the front steps I could see him as plain as day."

"Would you recognize him if you saw him again?" she asked.

"I'm sure I would. An odd fellow, about your boyfriend's height with the same hair, but a mean face. Your boyfriend's face is kinda sweet. You know?"

"Yeah, I know." Ronda sighed inwardly and imagined Nate's endearing smile.

"This guy had a long, thin nose and..."

"Oh my God," Ronda said and then asked, "Did he have a really square, prominent jaw?"

Mr. Carroll seemed surprised. "You know him?"

"No, I don't, but I have the feeling I will." She grabbed her suitcase and started to run inside, then thought she should say a little more to her neighbor. "Oh, Mr. Carroll, thank you for watching my house and don't let him see you, okay?"

"Will do," he said.

Ronda looked carefully around each corner before she

entered. She searched room-by-room, closet-by-closet, until she knew the house was empty and nothing was missing. What could the son of a bitch be looking for? She had nothing of value. She could have left her doors unlocked until all of this started happening.

She was somewhat insecure about taking a shower, but shower she would, even if it would be the world's fastest shower ever. At least this asshole only seemed to want to break in when no one was home.

Getting dressed was another rushed affair. She wriggled into her black, special occasion underwear and donned her little black dress. She swept her hair up into a sexy filigree clip, found some black high heels that she rarely wore and her double-strand pearl choker completed the outfit. Why, if he was looking for valuables, didn't he take the pearl necklace?

Looking in the mirror at the result, Ronda thought she might look attractive, if not for the wrinkled brow and the anxious look in her eyes. *Well, that's how I am today. Nate will have to take me as I am.* She also realized with warm, prickly delight that he probably would.

Ronda had planned to meet Nate at his place so he could spend maximum time getting it in some kind of order. She tried the doorbell and there was no answer. She tried to open the door and it was locked. His BMW was in his driveway so he had to be around. At last, he met her at the door wearing only a towel and a big smile. They kissed hello.

"You look lovely," he said, as he held the door open for her. The interior was neat and looked as if he had been living there for weeks, not hours.

"Wow, Nate, your house looks excellent. If I hadn't been

here earlier, I would never have believed you did it all in one day."

She took in the clean, minimalist yet cozy look of the place. There was even a tall plant in one corner.

He nodded and looked around. "Yeah, when I put my mind to something..."

"It's really wonderful."

"You helped pick everything out, remember?"

She laughed. "How could I forget that marathon shopping day?"

"Are you saying there's such a thing as too much shopping?"

"Maybe." She whirled around to face him. "Listen, I have to tell you something important before I burst."

"Oh, please don't do that. I just got the place all cleaned up."

She wanted to laugh but needed to get serious. "Nate, there was another intruder in my house this morning, possibly the same one as before. My neighbor got a good look this time."

"Oh no. What did he say?"

"It sounded like it could be the person I saw at the restaurant that day. He had a thin nose and a prominent square jaw, but he was wearing your hair color and style."

Nate put his arms around her and rubbed her back. "Was this neighbor the old guy who lives closest to you?"

"Yeah, the 'elderly gentleman'," she corrected, "in the house with no lawn. He usually sits on his porch in nice weather."

"Ronda, would you feel better if I stayed with you there?" He nuzzled her neck and kissed it. "I think we could make it romantic."

"N—No, that isn't necessary."

"You could stay here if you want to. I'll be out of your hair all week."

She bristled. "No! I don't want to be run out of my house, Nate." She was exasperated and Nate took a step back.

"Okay, I'll let you decide what you want to do. How about if I just get dressed and you can think it over?"

"I'm sorry. I know you're trying to help."

He nodded. "I'll be getting dressed," and left her alone.

She sat there, realizing her nerves were ragged. This thing was taking its toll on her. She wanted it to stop, but there seemed no end to it. If only she could go back to living in her own house, leaving her door unlocked if she wished, and not worrying about a thing.

Nate emerged wearing gray slacks, a white button-down shirt, and a tie, carrying his brown leather jacket.

"I'm sorry I don't have any suits up here."

"Don't apologize. You're right in step with the Maine lifestyle. No one wears suits on a date. I can't think of any occasion here requiring a suit except maybe a funeral."

"Well, I'll bring a black one up from Boston as insurance. If I have it, I won't need it—like having an umbrella keeps it from raining."

She chuckled. "Do you believe that?"

"No, but I thought you might."

She slapped his rear end, playfully.

"Ah, better not start that, Ronnie, or we'll have gotten all dressed up for nothing. So where's a nice place to go for dinner?"

"I don't know. I haven't been on a dressed-up date in Maine for a while. Now, if we were in New York... Can't you think of anyplace?"

"I'm not familiar with the Maine restaurants, but I could take you to Boston."

"Ugh, that's so far and I'm getting hungry."

"Okay then, how about Portsmouth? There are plenty of restaurants and it's a quaint walking town to kick around in afterwards."

"Hmm..."

Nate smiled. "Anything you want."

She rolled her eyes and said, "Fine. Portsmouth it is."

Dinner at the beautiful Wentworth-by-the-Sea hotel was followed by a play at the Portsmouth Repertory Theatre. Not wanting the night to end, Ronda suggested a walk afterward. It was a magical night where time ceased to exist, and the balmy breeze off the ocean created an almost surreal atmosphere. In oceanfront Prescott Park, Nate delivered another one of his masterful kisses.

"I love men who aren't afraid of public displays of affection."

Nate kissed her again and nibbled her lip before saying, "Well, the night is drawing to a close, Ronda. I'd like to suggest that you stay at my place tonight, so I can break in my new sheets..." She quivered when he kissed her with a fiery passion. His hand stroked down her back to her buttocks and squeezed. He slipped his other hand behind her head, and drew her into his strong, hard body. She was pressed up against his tremendous erection and her desire spiked. They were both breathless when he finally released her.

"You drive a hard bargain. The idea of returning to my cottage right after another break-in makes me queasy, plus the allure of a night in your bed, with sheets, pillows, blankets—and *that,*" she said nodding toward his hard on, "sounds pretty wonderful."

Nate was a better lover each time. She had completely forgotten that he was ever the guy from high school that broke her heart. People do change, she had decided, and he was living proof. No man had ever been more attentive to all of her needs and desires.

He knew how to please her. Thinking about how he satisfied her, multiple times, melted anything that was left of her guard. She loved making love with him, and they could go on for hours, days, weeks, for all she cared. Nate could make her forget she had a job.

It was as if he'd found buried treasure in the form of the black bra and panties when he uncovered them. Ronda made a mental note. *Must go shopping for more of those reactions.*

He explored her body thoroughly. Licking and blowing on her nipples, they became diamond hard immediately. When he placed his warm mouth on them and suckled she writhed with pleasure. Finding and cupping her electrified mons, he barely touched her and she arched into his hand as if pleading with him not to tease. He obliged her fully, rubbing her aching bud, bringing her to a shattering orgasm until she tore his hand away.

"I—can't take—much more."

Nate pulled her close and kissed her with such fervor that their chests rose and fell together. He continued to pleasure her until, after another luscious orgasm, she begged for him. She needed him inside of her.

Nate grinned and thrust his hard cock into her at last.

His slow, deep, rhythm was torture, yet gradually gave way to a faster, more passion-filled pace that could make fucking an Olympic sport. Both were passionately throwing themselves into it and Ronda could feel her pulse pounding. The joy of anticipation coursed through her knowing that another deeply rewarding orgasm wasn't far away.

She grabbed his damp shoulders and held on. The physical coupling of their bodies along with the growing love and trust between them led to an explosive internal release. It was the first time she had orgasmed from a man's cock hitting her deep inside. It was different that way. Deeper and more primal. Nate nearly collapsed when he too had reached a shuddering climax.

He gathered her in his arms and tenderly covered her mouth with his. Barely leaving her lips, he took in a deep breath and pushed her tousled hair away from her face. They kissed and gazed at one another as if they knew that what they had shared was already more than most people experienced in a lifetime.

Exhausted to the point of slap-happiness, they began cracking stupid jokes and laughing. They grinned until they fell asleep in each other's arms.

The next morning Ronda woke up first and wondered if she should get dressed and go home or invite herself for breakfast and possibly wind up staying all day. She mulled it over, until Nate woke up.

"I'd love it if you'd stay. Can I lure you with promises to cook for you?"

"But you don't have much in the way of food yet, do you?"

"Yeah, I know. I probably need to go to the store," he said.

Ronda smiled. "I think that's my sign to get home sooner rather than later."

"Let me take you out to breakfast, then."

Ronda wondered why she'd had a hard time accepting Nate. He said he loved her. That was certainly not something he had to say if he didn't mean it. She was sleeping with him anyway. Maybe she just needed time to believe in love again. She hadn't thought about the summoning ceremony for a while, but was inclined to laugh when she realized how silly it was to expect an immortal lover.

She made herself go home, although reluctantly. She

wanted to look around her house to see if anything was missing. She figured she could also get a little house-cleaning in while she was at it.

With those dual purposes in mind, she headed north, enjoying the scenery as if seeing it anew. Arriving at her house, she found Marci Jo's car in her driveway, and when she walked up to her screen porch, she saw her friend asleep on the loveseat.

Ronda unlocked and opened the door, fairly sure it would wake Marci Jo. She stirred and stretched long and slow, reminding Ronda of Talon, but frowned at the sun and the intruder who woke her.

"Mornin', gorgeous," Ronda said cheerfully.

"It isn't a good morning. As soon as I can think straight I have something to tell you." Marci Jo sat up and groaned.

Ronda noticed her friend squinting her puffy, mascara-streaked eyes. "Hung over?"

"Yeah. I bought us a pint of Southern Comfort. Can you tell who drank it?"

"You look like you want to get a rifle and shoot that bright yellow thing out of the sky."

"Mmm hmm." Marci Jo struggled to her feet as the empty liquor bottle fell to the floor. Stumbling into the house behind Ronda she asked, "Could you possibly take pity on me and brew some coffee while I sober up enough to tell you something terrible?"

"What is it?"

"Coffee first."

"Of course. Come into the kitchen. I'll even close the curtains for you."

"Oh, that would be sweet."

In the kitchen, Marci Jo dropped into a chair, Ronda closed the blue and white café curtains and made coffee.

"So what is it?"

"No. You have to sit down first."

"Marci Jo, you're making me nuts, now. What happened?"

"Ronnie, you can't tell this to your boyfriend. Promise?"

"Why?"

"Promise!" Marci Jo was now fully awake and fully intent on getting the story across in her own way and on her own terms.

"Okay, fine. Now tell me."

"Your co-worker, Jenna, is in the hospital fighting for her life thanks to her asshole boyfriend."

"No! That scum!" Ronda shouted.

Marci Jo slapped her hands over her ears and winced in pain. "Have mercy."

"Oh. Sorry."

"Tommy took it so hard. He assaulted Jenna's boyfriend and may have killed him."

Ronda's jaw dropped and she couldn't speak.

Marci Jo rubbed her red eyes. "We had had some wine with dinner, and we were reminiscing and laughing. Oh, Ronnie. It was going so well... We used to fuck, but it was just friends with benefits. You know? This time it was more than that. We decided we were ready to have a real relationship, and we were just heading for the bedroom.

That's when Antoine called. He had to let Tommy know that Jenna would need to be replaced indefinitely. I guess the last time the scumbag attacked her, Tommy got right up in his face and told him that if Jenna got hurt again he'd kill him. There were witnesses to that threat."

"I'm almost afraid to ask... Where's Tommy now?"

"I have no idea. They wouldn't let us see Jenna because she was in the ICU. In the hallway, though, we saw her boyfriend telling the cops that she was a pathetic klutz and fell down the stairs. Tommy managed to get outside, without going after him, but he insisted on waiting for him. I couldn't stop him or talk him out of it."

Ronda shook her head. "This isn't happening."

"Tommy did try to talk to him, but that twit just laughed and said, 'Prove it. There ain't a damn thing you or anybody can do'."

"Oh, Ronnie, before I knew what was happening, Tommy grabbed him and threw him against the brick wall, then he slammed his fist into his nose so hard, I—I think he forced it up into his brain. The guy just crumpled on the ground. I've never seen anything like it."

By now, Ronda was crying. This didn't even seem possible. "He's the kindest, gentlest man I know. He couldn't ... isn't even capable of it, is he? Did anyone besides you witness it?"

"The ICU desk clerk came outside for a cigarette just before Tommy ran. I know she saw the two of us, so I took off too."

"Why can't I tell Nate?"

"Do you want Tommy to go to jail for giving a slime-ball what he's been dishing out for years?"

"No, but what's going to happen now? To him? His business? His son? Why did he run? How long can he go into hiding, if he can hide at all?"

"Ronnie, I can't answer most of those questions, but there's one thing I do know. You're going to be taking over the business for him."

"Shit, you can't be serious."

"Just until Ty gets back. Please. It was the last thing Tommy asked before he tossed me his keys and dashed off."

"Oh, thanks, Tommy. Thanks a lot. Why did he take off on foot? Wouldn't he get farther in his car?"

"Not if the police are looking for it. I drove it back to his house and left it in the driveway. Here, let me give you the keys."

Ronda threw her hands up in the air and pushed her

chair back. "I don't want them. That would implicate me, wouldn't it?"

"Yeah, I guess it would. Well, I'll give them to Ty when he comes back."

Her mind raced in the moment of silence that followed. "How am I supposed to cover this up, Marci Jo?"

"You don't have to. Just try to hold on until Ty gets back and can take over. If the police want to talk to you, say you don't know anything, because you don't. You weren't there. For all you know maybe I'm making the whole thing up."

"I wish you were." Ronda got up, blew her nose on a paper towel and poured coffee with shaking hands. "I have to work tomorrow. How am I supposed to act?"

"Like it was any other day. The less suspicious you act, the better off everyone is. You can say that maybe Tommy left early for Ty's graduation. The only one you really have to tell is Ty, and I'd leave out the gory details."

"So the only ones who know the whole story are you and I?" Ronda put the coffee pot back and considered the facts and options.

"I think that's best for Tommy's sake."

"Marci Jo, what am I going to tell Antoine?"

"Oh... Antoine. He's kind of a loose cannon, isn't he?" Marci Jo let out a long breath. "I don't know. Let's think about that for a while."

"I wish I could tell Nate. I'll bet he knows how to devise a cover story."

"No! No one else." Then she got an evil gleam in her eye and said, "So, did you and your man make wild monkey-love all night?"

"Jesus, Marci Jo."

"What? I'm living vicariously."

"Well, stop it. I'm not in the mood."

"Bet you didn't say that last night," she teased.

Ronda dropped into her chair and burst into tears.

"I'm sorry, Ronnie. I'm sorry. I was trying to lighten the mood a little."

"I know, but you can't imagine how crushed I am right now. He was so... He was above that."

Ronda and Marci Jo went for a long walk on the beach. They had been out when Nate dropped by and left an envelope with Mr. Carroll. Ronda opened the envelope and was relieved to know he had received an urgent call from a client and had already left for Boston.

Now she didn't have to act like everything was normal and lie when he noticed it wasn't.

In the same envelope, she also found a key to his beach house.

CHAPTER THIRTEEN

Antoine had arrived at five to prepare the kitchen for the breakfast crowd. Ronda still had no idea what she was going to say to Antoine. She parked out back next to the only car there. Sitting in her car, she muttered a prayer for the right words and steeled herself for whatever would happen.

When she marched inside, Antoine was taking storage containers out of the large refrigerator.

"Ronda? What are you doing here so early?"

"I have to talk to you, Antoine. It's important."

Sensing the gravity in her voice, he stopped what he was doing and sat down.

"Did she die?"

"What? Oh, Jenna? No. This is related to what happened to Jenna, but it's worse."

"What could be worse?"

Finally, out of desperation and lack of ideas, Ronda decided to try it Nate's way and come out with the truth. "It's Tommy. He may have killed her abusive boyfriend—and now he's on the run."

Antoine was speechless. Ronda sat on the counter and waited patiently.

He shook his head. "It's my fault. I told him about Jenna. I should have waited until this morning or told him nothing at all."

"You know you had to tell him. It isn't your fault."

"Still I feel like I should have said it different or... Why did he run? How did you know about her? Did someone call you?"

Ronda ignored the questions and directed his thoughts elsewhere, hoping he wouldn't ask again. "Antoine, do you think you and I can keep this place going 'til Tommy comes back?"

He sat up ramrod straight, looking offended. "Why you and I? I've done it while he was gone before."

"This is different. We have no idea how long he'll be gone." She sighed. "There so much to do. There are supplies to inventory and order, daily bookkeeping, deposits, schedule changes, paychecks..."

"Jesus. I can't do all that and cook too."

"That's why I'm willing to do the office stuff until either Ty or Tommy get here."

"You can do all that?" There was an edge of suspicion in his voice and his eyes narrowed.

Ronda hadn't counted on having to defend her abilities, but she had come forward with this much truth. She might as well tell him.

"I'm a graduate of NYU, Antoine. Tommy and I thought it best not to say anything so the other waitresses wouldn't feel weird about it."

"You're kidding. What are you doing here if you have a college degree?"

"Right now? Trying to help one of the most decent people I know. I don't want him to lose everything he's worked for. Do you?"

"Of course not. I'd do anything for Tommy."

"So, can we work together until this nightmare is over?"

He nodded. "We can work together for as long as it takes, as long as you know who's in charge." He pointed to his spattered apron with his thumb.

"Of course. Now I have to swear you to secrecy. The more people who know, the more dangerous it is for Tommy."

Antoine raised his right hand. "I swear."

"Okay. Now one of us has to call Ty."

"Hey, I've got a kitchen to prepare."

"You're right. I'll call him." Ronda half expected that reaction. Before she left the kitchen, she turned to Antoine and confessed, "He's always so mellow. I just can't see Tommy doing anything like this."

"I've known him more than thirty years. He's better tempered than anyone I know, but everyone has their limits."

Antoine returned to readying the kitchen for breakfast, shaking his head.

Ronda entered the little office that was Tommy's private domain. Opening the lock with Tommy's key and surveying the surroundings, something was missing. *What am I looking for?*

Suddenly it struck her that she was looking for Tommy. He was as much of a fixture here as the gooseneck lamp. Ronda closed the door behind her gently. This would be her office for a while—only for a while, she hoped.

Calling Ty would be harder than telling Antoine. Ronda sat in silent meditation, hoping to find her place of inner calm before looking through the Rolodex for Ty's number.

She rehearsed possible scenarios in her head. Finding the number, she hoped it was current. Three others had been crossed out. Like most college kids, he had probably lived in a different dorm or apartment every year.

The telephone rang four times, and she was about to

hang up when a very sleepy voice picked up the receiver and said, "Hello."

"Ty?"

"Yes. Who's this?"

"It's Ronda Calhoun. I'm calling from your dad's restaurant in Maine." *It might be your restaurant now.*

"Do you know it's just after three a.m. here?

"Oh Geez, I'm so sorry, Ty. I have to talk to you, though. This can't wait."

"What's the matter? Is it my father?"

"Yeah. It's Tommy. He has allegedly beaten and possibly killed a man."

There was nothing on the other end at first.

"Ty? Are you there? Are you all right?"

"I'm here. I thought you were going to tell me he had an accident or a heart attack. Are you sure about this?"

"I swear I'm telling you the truth," Ronda said.

"I didn't think you were outright lying. Could there be some mistake? Who did he allegedly kill?"

"Jenna's boyfriend."

"Jesus. Don't tell me. The scumbag finally killed her?"

"No, but almost."

"Where's my dad now?"

"That's a very good question, but I don't have an answer for you." Ronda sighed. "He took off right after the incident."

"What? Why the hell..." Ronda heard his deep intake of breath as he paused. "Well, I know he's a survivor. He had some kind of special training during the war."

"Really? I never knew about that," Ronda said.

"Yeah. I think he was a Green Beret or Special Ops. He never wanted to talk about it."

"I wonder why not?"

"I don't know, Ronnie. Damn, graduation is only a week away. He was going to be here for it, if it killed him."

"He might just show up, Ty. Keep your eyes and ears open. I'd bet money he's heading west right now."

"You're not going to tell the police are you?"

"Ty, I would never ... I'm here to keep things running smoothly until you get here."

She pinched the bridge of her nose and squeezed her eyes shut. "Please promise me you're going to come home right after graduation and take this terrible responsibility off my shoulders. We need you."

"Of course I will. I'm grateful *you're* there right now."

Losing the battle not to, she began to cry.

Ty's voice took on a softer, soothing quality. "Hey, I know this must be hard. You were already dealing with a lot. Just let Antoine handle the petty squabbles and the sick calls, and you can do the nightly deposits and keep the deposit slips somewhere safe. Together you can order whatever supplies run low. Leave everything else until I get back."

"Okay." She sniffed.

"Ronda, thanks. We won't forget this, ever."

When Nanette arrived, Ronda had her first chance to pretend that nothing was wrong. Marci Jo arrived at the same time and offered her help. "I've done it before. Taking orders, making correct change."

"I guess that's considered experience."

"I'll give it a whirl," Marci Jo said.

Nanette approached Ronda and whispered, "I'm having a hard time understanding how Tommy could hire a new waitress and yet not be around to supervise."

Ronda told her about Jenna and said that Marci Jo was a temporary fill-in; Tommy was probably at the hospital or arranging for legal counsel.

Nanette wasn't shocked. With her teeth clenched she

said, "I always knew that dirt-ball was going to kill or maim her one day."

"How long has Jenna been working here?" Ronda asked.

"Over five years anyway. Tommy bought her a charm bracelet for her five-year anniversary. The dirt-bag flushed the bracelet down the toilet."

"What an asshole. I don't even know him, but I hate him."

"It doesn't get any better when you know him," Nanette said.

Marci Jo got along famously with the regulars, especially Ed who hoped she'd be there full time.

"What do you mean you have another job to go back to? Where do you work?"

"Vacationland Travel."

"Good. I'll go there and get you fired."

"No you won't, but all your pleading and threatening is good for my ego."

"Well, try to fill in more often, will ya?"

Ronda was glad Marci Jo was keeping the regulars occupied at the counter. She was working the back part of the dining area and her head was swimming with details she had to attend to. Finally she started writing herself notes on the back of her order pad so she wouldn't forget the priorities.

The first order of business scribbled on her pad was, "Hire new wait staff." Should she pretend that Tommy asked her to do it, or should she take Nanette into the ever-widening circle of confidantes? Ronda knew Nanette was too bright not to notice and yet there was something reactive and unpredictable about her. So, continuing to worry herself sick, she made no decision.

By ten a.m., Ronda was almost in a panic about hiring someone. Placing an ad wouldn't work. It would take too long to appear in the newspaper. In a welcome lull, staring out the window, she got a brilliant idea and wondered why it hadn't occurred to her earlier. Cousin Tommy's had a large sign visible from the highway. There was a huge rectangle underneath where sliding letters could be used to post specials. Still displayed on the sign was last week's special, chicken cacciatore.

Ronda walked into the kitchen to talk to Antoine. He was getting ready for the lunch crowd and barely glanced at her. "How come you only bother me when I'm busy?" he asked.

"When are you ever not busy?"

"Good point. What do you need?"

"I need to know where the letters for the big sign are kept."

"Screw the weekly special, Ronda. It can be the same thing again. I have plenty of chicken. What I don't have, though, is tomatoes. Can you call in an order?"

"I'll figure it out. You'll get your tomatoes. Meanwhile, we need another waitress right away. Marci Jo is only here to get us through one day. Tomorrow will be a disaster unless we get someone ASAP."

Antoine said, "Christ, I can picture the orders mounting up on the counter, getting cold, and I'll probably have to come out and deliver 'em to the tables myself. The letters are in Tommy's office in a cardboard box on the shelves behind his chair," Antoine said. "You want to advertise for a new waitress on the sign?"

"Yes, right away."

"I approve. Get Stretch to find the long arm and ladder for you. It's down in the basement. You're probably good at a lot of things, Miss NYU, but I don't think heavy lifting is on your resume as one of your talents. Get the kid to go up the ladder and change the sign for you. If he falls off, he's easier to replace than you are."

"My God. Was that a compliment, Antoine?"

He smirked, and she proceeded to the convenience store. No more time for teasing or pleasantries.

She had to tell the kid working in the store about Jenna and get him to go after the ladder while she found the letters in Tommy's office.

Stretch agreed to post the sign and said he felt badly about Jenna.

Ronda was in the office grabbing the box of letters when the phone rang.

"Ronda?" said an anxious voice on the other end.

"Ty? Is that you?"

"Yes. Listen, I was barely awake when you called last night, and I wasn't thinking straight. I don't have to stay here for graduation. I can be back there as soon as tomorrow night."

"No, Ty. You've worked too hard to lose out of your graduation ceremony. Besides, your dad may still be coming. Even if he isn't there, you know he wouldn't want you to miss it on account of him."

Stretch showed up at the door and Ronda, who didn't have time to go through the letters handed him the whole box. She placed a hand over the receiver and mouthed a silent "thank you." The kid smiled and strode off to accomplish his task.

"I don't know, Ronnie. I think he might just prefer I get my ass back home and help out there."

"We're fine, Ty. Everything is going smoothly. Marci Jo is filling in, and I have an ad for a waitress being posted as we speak." *I hope I sound more positive than I feel.*

"Are you sure?"

"Yes. I promise I'll call if anything gets out of hand."

"I want you to, Ronda. I mean it. Don't be like Antoine and refuse to ask for help."

Suddenly the thought of Antoine needing tomatoes popped into her head. "Oh, there is something you can probably tell me. How and from where do I order more food and supplies?"

"Are you sitting in Tommy's chair behind the desk?"

"Yes." Ronda felt funny about admitting it, but Ty continued, seeming to have no problem with it at all.

"There's a folder in the right-hand desk drawer. Everything is alphabetized. My dad's system makes sense only to him, I'm afraid. Look under 'O' for ordering—not 'P' for purchasing."

Ronda found the 'O' folder and flipped it open on the desk. Everything she needed was right in front of her.

"Oh, and deposit slips are in the checkbook under 'B' for banking," he added.

"Thanks, Ty. You're a lifesaver."

"No, Ronda. You're the lifesaver. I just wish I knew what my father was thinking when he took off. That can only make things worse, I'm sure."

"Well, if he shows up out there, Ty, give him a good hard slap upside the head and tell him it's from me."

"I'll do that."

They concluded their phone call and not a minute too soon. Ronda had just stepped out of the office and was returning to the restaurant to see two police officers and a detective questioning a trembling and tearful Nanette.

That reaction couldn't be faked and Ronda was glad she hadn't told her anything. Now Ronda hoped she could fake hers. She felt like she was walking in slow motion. Glancing over her shoulder, she caught a glimpse of Marci Jo slipping into the kitchen. As she approached Nanette, Ronda gently touched Nanette on the arm.

"What's going on?" she asked.

Nanette couldn't talk. The detective introduced himself.

"I'm from the P.P.D. Homicide Division. My name is Detective Sutton." He showed her his detective's badge. The other two uniformed officers were watching her intently.

Here goes, she thought.

"Homicide?" She gasped. "Did Jenna die?"

"No, ma'am," the detective answered. "Her condition is improving." He left it at that and just waited and watched her.

She managed to look confused and peered over at Nanette, as if wondering why she was so upset.

Finally the detective continued. "James Stone was murdered."

"Who?" The name didn't register so Ronda must have still looked convincingly confused.

"Jimmy," Nanette said, at last. "Jenna's boyfriend."

"Oh," Ronda murmured, then she turned to the detective and shrugged. "I'm new. I didn't know him at all, I'm afraid."

Nanette grabbed her shoulder and shook her. "They're looking for Tommy. He's a suspect!"

Ronda decided the less said, the better. "Tommy?" Her gasp sounded sincere too. Probably because she still couldn't believe it. "I don't know where he is," she said to the cop, truthfully.

"Has he contacted you at all?"

"No."

"When was the last time you saw him?"

Ronda looked around at the whole restaurant watching with rapt attention. She decided to try a diversion. "Is this really necessary, right out in front of all the customers?" she asked.

"We can always go to the station if you don't feel like answering a few simple questions now."

"Oh, no. I don't mean to be uncooperative. I was just thinking, you know, bad for business."

"If we get enough information without pulling teeth, we'll get out of your way," the detective said. "Now when did you last see him?" He was like a pit bull relentlessly hanging onto his question.

She tried to think of the last time she might have been seen *with* him.

"The art show," she said. "I ran into him Saturday morning at the art show in Gorham."

Detective Sutton wrote that down.

"Your name, miss?" he asked.

"Ronda Calhoun." When the detective looked up at her without raising his head, she was afraid he knew about her family and hoped he wouldn't say anything about her wealthy, dead parents. "I just assumed he was at the hospital. Did you look for him there?"

"Yes, ma'am." He reached into his breast pocket and produced two business cards, one for Ronda and one for Nanette. "If he contacts either of you, call the number on the card and ask for me."

Ronda was just about to let out a sigh of relief until she saw them heading further into the restaurant instead of leaving. They were aiming for the kitchen.

Ronda hugged Nanette and watched helplessly, knowing Marci Jo, her best friend and the only eyewitness, was in there.

"Nan, why don't you take a break while the police are talking to Antoine? I'll bring you a cup of coffee."

"I'm all right. I don't know why I overreacted like that. I'm sure Tommy's innocent. He'll probably stroll in here this afternoon and..." She suddenly lowered her voice. "Ronda, what if he isn't?"

Ronda guided her to an empty stool at the end of the

counter. "Don't even think that way, Nanette," she whispered. "We have to think positive. It's just a big mistake."

From this vantage point Ronda could see into the kitchen a little better. The restaurant was so quiet you could hear coffee splash. She poured Nanette a cup and heard Antoine answer the detective's questions, convincingly. She refilled coffee cups all down the line and tried to sneak a better look. She couldn't see Marci Jo.

Patrick, one of the newest regulars asked, "Do you think Tommy's involved in this?"

"Are you on crack?" Ronda hissed quietly, but she got her point across. "How could you even ask that? This is Tommy we're talking about. The same Tommy who hired me with no experience just because I needed a job."

Nanette looked up. "You had no experience?"

"I have plenty of experience now, don't I?"

Nanette just lowered her head and added, "This is the same Tommy who hired me even though I was on probation."

"You were on..."

Nanette shot Ronda a look that said, "Don't go there."

Patrick looked ashamed and said, "Yeah, the same Tommy who loaned me money when I was being sued and couldn't afford a decent lawyer."

Ronda looked up and saw the officers and the detective come out of the kitchen. This time they headed toward the convenience store. She glanced out the window and saw Stretch on the ladder. It seemed impossible, but they managed to miss him.

As they were coming back through the restaurant, Ronda glanced outside. He was down off the ladder, had it under his arm and was just heading to the back door of the convenience store. Then the detective stopped.

He looked back toward the convenience store and asked no one in particular, "Who works back there?"

Damn. One more thing to worry about. Ronda took a deep breath and admitted, "A kid named Stretch."

Nanette interjected, "Percy. His real name is Percy."

Detective Sutton muttered under his breath, "No wonder he goes by Stretch."

The cops returned to the convenience store and found Stretch entering the back door. They asked the same questions plus a couple more. Ronda sneaked toward the store, pretending she had an errand that involved the supply room. Her ears perked up, as she overheard the last question and answer.

"Who asked you to advertise for help on the sign?"

"Ronda did."

"Ronda Calhoun?"

"Yeah. The girl from in there," Stretch said. Ronda could feel her ears burning and pictured him pointing right to her.

"Interesting," the detective said, and, at last, they left by the back door.

CHAPTER FOURTEEN

Marci Jo—Where was she? Ronda hurried to the kitchen and demanded, "Where's Marci Jo?"

Antoine opened the large freezer door and released a shaking Marci Jo.

"Are you okay?" she gasped.

"IIIII'll livvve," Marci Jo quivered. "Cooooffeeeee."

Ronda helped her over to the counter and seated her between Ed and Patrick. She poured her a cup of coffee and the guys rubbed Marci Jo's arms to warm her.

Nanette looked on from her stool at the end of the counter. "Why did you hide like that?"

Marci Jo must have anticipated the question and rehearsed her answer. "Look, I'm only here for one day. I don't want to get involved."

That answer seemed to satisfy everyone.

As soon as she could, Marci Jo took Ronda aside and whispered, "I got a call on my cell phone."

"While you were in the freezer?"

"Yeah. I grabbed my pocketbook while I was looking for a place to hide. Good thing too. It was kind of private." She lowered her voice and whispered. "Family emergency. I've gotta go. I'll be away for a few days. I'm really sorry, Ronnie."

Ronda raised her eyebrows, but her friend's expression told her she'd get no more information.

"I have to leave now, Ronnie."

"Of course. Thanks for this morning," she said. *If only I could let out a primal scream.*

How were they going to make it through other days like this? She tried to think of ways she could make it easier on herself. She couldn't think of a thing other than cutting some steps out of her morning routine, which would allow her to sleep until four forty-five and arrive at five-thirty. *Good Lord, what a life!* She could take shorter showers. She could skip all the make-up.

And as hard as it was for her, on the way home she'd have her hairdresser cut off her beautiful long hair. Blow drying took too long and if she let her waist-long hair dry naturally she'd look like she'd just walked out of the ocean.

That way it would just be lather, rinse, and repeat the insanity every morning.

Despite the cute, pixie haircut and easier morning routine, she was still in for less than easy days, and she knew it. The sign that Stretch created had an almost immediate response. Antoine said he could interview potential waitresses between two and three o'clock.

Nanette held down the fort while Ronda hurried into the office and figured out how to order the list of things Antoine had asked for. The request grew from tomatoes to the weekly grocery shopping. She figured it would be better to call in one large order rather than several small ones, so she asked him to write down everything he might need.

As soon as she was through ordering from the distributor, the phone rang.

"Hi, Ronnie. How's everything going?"

"Oh, Ty. If you mean the restaurant, everything is fine. I've called in the weekly order, and we have three potential waitresses scheduled for interviews with Antoine between two and three."

Then she took a deep breath and came right out with it. "But the police were here yesterday, looking for your father."

"Jesus. They didn't waste any time."

"No. I guess not. The detective said he was from Homicide and his name was Sutton. They were looking for your dad and he questioned every employee, but I don't think he got much out of us." She raked her fingers through her short, sporty hair.

"I'm glad of that. Ronda, honestly, I'll come back if you need me to. Just say the word."

"No. Please stay there. We're okay, I promise."

"If it were anyone but you running the place, I'd come back tonight."

"Wait for your dad. I'd feel better knowing he's okay, and I'm sure he must be heading your way as we speak."

"By the way," Ty added, "I'd get a burner phone if I were you. The police could tap the restaurant office phone pretty easily."

"Oh my God. I didn't think of that."

"You can't be expected to think of everything. I'll give you my number and you can call me with yours when you get one."

"Okay. I have a paper and pen ready..."

Ty gave her the number and was about to hang up when he remembered one more important piece of advice.

"Oh, and Ronda? You might want to sit in on the interviews and have a say in the hiring process. Antoine will just pick the prettiest one."

She shook her head and had to laugh. "Oh God, you're probably right. Thanks for the tip."

Ty wished her luck and hung up. Ronda pulled the crumpled paper which served as her brain from her pocket and added "burner phone" to the growing list of things to do.

Now she had to tell Antoine that she wanted to be in on the interviews. She returned to the restaurant, trying to think of a tactful way to present it without insulting him. As it happened, Antoine was looking for her through the serving window and as soon as he saw her, he waved her into the kitchen.

"What the hell did you say on the sign?" Antoine demanded.

"I didn't tell Stretch anything specific. Just that we needed a new wait person pronto. Why?"

"Because two more people have come in. I can't interview five people in one hour, and I can't stay late today. I have an appointment after work."

"Want me to help?" Ronda asked, innocently.

"Yeah. Why don't you do the interviews and just let me see the best candidate for a final decision."

"I can do that."

"And go find out what's on that friggin' sign."

"I'll do that right now," Ronda said.

The sign was visible from the highway, but not from the restaurant, so she had to go outside to read what it said. There, in glaring capital letters pointed directly at the oncoming interstate traffic, she read, "WAIT PERSON NEEDED DESPERATELY. LIKE RIGHT NOW."

Oh, man.

A car door opened, and caught her attention. Just stepping out of the economy rental car was Monica, the paranormal researcher. Ronda slapped her forehead. She had forgotten all about them.

Monica walked over to her and smiled sweetly. "Hi, Ronda. So, did you come to a decision?"

"I'm so sorry, Monica. It seems the decision has been made for me. My boss has ... been called away and has left me in charge of the restaurant. I'm busy beyond belief."

"Well, I understand things that are beyond belief. Will you keep my card and call me if things free up for you?"

"I will. I really will. I think your research is interesting and important work."

Monica smiled warmly, shook Ronda's hand, and returned to her car.

What other things might be falling through the cracks?

The interviews were short. Ronda had several inappropriate applicants to send away as nicely as she could. One woman had a number of health problems that would necessitate working no more than four hours per day, twice per week.

One man was rude and abrupt and Ronda had to tell him that it just didn't seem like the right fit. He exited the interview with his middle finger raised.

Another woman was a displaced housewife. That was fine, but she described, bitterly, how she found herself dumped and desperate. Then she did some man-bashing. Not the best candidate for a place where the men far outnumbered the women.

Ronda was about to give up hope when the fourth candidate came in. Susan was pretty enough for Antoine, plus she seemed bright and energetic with a good sense of humor.

Ronda thanked her lucky stars. "So, you have experience waitressing and you're available now... That's great. Our sign has brought in some pretty unsuitable people. Pardon me for asking, but is there anything more I should know about you in advance, Susan?" She waited patiently, while mentally crossing her fingers.

The young woman seemed to be mulling something over.

"Any trouble with the law?" Ronda figured that was a safe question since some job applications asked if the applicant was a felon. *Ironic, since the owner is one.*

"Not for years. I hung around with the wrong crowd when I was younger and I did a couple of months in Juvie. That scared me and I haven't been in trouble since."

"What did you do?"

She took a deep breath. "I jumped on the back of a cop who was threatening my boyfriend at the time. They called it 'assault'."

Ronda thought about the officers who were there the day before. She would have liked to jump on them and ride them right out of the restaurant.

"Susan, can you start tomorrow at 6 am?"

The young woman looked surprised, probably expecting a "thanks, but no thanks" or "we'll be in touch" reply.

"Yes. Absolutely. Call me Sue, everyone does."

"Wear some comfy sneakers and I'll get you a uniform." She recalled Tommy saying those words to her. Tommy probably thanked his lucky stars too.

Ronda breathed a sigh of relief and looked forward to the day when Ty would take over.

She finished up the paperwork, collected the money from the weekend, counted it, and soon the second day from hell would finally be over.

Ronda left her phone number with Dan, the evening cook, and Sherri, the senior evening waitress. She simply told them that Tommy was away. They seemed to accept the minimal info without question, so she headed to the bank.

At the bank's drive-up window Ronda noticed several cars in line and heaved a heavy sigh. As she pulled in behind the last car she leaned on her elbow, chin in hand. A white car behind her pulled over to a parking space and sat there. Being observant as well as bored, she checked her side mirror and waited for the driver to get out of the white sedan. He didn't.

She couldn't help being curious and kept checking, slowly proceeding to the front of the line. She was able to make the deposit without fanfare, but as she pulled away, the mysterious white sedan pulled out of its parking space and came up behind her at a traffic light.

Driving toward home and watching the other car's progress, she thought that maybe she was being followed. She turned left to take a more circuitous route. If the car followed her to Old Orchard Beach by way of Pine Point, she'd know something was up.

Ronda led the other car down a winding path and along the sandy roads—the back way to Old Orchard. Of course, she hadn't forgotten her other mission. To pick up a burner phone. However, if the cops were following her, and she suspected they were, she would prefer the boys in blue not even know she had one.

Okay, I'm getting tired of this low speed chase. She parked on the road, in front of the little yellow house next to hers and crunched up the gravel walk to visit her neighbor and Talon. The sedan had parked on the opposite side of the street half a block away.

She opened the unlocked screen door and tried the old brass doorknob that allowed her to enter the home. The fact that the inner door was unlocked didn't surprise her. Mr. Carroll left it that way so he could go back and forth from the porch to the bathroom frequently, as elderly men with enlarged prostates do.

Talon greeted her nosily. Ronda had a funny feeling that something was wrong. "Mr. Carroll?" she called out.

No answer. Talon continued to meow and Ronda picked her up to soothe her. When she walked into the kitchen she froze, horrified to discover her elderly friend lying on the floor. She rushed to his side and tried to find a pulse, but couldn't. She knew that she had to get help as quickly as possible, so she charged out of the house, ran straight to the white sedan, and banged on the driver's window. "Are you a cop?"

The gentleman, sporting a buzz cut, rolled down the window. "Who wants to know?"

"Look, I don't have time for this. If you know CPR, help me. My friend is unconscious on the floor."

"Shit," said the man. He threw open the car door, trotting behind her into the yellow house and over to the body on the kitchen floor.

"Call 911," he shouted. "Give the address, and ask for an ambulance." Going to work on the old man using mouth to mouth resuscitation, he ripped open Mr. Carroll's shirt and began chest compressions.

Ronda did as she was told. When the ambulance arrived and took Mr. Carroll away, the guy called the police and requested an investigation.

"You need to stick around and talk to the police, ma'am. This looks like a crime scene."

"What? What makes you think...?" Her lower lip quivered. *Poor sweet old Mr. Carroll, a victim of crime?*

"Bruises on his chest and back, plus some broken ribs. I doubt if they're self inflicted."

"No, of course not." Ronda's mind went numb waiting for the police to arrive. It took her a few minutes to notice Talon's absence. "Wait, my cat. She's not here. Mr. Carroll was watching her for me and now I don't see her. I have to look for her," she said in a panic.

"Sorry. You're not leaving the house, and I didn't see any cat."

"She must have run out when I went to find you."

"Same answer."

Ronda suspected from his authoritative tone that he was definitely a cop. She also figured if she tried to leave to look for Talon, she could wind up in handcuffs.

Looking around, but not touching anything, he said, "I wouldn't leave this room if I were you."

Ronda pulled a chair away from the kitchen table and was about to sit on it, when the man snapped, "...and don't touch anything."

"Jeez, man. You know I didn't do it. If I did I wouldn't have run out to get you."

"They'll be dusting for fingerprints. Keep yours off of the blunt objects, will you?"

"They don't take ass prints yet, do they?" she asked angrily and plunked herself down on the chair.

The mystery man simply looked at her, betraying nothing. Once the police arrived, he met them outside.

As soon as one of the uniformed cops was able to take Ronda's statement, she went off to look for Talon.

She walked all over the neighborhood calling, "Here, Talon... Here, kitty." *Shit.* Suddenly, she realized that she had another abandonment or two to deal with and tried hard not to cry. "Here, Talon... Here, baby," she called out, her voice now shaking.

Ronda returned home after hours of searching and calling for her feline companion. She had combed the neighborhood and beyond, going into people's backyards, looking under porches or anywhere that Talon might be hiding.

Absolutely sick about her latest losses, she returned home. She poured a tall glass of beer and brought it out to her porch. Mr. Carroll's yard was now draped with crime scene tape. It hurt too much even to look at it, so she went back inside.

Drowning her sorrows in beer was something she had done occasionally in the past year, but she didn't want to make a habit of it. As she was heading to get her second glass, she decided that this was the proper occasion to get completely intoxicated. Maybe not as bad as she did at the summoning, but still...

As the second glass disappeared, she said out loud to no one, "Leave it to me to be proper about getting drunk." Her next beer flowed over her lips straight from the can. Remembering that it wasn't exactly proper to get buzzed alone, either, she felt oddly better.

As she was drifting off into oblivion, she had a vision, or dream of Mr. Carroll, raising a glass to her from his rocker on the front porch. As she gazed at his image, sipping his foamy beer from his frosted mug, she knew she had to call the hospital.

She looked up the number of the Biddeford hospital, where the EMT said they were taking him, and asked to be connected to the ER.

"Hello. I was wondering if I could speak to the doctor in charge?"

"Can the charge nurse help you? The doctor is rather busy right now."

"Yeah. That would be fine."

In a few moments the nurse came to the phone and answered her question.

"We were able to stabilize him and transfer him upstairs, Miss Carroll. I believe he's out of danger. They transferred him to the third floor ICU for close observation tonight, but he'll probably be in a regular room sometime tomorrow."

"Thank you," breathed Ronda, letting go a deep sigh of relief. She didn't correct the nurse's assumption that she was family. That might help her get in to see him later.

She wanted to talk to Nate, but Marci Jo didn't want her to. "Damn it. Where's Marci Jo now?" As she let the tears flow freely, she felt a soft touch on her leg. She sat bolt upright and saw a purring Talon rubbing up against her.

"Oh, my baby. My sweet kitty," she cried and scooped Talon up into her arms. She buried her face in the soft fur and didn't even care that the fine dander tickled her nose. She held her pet close, walked inside the house, locked the door, and patted her as tears continued to roll down her cheeks. Ronda didn't know how Talon had possibly made it onto the porch without her knowing about it.

"Thanks, Sarah ... or whomever," she whispered. "Thank you for knowing what I needed right now."

At that moment the phone rang. She answered it hesitantly. "Hello?"

"Ronnie, it's me, Nate."

"Wow, what timing you have."

"Really? I was just calling to see if you'd like to meet me in that park in Portsmouth. I'm missing you so much that I just want to touch you and kiss you."

She tried not to cry, but it was impossible. Ronda began sobbing into the phone.

"Ronnie? What's going on? Are you all right?" He sounded panic stricken.

"I'm okay, Nate. I'll be all right." She took a couple of deep breaths and composed herself. "I just had the worst day, and as much as I'd like to I can't drive to Portsmouth in this condition. I've been drowning my sorrows. My next-door neighbor is in the hospital. He's going to be all right, but I was so scared."

"I'm sorry, sweetheart. Can I do anything?"

"No. Nobody can do anything, unless you can turn the clocks back to yesterday morning."

"I'll come up and hold you if you like. I promise that's all I'll do, if that's what you need."

"You would do that for me? I could really use a friend right now, but I don't want to make you go out of your way. Just your voice is comforting."

"Whatever you need, love. I'll do anything to help. You know that."

"Okay. I guess I'll let you help me through this," she sniffled.

"It's about time." He sighed. "I'll be there in an hour. You can tell me all about it, then. Just hold on."

She managed to smile. "Are you sure?"

"There's nothing going on here. I'd love to come up and be with you."

"You're amazing ... and Nate? I never told you this, but you really deserve to know—I love you too."

There was a long pause on the other end. She wasn't sure what to think. Maybe he had already hung up, but there was no dial tone. Maybe he had dropped dead from a heart attack.

"Nate, are you there?"

"I'm here, Ronnie. I was savoring. Do you know how much I've wanted to hear you say that?"

"No."

"I'll tell you when I get there. I'll be with you as fast as I can. Don't move, okay?"

"The only place I'm going is straight upstairs to bed. I'll leave the key under the mat. Meet me between the sheets, will you?"

"Count on it, love."

Nate would be there. She blew out a long breath of relief. Before she went to bed, though, she wanted one more beer to ease her into sleep. She popped the top, and raised her can in the direction of her neighbor's house. "To your health, you dear old man." She was finally calmer, knowing he was going to make it, and knowing how much Nate cared. She could feel it now. He was a warm presence in her heart.

As oblivion settled over her, she fell asleep on her sofa, and that's where she woke up the next morning—late.

CHAPTER FIFTEEN

Holy Christ. What time is it? She had only ten minutes to get to work and the commute, even under perfect conditions, took thirty. She was still wearing her uniform, having never changed out of it the day before.

Her brain and her mouth were sharing the same cobwebs. Her uniform was wrinkled, but there was no time to worry about that now. She smoothed it the best she could and bound her hair in a plastic clip. She could buy deodorant when she got there. *I just need to get there!*

Grabbing her purse, she ran for her car. There was something stuck in her front door but she was moving so fast she didn't stop to look at it, so whatever it was fluttered to the floor.

As soon as she reached the highway, she let the new Jeep show her what it could do. Flying down the highway, well over the speed limit, she spotted the blue lights in her rearview mirror. *Crap.* She forgot that cops stop red vehicles more than any other color.

Shit. Just what I need this morning. Ronda pulled over and thought if she tried the Calhoun charm, she might get away with a warning. She grabbed her license and registration before the officer walked over to her open window.

"Morning, ma'am. Do you realize how fast you were going?"

"I'm sorry, Officer." She opened her blue eyes wide and hoped she looked young and innocent. "I was hurrying to work. I hate to be late when I'm supposed to be setting a good example."

Her sweetest smile didn't seem to make any difference. The officer said he would be back in a moment with her citation. He had clocked her at eighty-nine miles per hour and the ticket was going to be expensive.

Damn. The Calhoun charm never fails. She glanced in the rearview mirror to see puffy eyes wearing streaked makeup looking back at her. *No wonder.*

When Ronda reached the parking lot, she was almost half an hour late. In the restroom, she wiped her face and armpits with damp paper towels, applied deodorant, and hit the floor running.

Susan seemed to be handling the counter and the regulars quite well under the circumstances.

"Don't give the new waitress any of your first day baloney, guys."

"Don't worry," Roy said. "We'll be good." As soon as he had said that, he turned to Sue. "Hurry it up, sweetie, I've got three shags waitin' for me."

"I know what a shag is, guys. My uncle drives a twenty-wheeler with a drop down axle. So, you've got three trips under a hundred miles each, today, huh?"

"Hey, this little girl's no deadhead," Pat said.

"Thanks, and I know that means driving a truck with an

empty load, not a follower of the Grateful Dead." The chuckles indicated that Sue was making some fast friends.

Nanette whirled around and glared at Ronda. "Couldn't pull yourself away from Mr. Sexy this morning?"

"I got stopped." She pulled the ticket out of her pocket to prove it, but Nanette seemed unimpressed.

"What did they do, search your car? It doesn't take half an hour to get a ticket."

"Listen, Nanette. I was already late, and I was speeding. There was no 'Mr. Sexy' involved. I'm sorry. That's all there is to it. Now can we move on?"

"Don't get huffy with me. How would you like it? I've been so friggin' busy I haven't even had time to get more friggin' napkins out of the friggin' supply room."

"I'm sorry. I'll get them in a minute, okay?"

Nanette stormed off, unappeased, but they were both too busy to argue. Ronda picked up half of Nanette's tables.

Antoine was in full cooking frenzy when Ronda came to the window for her first order. He didn't say anything, but he glowered at her with narrowed black eyes.

She picked up the orders and retreated hastily.

Nice work, Ronnie. You blew it, big time.

When the morning rush died down, Ronda had a chance to apologize to Sue for the baptism by fire. Sue seemed fine with it and still managed to stay downright cheerful. "What were you supposed to do? Lead the cops on a high speed chase just to get to work on time?"

"Thank you for understanding, Sue."

Okay, one last apology before she called Nate and tried to explain. She steeled herself for Antoine's reaction. Remembering how he hated lateness, she marched into the kitchen.

"Antoine, I'll get Stretch to take down the sign if you think Sue is working out."

"It's already down," he answered curtly.

"Oh, well, good. That's good." She wracked her brain for something to say or do that would make it all right again.

Antoine finally broke the uncomfortable silence, shaking his pancake turner at her. "Tommy would never have started a brand new waitress with only one other waitress on. Being late was unfair to the new girl as well as me and Nanette."

"I know. I'm sorry." After about the third heartfelt apology he told her that it was too late to do anything about it and to get back to work.

She took the tongue lashing quietly and was on her way back to the dining room when she heard the phone ringing in the office. She used the key in her pocket, opened the door and answered it.

"Good morning, sleeping beauty," Nate said. He didn't sound the least bit upset.

"Oh, Nate. Did you come up? I am so sorry. I'm afraid my... Well, I must have passed out."

"Yeah, you looked like you were out cold when I peeked through the curtains."

"Oh God, I'm sorry you came all the way up."

"No big deal. I knocked on the window but you didn't even stir. At least I could see that you were still breathing. I figured it was better to let you sleep, so I left a note and drove to the beach house."

"Damn. How can I make it up to you?"

"I'll think of something," he said wickedly. They both chuckled knowing what that would be, but then he added, "Actually, hon, there is something I'd like you to do."

"What's that?"

"Move into my beach house with me. I've decided to use my branch office more, and my Boston office a whole lot less. I'd love it if we could be together. 'Live with me and be my love'?"

She swallowed hard. "Are you serious?"

"I couldn't be more serious."

"I—I think I like that idea, Nate, but let me mull it over."

"Think about it, and try to have a better day, sweetheart. Okay?"

"It's a whole lot better already." She smiled despite being more overwhelmed than she was five minutes ago.

They whispered, "I love you," at the same time, chuckled, and as soon as she hung up the phone rang again. This time it was Ty.

"Do you have E.S.P. or something?" she asked.

"Probably not. Why?"

"Because every time you call, I'm right next to the phone."

"A convenient coincidence, I'd guess. Listen, did you get a burner phone yet?"

"No. I had one emergency after another yesterday. The craziness didn't even stop after I got home. I'll get one after work tonight, I promise. Have you had any word?"

"Yeah, actually I have. He left a cryptic message with a trusted friend. First tell me about yesterday."

"No. You don't want to hear this." She closed her eyes and pinched the bridge of her nose.

"Sure I do. Now, tell Cousin Ty."

"Ha. You sound just like your father. Okay, I guess I'll spill my guts." She took a deep breath, hoping she could get through the explanation without crying. "First there were five applicants for the job and Antoine asked me to do the interviews, which was fine. We have a terrific new waitress, named Sue. She's a treasure."

"Good. Keep her happy. What else?"

"Well, I think a cop followed me to the bank, and then all the way home."

"You're kidding."

"No, and that's not all... I had to go and ruin his stake out when I discovered my neighbor on the floor of his kitchen, unconscious." Her voice wobbled. "He's the nicest old guy. Apparently it was a home invasion."

"My God, that's horrible. I hope he's okay."

"Yeah, he's in the hospital, but they seemed optimistic about his recovery when I called."

"Well, that's good. So, how did you ruin the stake out?"

Ronda sat up a bit straighter. "I quickly grew a pair of masculine jewels, marched down to the unmarked car and demanded help."

Ty laughed out loud. Finally he coughed and became more serious. "You had a world class bad day, yesterday, Ronda."

"It gets worse."

"Jesus. What else?"

She closed her eyes and sighed. "Well, this is my own fault, but after everything that happened I needed a few beers to calm down. I'm kind of a lightweight, so it doesn't take much and I passed out on the couch. My boyfriend came all the way up from Boston to comfort me, knocked on the window, and couldn't wake me up. I woke up late this morning since I didn't hear the alarm."

Taking a deep breath, she continued. "Because I was late, I was speeding. Because I was speeding, I got a ticket. Because I got stopped, I was much later for work than I already would have been—about half an hour, and now Antoine and Nanette hate me."

"Oh, my God, Calhoun." Ty laughed. "A whole half hour late? You're fired."

"Sure. Why not? That would just top it off. So what about Tommy?"

"I guess I can tell you some of it..."

"I'm dying to know anything you can tell me."

"Okay. They're safe. He's with his travel agent and they won't be back anytime soon. It's you and me running the place now, Ronnie."

Ronda was shocked speechless and almost dropped the phone. His last sentence didn't even register, until the fact that Tommy was out of the country and had taken Marci Jo with him sunk in. *Christ. Now I've lost my master teacher and my best friend too.*

Leaning forward, she pinched the bridge of her nose and asked him about the remainder of his statement. "Hey —What do you mean, you and me? You're able to take over when you get back, aren't you?"

"Ronda, I won't lie to you. I'm not my father and I don't want to be a slave to the place seven days a week. I'd like to have a life too. So, I'm asking you, please, to stay on as the manager. You'll get a significant raise, and we'll get every other weekend off. It's a win-win situation."

"Well, give Antoine and Nanette raises too, if you can. They deserve it."

"Done. We'll give them whatever you think they deserve."

She twirled the phone cord and put her feet up on the desk. "Really? A hundred dollars an hour?"

"Hmmm, maybe we should discuss the budget first."

"What makes you think I'm restaurant management material, anyway?"

"What, are you kidding me? After what you've been through and you're still there? That kind of dedication, your intelligence and tactful people skills make you perfect for it. Hell, I'll even discuss tuition reimbursement for you to get an MBA if you want one, but I can teach you all you need to learn."

A lump formed in her throat. Suddenly Ronda knew what she wanted to do with her life. If she hadn't stumbled into this job, she might never have found it.

Her gratitude would have continued had it not been for Antoine appearing in the doorway, looking furious. "Are you planning on working at all today?" he growled.

"Put him on the phone," Ty said. All the way from California he could tell what kind of mood Antoine was in. Ronda was glad Ty heard him and knew what to do.

She handed the phone to Antoine without saying a word and returned to the dining room.

———

Nanette was still pouting and refused to make eye contact.

"Hey, Nanette. That was Ty. I told him that you and Antoine deserved raises after all your hard work here, especially lately."

"Oh, you did, huh?" Nanette sounded like she thought it was bull.

"Yeah, I did. So, how much of a raise do you need to get that smile back on your face?"

"Oh, I need more than a raise, Ronda."

Uh oh. "So what do you need?"

"I need you to keep working beside me here, and I need a dollar an hour more. How about that?"

"I think that can be done," she said, relieved. If she lost Nanette, the restaurant would be finished.

"Antoine told me about your degree by the way. I imagine you can get any number of better jobs and you'll be out of here soon."

"I'm not going anywhere, Nanette, and you're wrong about something."

"You aren't a college graduate?"

"That's not it. You were right about that, but you were wrong about there being a better job anywhere."

Nanette smiled and impulsively hugged her, then hurried away as if embarrassed.

Ronda was only partially relieved. I hope she's still as happy when she finds out that Ty is making me her boss.

Ronda finally got out of work, dropped the deposit at the bank, and was off to buy the burner phone she desperately needed—if only to contact Marci Jo and rip her a new one. Before heading home, however, she wanted to visit her co-worker and friend, Jenna, in the hospital.

She drove straight to Maine Medical where Jenna was recovering.

"Are you a family member?" the receptionist asked.

She answered, "No, I'm a friend and co-worker."

"Your friend is still in the Intensive Care Unit and can't have visitors outside of family."

"I feel like family," Ronda said.

The receptionist just smiled and said, "Sorry."

Ronda asked if she could talk to Jenna's doctor, but the receptionist said he wouldn't be able to give her any information unless she was family.

"I'm her boss," Ronda said assertively. "Can I ask him when she's apt to be coming back to work?"

The receptionist's smile faded. "Sorry."

As Ronda was about to leave, she thought of someone else she knew who happened to be in this hospital. "Michael Lawson. Is he still here?"

The receptionist looked at the computer and said, "Yes. He's on Five West. Check in at the nurses' station first."

"Thank you," Ronda called over her shoulder as she headed for the elevator. Once she found the fifth floor and then the nurse's station, she looked for a nurse—even a secretary or janitor would have been nice. No one was around.

Note to self, Ronda. Stay out of hospitals until they're fully staffed.

She could see the patients' names scrawled on an erasable board beside each door, and the room right in front of the nurses' station said "Lawson." She entered the semi-private room, timidly. The man in the first bed was most definitely not Michael Lawson, unless the former love of her life had changed his race. The African-American man was snoring, although she wondered how anyone could sleep in a stark white room with overhead lights glaring. She attempted to be very quiet as she crossed the room, around the curtain divider, to the other bed.

Michael's face was badly bruised and swollen. She could see that he had a cast on one arm from his shoulder to his fingers, and he was in traction. She felt a pang of something. What was it? Sympathy? Love re-warmed like leftovers? No, it was pity.

He must have sensed her presence because he opened his eyes, or rather, the one eye that wasn't swollen shut. It opened wider when he saw her and he tried to speak. Because his jaw was wired shut, he could only formulate garbled sounds that didn't even come close to perceptible words.

Ronda witnessed the attempt to communicate, and out of compassion, reached for his one free hand.

"Michael, I'm so sorry this happened to you," she said, softly. She meant it, despite what she expected would be secret satisfaction.

Michael squeezed her hand, and a method of communication occurred to her. "Squeeze once for 'yes' and twice for 'no,' okay?"

Michael squeezed once.

"Do you know who did this to you?" she asked.

He squeezed once.

"How many men attacked you?"

He squeezed twice.

"Oh, right. Sorry. I'll rephrase...Do you know why they did it?" she asked.

Michael dropped her hand altogether and pointed right at her.

"Me? Because of me?" she asked, incredulously.

He took her hand again and squeezed once.

"Can you write?"

He squeezed once, so she rummaged in her pocketbook for a piece of paper and a pen. When she placed it on the over-bed table in front of him, she realized his unbroken hand was his left. He was right-handed, so it would be even harder for him to write legibly. He scrawled something on the paper as Ronda anchored it for him. She couldn't quite make out the message.

Michael wrote again. This time the words were very legible. "Get out."

A nurse entered the room and looked shocked to see her there. "How did you get in here?" she demanded.

"I—I was just going," Ronda stammered. Crumpling the paper and stuffing it into her purse, she wasted no time sailing past the nurse and down the nearest stairwell.

The nurse called after her. "In the future, you *have* to stop at the nurse's station first. We keep track of all visitors in this room."

Ronda drove to Nate's beach house, and on the way she called him. He would have to call her back, of course, so she left the new number on his voice mail and detoured to pick up groceries on the way.

She had thrown a few items in her cart and was aiming for the registers when she spotted a familiar woman wheeling a cart toward her—Janice. She never thought about clairvoyants having to deal with something as mundane as grocery shopping, but there she was.

"Janice!"

Janice looked past the tomato display at her, and her eyebrows shot up. "Oh, my dear, I tried to call you, but your line was being checked for trouble."

"Really?" Ronda was stunned. She had used her phone the day before to call 911. "When did you try?"

"This morning. I received another message for you. I'm sure it was for you." Janice looked around and lowered her voice. "There's something more your family is trying to communicate and I'm just not getting it. I don't usually do this in the grocery store, but they are insisting that I tell you to be careful."

"What about, specifically?"

"They said it before and they are saying again, that you are being deceived. Be careful whom you trust."

Ronda's first thought was, *How do I know I can trust you, then?* Janice had been nothing but supportive and sincere and she was ashamed for her inner sarcasm. It was an old habit. "I'll try to find time to see you in your ... What do you call the room in your house that you use for readings? Your office?"

Janice chuckled. "I do my channeling in my sacred space, but you can call it anything you like." Then she said goodbye and excused herself to continue shopping.

Ronda went through the check out and had much to mull over on her way to Nate's. Should she tell him about going to see Michael? Everything seemed threatening and confusing. What good was having a private eye boyfriend if she wasn't a hundred percent sure she could trust him?

Marci Jo had insisted that she leave Nate out of the loop. Did she know more about Tommy and that was why she helped his sudden flight out of the country? How could Marci Jo really chuck her friends and relatives, all her investments, and her career to run off with him?

Once at Nate's out-of-the-way beach house, she decided to take stock of the people she trusted. Drawing up three columns on a piece of paper, she would write it out logically. Perhaps that way she could stop her head from spinning.

There was Marci Jo, her best friend. No question of loyalty, love or trustworthiness there. Sanity, maybe, but she wrote her name in the right-hand column.

There was Nate. She had questions once, but they had been dispelled, hadn't they? Was she really looking at him impartially anymore? Hmmm. Maybe she should be careful, as Janice had said. Yet here she was in Nate's house and his life. She didn't know what to think, so Nate's name landed in the middle, in the cautious trust column.

Tommy. Once, she would have placed Tommy in the right-hand column, but now he had to go in the left. She looked at that and wondered why she was sticking her neck out for someone she didn't trust. Oh well, she'd look at that later and just continue the exercise for now.

Ty she placed in the middle column. She just didn't know him well enough yet. He was going to be working alongside her, and she'd get to know him quite well after his graduation, but for now—middle column.

Michael was in the left hand column. She realized that total trust was missing from their relationship. If she didn't trust him, why had she believed in him enough to consider marriage? She decided to look at that later, too.

Lorena she didn't know at all, so she didn't even write her name down. Nate had said she was probably in on it, but Ronda still remembered the girl's desperation. Lorena loved Michael with all her heart, but Ronda was having doubts about Michael's ability to love anyone other than himself. She'd leave Lorena up to Nate.

Janice's name landed in the middle column, for provisional trust. Ronda wrote Monica's name, representing the whole paranormal research group, in the middle too.

Antoine and Nanette, her remaining closest co-workers, needed a little more thought. Both of their names appeared in the middle but leaning more to the right.

Poor Mr. Carroll. She added his name to the right column without hesitation and wondered how he was doing. She still hadn't had the time to go to the small local community hospital and check in on her neighbor and friend.

Ronda looked at all of this and still couldn't make heads or tails of it. They probably *all* should be in the middle. That's what Janice was trying to tell her, but believing Janice would place her in the right-hand column. Ronda got so frustrated she crumpled up the paper and crammed it into the bottom of her purse, which was beginning to look like a wastebasket.

Her cell phone rang. She was afraid to answer it, thinking it was probably Nate, but what did she want to tell him now? Caller ID told her it was okay. It was the restaurant.

She breathed a sigh of relief until she heard Dan, the evening cook's voice shaking, with incredibly bad news. The cops were there again and were asking questions about Tommy, Ty, and even about Ronda's involvement in connection with the recent murder of Jenna's boyfriend, Jim. Dan wanted to know what he should tell them.

Damn the phone at the restaurant. It must be tapped. Perhaps that's why her home phone was being "checked for trouble." They wanted her to use the phone at the restaurant for personal calls.

"Dan, cooperate to the best of your ability. If you know anything, tell them. If you don't, tell them that you don't. That's all any of us can do." She was hoping that he knew nothing, but she didn't count on the next question.

"They want to know why you're in charge and yet you're one of the newest waitresses. In fact, the girl who started yesterday is the only one newer than you."

She took a deep breath and decided to tell a partial truth. "It's because I'm good with numbers and good with people. I can handle things there. That's all."

"But Antoine is..."

"Not good with numbers and not good with people. He's good with food. That's about it." She berated herself about being so abrupt. She hoped she wouldn't regret it.

"Okay. I guess I can tell them that," he said and hung up.

Should she bother protecting her cover story anymore? Would having one cause even more suspicion?

She pinched the bridge of her nose. The cell phone startled her, and this time it was Nate.

"How are you?" he said.

"I'm planning my nervous breakdown." The stress temporarily disabled her brain and she forgot that Nate knew nothing about her "battlefield promotion," and her boss's absence.

"What happened? Is Mr. Carroll...?"

"No. At least I don't think so. I've been too busy to check on him."

"Ronda, what else is going on that you haven't told me?"

He wouldn't buy anything she could fabricate on the spot. Provisional trust. Cautious trust. She had some form of trust there and decided to listen to her own gut feelings rather than Marci Jo's advice at this point.

"Yes, Nate. There's a lot going on that I haven't told you."

She filled him in on the fact that Tommy was missing and what he was accused of, according to police. She left out the part about knowing he had skipped the country and Marci Jo's eyewitness account, hoping that would placate her friend.

She told him that she had been managing the restaurant

and that all of her time had been involved in keeping it afloat until Ty could get there. She told him that she was followed home the day before by a plainclothes cop. She told him that she had to refuse to let the paranormal researchers into her parents' home because she just couldn't deal with it all.

Then she turned the conversation back to Nate. "What have you been able to find out about Michael's attacker?"

"Don't worry about that now. You have enough to worry about, Ronnie. I'm glad you're at the beach house. I wrapped up the case I was working on. I'm free to come up anytime."

She hadn't said she was at the beach house. She wasn't the only one to slip up. How did he know where she was? *What the hell?*

"Ronda? Are you there?"

"Yeah. I'm here, Nate. You don't have to come back until the weekend. I'm fine. Really."

"I'm not convinced of that."

"Well, I am."

"Okay. I'm just concerned, honey. I love you so much, and I don't want to let anything happen to you."

"Yeah. Bye, Nate." She sank to the floor as she hung up, a wave of nausea engulfing her.

Tears sprung to her eyes and she didn't try to stop them. Pounding the floor until her hand hurt, she wished she had someone to blame for everything that had happened and everything that was still happening. She shook her head violently and tears flew. *Why? Why can't I have one person I can love and trust—completely, unconditionally, and at all times?*

Grabbing a few necessities, she ran for her vehicle. She didn't know where to go, but she'd figure it out on the way there.

CHAPTER SIXTEEN

The next morning she woke up early. Sleeping in her SUV wasn't the best situation, regardless of finding a beautiful lot with a view. She still felt safer there than at home.

Antoine was in the kitchen when she arrived, filling his stainless steel containers with the ingredients for breakfast.

She needed to look at the books in the office and log in the last deposits. After that she'd try to figure out the payroll system to guarantee the staff got paid. She knew they all depended on their paychecks, even though they joked and called it their "allowance".

She found Tommy's accounting books easier to read than she thought they'd be. His simple, straightforward method of handling the business was coming in handy and she entered the deposits for the last two evenings. Out of curiosity she flipped back to check if he paid his taxes quarterly, or if he left it all to the end of the year for tax accountants. She saw that he did quarterlies, and thankfully the next one wasn't due for another month. She looked at the year's total in the profit column and her mouth went dry. *Wouldn't it be hard to run out on a juicy profit like that?* Whatever made him run must have been pretty powerful.

She looked in the drawer under "P" for payroll. It was there. She saw what everyone was making and was shocked to see that all the wait-staff were earning the same hourly amount. She had told Susan to expect the same amount that she was making because they were both so new, but she never expected to learn that Nanette was making the same as the new waitresses, even after three years.

She'd be in deep trouble if Ty didn't get back soon. Her name wasn't on the checkbook so she couldn't sign paychecks and Thursday was payday.

Ty's name was on the account since he would someday be running the business. He wanted to set up electronic money transfers among other conveniences, and she could have done everything with a few numbers and a password. It hadn't happened yet, so she had to think of another way to pay the staff.

If she set aside a couple of deposits she could pay them with cashier's checks. She'd open an escrow account with the deposit that afternoon. With that decision made, she locked up the office and double-checked that the dining room and counter were restocked and ready.

Susan was the first waitress in. She was humming as she set the tables in the dining area.

"So, do you like it here?" Ronda asked.

"Yeah, I do. The customers are great."

"They can be a lot of fun, can't they?"

Sue finished the tables. "I don't know if I offended Nanette, though. She seems mad at me or something."

"I don't think it's you, Sue. I'll talk to her. I've noticed a negative attitude lately, but I really don't think it's directed at you." Ronda wrote *Nanette* on her order pad. "Just try to keep that smile on. I'll see if there's something I can do to lift Nanette out of the blues."

"You are really nice to work for. I don't know Tommy, but I hope he's as nice as you."

Ronda smiled, a little embarrassed. "He's the best, Sue. I know you'd like him and vice versa."

Ronda thought about her "master teacher". Tommy had been an example of tolerance, reason, and patience. She suddenly felt ashamed for putting him in the untrustworthy column.

She also realized why she was keeping this place together. Would a master teacher put her in this position? Hell, yes. He'd entrusted her with his proudest accomplishment, knowing she could figure it out. That meant something.

"What I don't understand," Sue was saying, "is why he would just take off because the police want to talk to him? Everyone says he couldn't have done it."

"People might not understand his reasons for running off, but once he disappeared, he may have been worried about looking guilty on that basis alone." *I'm pretty sure he had another, better reason, and it must be a doozy.*

"I guess we'll have to wait and see. I'm sure it's a big misunderstanding. Maybe he thought no one would believe him."

It was too early to call Ty, yet she was longing to hear more about Tommy and Marci Jo. She had to know that they were safe and sound.

Tommy hadn't had the chance to teach her much about running the multiple businesses known as "Cousin Tommy's". The restaurant was the backbone of the business, but there was also a convenience store, gas station with both regular and diesel fuels to keep track of, and a mini arcade with coin-operated games. Even the one washer and dryer were coin operated. Who collected the coins? How did she know if they were low on gas? Waitressing for only a couple of months hadn't prepared her for any of that.

She promised she would speak to Nanette but the more she fixated on it, the more she dreaded it. Perhaps the only reason Nanette worked there was because of Tommy. Tommy's disappearance had hit her like a rock in the face.

All three girls worked together that day. The job was actually pleasant until the dinner shift arrived. Antoine stayed in the kitchen talking to Dan long after he usually departed, and Ronda thought it was a bit strange. Still, she had things to do, so she pushed it to the back of her mind and loaded up the deposit bag.

Carrying that much money to her car, her muscles tensed and her mind sharpened to hyper-alert.

Ronda looked around carefully, then strolled into the bank trying to look nonchalant. When she asked to open a separate escrow account for the restaurant, under her own name, the manager looked at her for a long moment.

"Did Tommy take on a partner?"

"Oh, you know him?"

"Well, we see him almost every day. He's been doing business with us for years."

"Then you probably know he hasn't been in this week."

"I guess you're right. I haven't seen him lately."

"He was called away. Family emergency."

"Oh. Does that have anything to do with the detective who came around this morning asking questions about him?"

Ronda was startled. "Sutton? Was his name Detective Sutton?"

"No. Smith, if I remember correctly."

She couldn't believe her ears. "Nate Smith?"

"Yes. I believe his name was Nate Smith. We couldn't tell him much. Is Tommy in trouble?"

She shook her head, finished her business quickly, and

secretly vowed to cut Nate into little pieces and feed him to the seagulls. Didn't she ask him to stop interfering?

As soon as she left the bank and jumped into her Jeep, her cell phone rang. It was Dan at the restaurant. He sounded upset.

"Ronda, Antoine quit. I'm really sorry. I wasn't thinking, I guess."

"Wasn't thinking about what?" She dreaded the answer.

"We were talking about the police asking everyone about Tommy, and I—I told him what you said to tell the police when they were asking questions about why you were put in charge. Shit. He promised he wouldn't get mad before I said it."

Oh God, what would the master teacher do now? "Dan?" she said, as calmly and evenly as she could. "You like Tommy, don't you?"

"Of course I do. He's the best. I'd do almost anything for him."

"Well, here's your chance to help him. Antoine has to be replaced. We can't have a restaurant without a cook."

"You want me to do Antoine's shift and mine too?"

"Just tomorrow, Dan. I'll talk to Antoine and get him to come back, but until he does, Tommy really needs you. This isn't for my benefit. If we close the place, I'll just go and get another job. But it's Tommy's dream."

"I don't know..."

"Time and a half."

"Okay, Ronda. You've got it. I just hope I can get up early enough in the morning."

"I'll give you a wake-up call."

Dan gave her his phone number and she wrote it down on the pamphlet the bank insisted on giving her when she opened her account. "I can't thank you enough, Dan. You're the best."

Once she had bolstered his ego, he sounded like he would rather die than let her down. That was something else she had learned from the master.

At last she was on her way home. She would grab a takeout dinner, swing by her cottage and pick up the mail, change her clothes, grab a fresh uniform and maybe go to Nate's cottage. If he was there, she intended to kill first and ask questions later.

Much to her displeasure, Nate was sitting on her front porch.

She sidestepped his kiss and grabbed for the door. As soon as she unlocked it, she said, "Come in. I'm going to yell at you, and I don't want the neighbors to hear every word of it."

Nate raised his eyebrows and cautiously followed her inside. "What did I do now, Ronnie?"

She closed the door and whirled around to face him. "Nate, I'm furious with you. I don't know if I can say this without exploding. First of all, how did you know I was at the beach house last night? Are you following me? And why were you nosing around the Seaside Bank this morning, asking questions about Tommy? Whatever you say had better be the truth, or we're through."

"Whoa, Ronda. You're not making this easy. Look, I really do love you and I just want to know you're safe. There was so much happening around you...dangerous stuff. The break-ins, your neighbor being attacked in a home invasion..."

"How did you know it was a home invasion? I didn't tell you anything except that he was in the hospital."

He hesitated, letting out a deep breath. "I paid a

colleague of mine to keep an eye on you while I wasn't around."

Ronda sucked in and held her breath, but exploded despite her best efforts. "You hired a PI to spy on me? How dare you do that without telling me, and what the hell makes you think you know what's best for me? Huh?"

He cocked his head to the side. "I thought you were going to postpone that nervous breakdown."

"My God, Nate. How dare you be so arrogant? I can't stand this invasion of my privacy, and right now I can't stand you!"

She pushed past him, hitting his shoulder as hard as she could, and left him standing in her living room while she ran and jumped into her Jeep. She hadn't taken the time to grab her purse, but she still had her keys in her hand so she fired up the engine. She glanced in his direction and saw him standing in the middle of her walk, frowning, with his hands on his hips.

She wasn't sure where she could go without being followed or bothered. He would probably look for her. Hell, he'd probably have all of his cronies looking for her. She had to find a place where she could stay until she cooled off. She drove around until she was low on gas. *To hell with him. I might as well hide in plain sight.* She drove to Cousin Tommy's for a free meal.

"He must be a scary dude to have you on the run. I've never known you to back down from anyone," Roy said.

"Yeah. Sometimes he intimidates me. Not the man himself. I'm more upset by his skills. He's a private detective and finds me wherever I go. Right now I just need to be alone."

Roy's pie and check arrived. The two unlikely friends were both quiet while they ate.

"A private dick, huh?"

"Yeah, sometimes..." Ronda chuckled. "At other times he can be really sweet."

"Listen, I don't want to get in the middle of a lover's spat, but if you're being stalked you can follow me to my place and sleep in my rig."

Ronda hadn't considered the possibility that she was actually being stalked, but thinking about it ... well, there was that element.

"Thanks, Roy. I might take you up on that. Let me think about it. In any case, I'll pick up the tab because you've been so sympathetic, okay?"

He started to protest, but when he saw her rip up the check he just laughed. Ronda reached into her apron, slapped a five-dollar bill on the counter for Sherri's tip and said, "You know, Roy, I think I'll take you up on that offer. Why don't you take my SUV to your place, and leave your rig right here in the parking lot? That might throw him off."

"Why not? I'll be here first thing in the morning anyway, and you'll have a dandy commute."

"Sounds wonderful. I'm exhausted, and I can use all the sleep I can get."

"If you oversleep, I'll knock once and then again three times. If anyone knocks different, don't answer it."

Ronda reported for work a little early, looking almost as disheveled as she did that Monday. Her hair was wild and her clothes were rumpled. The only thing missing were the bags under her eyes. She made a mental note to buy a couple of lockers even if she had to wedge them into the office somewhere. For now she'd just have to take another brand new uniform.

As she strolled through the parking lot, she sensed that something was wrong. Suddenly she realized that there were no cars parked by the back door. *Dan.* She forgot all about his wake-up call.

She grabbed her keys, including the back door key she had never tried before. It looked brand new and perhaps it had never been used. When she attempted to fit it into the lock, it didn't seem to work.

Ronda stamped her foot and yelled, "Damn." She tried it again, and it slipped in but wouldn't turn. Before the third try she shook her fist at the sky and yelled, "A little help here, please?" The key turned. She was in. "Thank you," she muttered sheepishly to whatever invisible force had lent a hand.

Calling Dan, she woke him from a sound sleep. He said he could be there in half an hour. Then Ronda knew she had to call Antoine. *I might as well get it out of the way.* He was probably awake, having worked this shift for twenty-plus years.

She was right. Antoine was awake and expecting her call. He didn't know, however, that she had Dan coming in and thought she was out of luck. He sounded disappointed when she told him that a cook was on his way.

"Antoine, please understand that I didn't mean what I said. I only said it to satisfy the police."

"I'm not convinced," he pouted.

"How can I convince you?" she pleaded. "Tell me what to do to allow you to forgive me and come back. Please?"

"I want a refrigerated display case for my desserts," he said. "And I want the restaurant to take special orders for my decorated cakes."

Ronda blanked. She wasn't expecting that. "A refrigerator? Like for pastry?"

"Yup. I want a real nice one."

"How much do they cost?"

"I'm guessing you can get one for a few thousand."

Stunned, she didn't dare say "no," yet she came up empty wondering how to get her hands on that much money. "Antoine, can you please wait until after a couple of paydays for it—and understand that I have to ask Ty?"

Antoine was quiet.

"Can't Miss NYU get the money from some wealthy friend or relative?"

"No, I can't. Antoine, I'm coming into a little money but not for another few months."

"What, you don't have a trust fund you can dip into?" he persisted.

"No. Look, if you must know, I lost my parents in a plane crash recently. I'm sure they would have set up a trust, but not knowing they were going to die in their fifties, they just hadn't gotten around to it. There's some money, but it's all tied up in probate court."

"Oh," he said, as if he wasn't sure he should believe her.

"Look, would I be working as a waitress if I had a big bank account?"

"I guess not." She heard disappointment in his voice.

"Antoine, can I please beg your forgiveness and promise to look into the refrigerated case? Will you come back then?"

"I might..."

There was an uncomfortable silence while she waited for something more.

Pinching the bridge of her nose, exasperated, she asked, "What will it take, Antoine? What?"

Antoine raised his voice. "You keep saying, 'If I apologize ... Can I beg forgiveness?' but you haven't apologized yet. At least I haven't heard an apology."

"I'm so sorry, Antoine. I didn't mean it. I should have

thought of something else to say. I panicked. It was a very poor choice of words on my part, and I beg your forgiveness."

"All right," he said. "That's enough, but you won't ever say anything like that again, right?"

"No, I won't. Of course I won't. Not ever. It was callous and stupid. I've learned my lesson. I promise," she said.

"Okay, okay. I'll come back tomorrow, but just so you know. I think we're low on chopped onions. You'd better start chopping whole onions for the omelets and such. Whichever cook you got to come in won't have time for it when he gets there, and he's going to need a ton of it. The onions are in the pantry next to the fridge and the containers are on the shelf."

"Oh, sure, I can do that. Anything else?"

"No. Your cook will be able to figure it out once he gets there, but I know we were low on chopped onions yesterday."

Ronda said goodbye, thanking him profusely and proceeded immediately to the kitchen. She found the bags of onions, grabbed eight of them, hoping that would make enough, found the sharp knife that she had seen Antoine use, and peeled off the onion skins.

She had just finished chopping the last of them when Dan came in and saw her eyes full of tears.

"Oh, don't cry, Ronda. I'm here now."

She smiled. "I'm okay. It's just these onions Antoine said you needed. I'd probably cry a lot more if you didn't come in this morning."

"Onions?" Dan said. Then he walked over to the large refrigerator and removed a stainless steel container, took off the plastic wrap and showed her a full six cups of chopped onions. "Like these?"

Ronda just hung her head and smiled. She could almost hear Antoine laughing.

Ronda and Nanette were setting out the cups, silverware, and napkins when Nanette spoke to her, looking smug.

"I see that Antoine isn't here today."

"No. He won't be here until tomorrow," Ronda said, without further explanation.

"Oh. Day off, is it?"

"Something like that." Ronda turned to face her critic with one hand on her hip. "Nanette, is there something you're dying to say?"

"Like what?"

"I don't know. It just seems like there's something on your mind."

"Nothing is on my mind. I, of course, don't have a brilliant mind, like you…"

"Okay, so you heard I have a business degree. What of it?"

"How can you do all of that and waitress too? Unless you're too good to wait on tables anymore."

"Nanette, knock it off. As soon as Ty or Tommy comes back, I'll be out here all the time."

Nanette sighed and seemed less petulant.

"I know you've been holding this shift together. I've told Ty how much we're indebted to you." She propped her butt against the counter and crossed her arms.

"Yeah, I do care about Tommy's. But what I don't get is why you do." Nanette grabbed a wet cloth and proceeded to wipe the counter raw. When she came close to Ronda, who didn't move, she tossed the rag in the sink.

"Because, like everyone here, I care about Tommy too. Even though I only knew him a short time, I felt close to him. Almost like he was a father figure. You know?"

"Well, I don't know about the father figure." Nanette let

out a sigh. "I kinda liked Tommy as a *man* figure, if you get what I mean..." She came close to blushing.

"Oh, I understand," Ronda said. "Yeah. I can see you two together. You'd make a really good couple."

That scored some points. Nanette smiled for the first time that day, and it looked like her cold shoulder was beginning to thaw.

"I really wish I knew where he was and what he was doing." Nanette picked up the wet rag again and wiped the counter that she had just thoroughly cleaned. "I'm worried sick."

"Me, too. I hope he's okay. I think he is. Ty said he used to be a Green Beret or something. He knows how to take care of himself."

"Really?" Nanette smiled ear to ear. "A Green Beret? I didn't know that about him, although I can totally see it."

Her mood had brightened considerably, and Ronda presumed that she was picturing Tommy in his camouflage fatigues, wearing his sexy beret.

The girls served breakfast to the regulars who traipsed through, as well as the occasional tourist who saw the thirty-foot sign promising good home cooking.

At long last Ronda felt she had a free moment to go to the office and look into the cost of a dessert display case. As she was leafing through the brochures on restaurant equipment, there was a soft knock on the door.

Ronda said, "C'mon in," without looking up as the door opened.

"Hello, angel."

"Ty?" She stared, flabbergasted. "What the..."

"Yup. I couldn't leave this all in your lap, Ronda. It just isn't right."

"What about your graduation?"

"I'll go back on Saturday, stay for the day, and fly home

right after it's over. I already gave away everything but my clothes."

Ronda couldn't help herself. She got up and charged, hugging him tightly. "Thank you. I've been okay, but I think everyone would feel better with you in charge."

"*We* will be in charge, Ronda, as equals. I really need you."

CHAPTER SEVENTEEN

"You're kidding. What do you need me for?"

"When I said that I intended to have a life other than the truck stop, I meant it. Can you help me out?"

"You've got it, Ty. By the way, can I make a couple of recommendations right now?"

Ty smiled and said to go ahead.

"A new refrigerator case for desserts. Antoine almost quit and said he needs one in order to come back to work happily."

"Yeah, I saw Dan in the kitchen this morning. He'll be glad to hear that Antoine is returning. When is he coming back?"

"Tomorrow, provided I do what I can to get him his new display case."

"Okay. I guess you're looking into that." He nodded toward the restaurant supplies brochure open to refrigeration.

"Yeah. The other thing, Ty, is even easier."

"Good. Glad to hear it. What's that?"

"Nanette needs a title and a few dollars more per hour. She's been holding the place together and up until now she's been making the same amount as me—even the same amount as Sue who started yesterday. We could use a part-timer too, so I can come back here and help you out."

"Yeah. I'm sure my father was trying to keep his book-keeping simple, but I agree with you. She needs some recognition. What won't sound stupid?"

"I don't know. I never liked 'employee of the month'. How about lead wait person? Does that sound too much like head waiter? I don't want the regulars to start razzing her about the need to make reservations."

"I like it. You can tell her that you recommended the higher position and that it comes with a hefty raise and she'll love you for it. You may need her to love you someday."

"You're pretty smart, Ty. I'm so happy to have you back I could cry."

"Oh, don't do that," he smiled. "Our regulars are counting on you to be cheerful."

Ronda gave him another big hug, "I can do that now." She smiled and practically skipped into the restaurant to do her usual good job.

By afternoon Ronda had told Nanette the good news— five dollars more per hour and the right to bitch at the other waitresses, not that she wouldn't have anyway. It looked like Ronda was in her good graces for life after that. Nanette was not only glad to see Ty but also thrilled to have Ronda back in the dining room nearly full-time.

Sue caught Ronda at a good moment and said, "I guess you were right. Nanette isn't mad at me at all."

"Yeah. I think she's feeling better."

"Has she been sick?"

Ronda shook her head. "I don't think so." *Not physically. Love sick, maybe.*

She found a quiet moment later in the day and explained to Ty about the escrow account. He agreed it was a good idea and decided to add to it, so she could cover emergencies in case Ty was away. He said his father kept an escrow account for emergencies, but there was nothing in it. He'd checked. It had been emptied. They both hoped it would be enough to keep Tommy safe.

When things were running smoothly, Ronda could take a deep breath and attend to other matters. It was bothering her that she hadn't been to visit Mr. Carroll in the hospital. Now that she didn't have to go to the bank after work and run from her boyfriend, she could concentrate on other important things.

At last, Ronda remembered why she was holding on to the job. It was downright enjoyable most of the time. When she left for the day, she felt carefree and ten pounds lighter. In truth, Ronda had lost some weight from stress and irregular eating habits.

She decided not to stop at her house but to go straight to the hospital. She didn't want to be sidetracked by Nate again. She would deal with him when she was good and ready.

She missed knowing her next-door-neighbor was always there. She missed his wave, his greetings, his teasing remarks. It was as if she could say, "Honey, I'm home" to someone. Well, she still might, someday.

She stopped at the receptionist and asked for his room. She was directed to it with a smile. It was a very different reception from the one she received in the city.

Ronda proceeded directly to his room and was met by an orderly, stripping the sheets off the bed.

"Where is Mr. Carroll?" she asked.

The orderly didn't know, so she walked with foreboding to the nurse's station.

"Oh, he's been taken to surgery again." The nurse informed her. "Are you a relative?"

"I'm all the family he has," she said, vaguely. The nurse didn't question it. *And he's all the family I have,* Ronda added, silently.

"Well, he had some more internal bleeding. You can leave your telephone number, and I'll have his doctor call you when he's out of the recovery room."

"Thank you. Please tell him that Ronda was asking for him."

Ronda's mind was ablaze on the way home. She was angry and in mental overdrive.

If Nate wasn't on her shit list at the moment, she'd have him look into the home invasion. She wondered why Nate made her so angry. All he did was to come to her house uninvited, try to tell her what to do, admit he was having her followed, and then accuse her of having a nervous breakdown. She snorted. *That would piss off anyone.*

When she reached her home the phone was ringing. She rushed in to pick it up before the old fashioned answering machine did. Apparently the line was no longer being checked for trouble. It was Mr. Carroll's surgeon.

"I'm sorry to have to tell you this, but your dear uncle didn't make it through the surgical procedure. He expired at 3 PM today. I'm so sorry for your loss."

Ronda heard the buzzing in her ears that meant she should probably sit down. Instead, she burst into tears and held onto her kitchen counter for support.

"Are you going to be all right? Can I send someone over? We have grief counselors."

"No, I'll be all right. Thank you." She hung up. Sliding down the wall, she curled into a fetal position and bawled her eyes out.

She had a heartfelt cry, and then prayed that he was at peace and happy wherever he was. Crime scene tape still roped off the stone yard of the house next door. Ronda couldn't bear to look at it. That evening it rained hard, reflecting her mood.

She didn't want to overdo the drinking again, so she dragged herself to bed early—drained, old, and tired. Her dreams were odd, but strangely comforting. She saw her dear old friend sitting on his porch.

"Mr. Carroll? Are you still here?"

"I'm right next door, Ronda."

"Just like always?"

"Just like always," he said in her dream.

The next morning Ronda was relieved to see Ty at the restaurant first thing in the morning. It was payday and he was making out the checks for the week's wages by hand, like his father always had.

Ty looked up when Ronda poked her head in.

"I think I'll get that computer system soon," he said.

"Which one? The super high-tech one or the compromise?"

"I'll get the compromise, out of respect for my father and also as a statement of faith that he'll be back."

"I like that. I'm still thinking positive. But there's one 'what if' that I keep coming back to."

"What 'what if' is that?"

"What if he just wanted everyone to think he was out of the country, and he's in LA for your graduation? What if he's planning to get in touch with you? I can't imagine him leaving without seeing you in person and explaining himself."

"I'm not sure what he's doing. As I said, he's a survivor. He may try to find me. He knows I'll be there."

"You wouldn't miss it for anything, I imagine."

"No. I'd lose my deposit on the cap and gown."

She chuckled. "You have a dry sense of humor. I wouldn't have guessed that about you, Ty."

"There hasn't been a lot to laugh about lately."

Ronda looked at her feet. "You can say that again. My next-door neighbor passed away yesterday."

"Man, I'm sorry to hear that, Ronda. Hey, if there's anything I can do..."

"Yeah," she said, believing it to be just the same empty offer made by well meaning, but ultimately busy, people.

"No. I really mean it," he said. "What did you do last night?" he asked.

"I went to bed early."

"Ronda, how about if we do something together tonight? I could use the company."

She was surprised, but the prospect sounded good. "I'd like to," she said. Before she went to work, he handed her an envelope with her paycheck in it. "Oh, good. Maybe now I can afford to go to a movie or buy more beer or something."

He simply smiled. It was much later in the day when she finally opened her paycheck and discovered that she had earned more than she could have anticipated. She poked her head into the office, but Ty wasn't there. Looking around, she found him restocking shelves in the store.

"What's this?" she said, holding out the check.

"Your manager's salary for this week."

She was astonished. "Wow. I don't know what to say."

"Say, 'I earned it'. In fact, you more than earned it. Now maybe you can go to a movie *and* buy beer."

She smiled and stretched up to find the warm cove of Ty's neck. She didn't care if there were a dozen eyewitnesses to the long hug they shared. Ronda gave him a peck on the cheek and returned to work in the dining room. All was well until Nate walked in.

"Ronda, we need to talk."

She grabbed a cloth and wiped the counter, refusing to make eye contact. "Funny, I have nothing to say to you."

"I think you do. In fact, I think you ought to be damn glad I've come to straighten your ass out about a few things."

Ronda heard a sharp, stinging tone that she had never heard in his voice before. "Like what?" she snapped, only then becoming aware of her own anger over yet another loss —the loss of her lover. Nate wasn't just a physical fuck buddy. He was a real lover on all levels. That hurt.

"Like how irresponsible you were to just leave your house the other day, unlocked, for anyone to walk in. Did you forget you've had two break-ins recently? What if I hadn't been there to close up for you?"

"Then I wouldn't have had to leave in a hurry, would I?"

By now the restaurant was deathly quiet and listening to every word. Mark and Ed stood up.

"Nate, it's my house, and I can do what I want with it."

"Okay, fine." He raised his voice. "But, there's more, Ronda. Much more. Did you know that your precious Tommy has been using an assumed name for the last three decades?"

"What do I care? He can call himself 'Madonna' if he wants to. I think it's part of our first amendment rights," she said through gritted teeth.

She saw Ty out of her peripheral vision and wondered if he had heard what Nate just said, but all he did was walk to Ronda's side, placing himself between them. She decided that if Ty was able to keep his cool, then she probably could too. Trying to ignore Nate, she reached beneath the counter, pulled out a container with a spout and proceeded to squirt more catsup into the nearly full bottles.

"I guess you don't care that he's wanted for murder, either," Nate said, glaring at Ty. "Hell, you're probably in on it. Your lack of reaction has 'premeditated' written all over it."

Ronda slammed a catsup bottle on the counter. "Please leave. You aren't welcome here." Her voice was shaking and she clenched the bottle with white knuckles, wanting to hurl it at him.

"Go ahead. Defend your new boyfriend! Just watch your back." Nate didn't look as if he planned to leave until every trucker in the restaurant stood and walked toward him, slowly but deliberately.

"This isn't the end of it, Ronda," he called over his shoulder as he strode out.

She took a deep breath and hung her head, elbows locked, bracing her weight against the counter.

"Thanks, you guys," she said.

"Anytime, Ronnie." Ed patted her hand.

Nanette walked behind the counter, shaking her head then hugged her. Saying nothing, Ty returned to the office.

Ronda found him there during the next lull.

"I'm really sorry about Nate's tantrum, Ty. I'd like to promise it won't happen again, but I'm not sure it won't." She dropped into the chair opposite him and hung her head. "It might be better if I leave after you're back permanently."

"Leave? Because of a boyfriend's lovesick outburst? Don't you dare."

She let out a deep breath. "I'm glad you feel that way, because I'd really miss the people here—and don't listen to Nate. He was probably bluffing to see our reactions."

"Don't worry about your job, Ronnie. You have tenure and can stay as long as you like. We'll talk more tonight."

"Are we still going somewhere tonight?"

"We can if you want to."

"I'd like the company, but I'm not sure I'm in the mood for a night on the town."

"I don't blame you. Why don't we just go to my house? I'll pick up some live lobsters on the way home."

"You don't have to cook for me."

"I miss Maine seafood and I miss cooking. Believe it or not, I'm a good cook."

"Sounds wonderful. Are you sure it's no trouble?"

"Will you get back to work, Calhoun?"

She finally smiled and left the office. Doing her job for the rest of the afternoon made her relax, and eventually she was even humming.

Ronda returned home to shower, change, and gather up her mail. Things appeared to be normal. The mail was scattered all over the floor, the water pressure was low, and she didn't know what to wear.

She settled on jeans and a football jersey with the sleeves rolled up. She felt like being completely casual since they were just hanging out.

Ty was in the same casual mode. He wore jeans and a Lakers T-shirt. He made a great indoor clambake and Ronda ate more than usual—not even caring about the calories.

"Are you a basketball fan, Ty?" she asked.

"Yeah. I played, you know." He leaned back and draped a long arm behind his chair.

"No, I didn't."

"Yeah. I had a basketball scholarship as a freshman. Had to quit the team to pass academics though."

"That's pretty cool, Ty. Right now I'm glad you took the business route."

"Me too. Let's move to the living room."

They settled themselves on the couch. "In my fantasies, back in high school, I hoped to go pro. Do you like basketball?"

"Not as much as football. I watch every Patriots game."

"My dad and I love football too. I was built for basketball, though."

"No regrets about coming home to Maine, then?"

"None. I love Maine. Why?"

"Only rumors. Some people think LA must have been so exciting that Maine would just bore you now."

"Maine, boring? The land of Stephen King? Never," he said, grinning. "Besides, I have a lucrative job waiting for me here."

"I have to confess, I peeked at the books."

"Ronda, I'm a business major. If it weren't a little gold mine, I wouldn't be interested in it."

She jumped up. "Well, enough of this crass money-talk. I saw a chess set. Do you play?"

"Yes, but I'm pretty good and I play to win."

"Good. Me too."

They moved the chessboard and pieces to the coffee table and became embroiled in a competitive game of chess.

An hour later, Ronda was down to one knight, two bishops, and her queen. Ty had the advantage of having his queen to do the final beheading. They congratulated each other on a good game.

"I want a rematch sometime. I don't want to play another game now, though," she confessed. "I have too much brain drain already."

"Yeah. Me too. I keep wondering about my dad and what that detective friend of yours said."

CHAPTER EIGHTEEN

"I wouldn't listen to anything he's saying right now. I think he's just trying to hurt me. I pushed him away, because I don't want him showing up everywhere without calling, having me followed, and deciding what's good for me."

"Shit. I'm still just getting to know you, but I can't imagine you'd let someone else take over your life."

She chuckled. "You know me better than you think you do, then."

"Ronnie, I have to wonder about the information he might have if it concerns my father. If he has something damaging, I don't want to be caught off guard." He stood and paced.

"You play life like you play chess," she said. "Three moves ahead."

"Yeah, if I can. Is there any way you could find out what he meant?"

"Not if it involves being in his presence, talking to him, or even reading his warped mind."

"I guess it's really over, then?" Ty stopped pacing.

She nodded but couldn't help feeling sick about it.

"There might be another way to check out his information. Are you in touch with anyone from your dad's childhood?"

"No. He said he was an only child and that his parents died before I was born." Ty sat on the chair, across from her. "He grew up in Florida but said he moved a lot."

"Do you have a picture of your father in uniform?"

"Yes. There's one of his whole unit." Leaning over to the end table, he rummaged through a drawer. "As far as I know, it's the only picture he has from overseas. Why? What are you thinking of doing with it?"

"I know a man who thinks he remembers him from that time. Could I borrow the picture and show it to him?"

"Damn. It isn't in here." He shut the drawer. "I'll look for it later."

"It would be worth a shot, though, don't you think?"

"Yeah. Could I come with you when you go to see him?" he asked.

"Sure. Of course."

They planned to see the used-car sales manager the following afternoon after Ty left for the day. It was Ronda's day off. She explained to Ty some of the events going on in Kennebunkport and said that she had to go there first to check on the house and talk to the police.

Ronda drove back to her cottage nervous and unsettled but glad that she had talked to Ty. She believed him to be a trustworthy friend.

The next day, Ronda's trip to Kennebunkport didn't tell her much that she didn't already know. The house was locked up tight. Nate had replaced the basement door and installed a deadbolt after the police found the researchers and escorted them out. *Oops, I never thanked him for that.*

Captain Millman said they checked Nate's credentials

and he was a licensed investigator in Massachusetts and had received his reciprocity license in Maine. The captain didn't read much into Nate's overprotective behavior. He seemed to think he would get over it now that the relationship was on the rocks.

Ronda walked into her parents' home and resumed the job that she had started before. She had to go through each room and rediscover old memories while she sorted and piled special belongings on the beds.

Four hours of memories later she couldn't stand it anymore and left everything where it was. She relocked the front door and absently wandered out to the driveway. She was tapped. Still, she had to make the trip to the car dealership.

Ty was there at the agreed-upon time and he admitted, "I'm a little nervous about what we might learn."

He showed her the picture, which was in a plain silver-tone frame. Ronda looked at it closely.

Tommy was in Army camouflage pants and a T-shirt, with dog tags hanging from his neck. He was sitting in the bottom left hand corner of the picture. No beret adorned any of the soldiers' heads.

"It's odd to see a very young Tommy, with light brown hair. He looks much handsomer now with the distinguished gray in his temples."

"Tell me that when I'm his age. But now, I guess we'd better get this over with."

They walked inside and asked for the manager.

"Is everything all right with your vehicle, Miss Calhoun?"

"Yes, it's great." He looked at Ty and seemed a bit startled. Ty ignored the reaction, if he saw it and handed the picture to him.

"Do you see the Tommy Kelley that you served with in this picture?"

"Yes." The manager smiled. "He's right here." He pointed to the man in the middle of the photo.

That's odd, Ronda thought. Then she pointed to the picture of the man she knew as Tommy and asked, "Do you know who that is?"

"Sure," he said. "That's Don. Corporal Berry." Glancing up at Ty, he added. "You look like him. Are you related?"

Ty nodded but remained silent.

"We called him 'the Don', like a Mafia Don. No one called him 'Don' without 'the' in front of it."

Ty looked at Ronda unable to hide his stunned expression any longer. "Are you sure?" he asked.

"Positive. Look here. That's me." He pointed to a private on the right side of the picture. The similar features were unmistakable despite years of aging and thirty or so extra pounds. He tapped the picture of Don Berry. "I always wondered what happened to him. I saw him standing with the MP's one minute, and when I turned back, he was gone."

"Was 'the Don' in some kind of trouble?"

"Hell, yes. He was about to be taken away and tried for murder. The Army wanted to make an example of him." The gray-haired man leaned against one of the vehicles in the showroom. "You have to understand, those were real tough times, and lots of guys resented his ability to cope without drugs. Well, he may have finally caved, or someone slipped him some acid. Anyway, he went on a "bad trip" and shot and killed one of our own. He thought he was the enemy, but he was his best buddy."

"Holy..." Ty's jaw hung open.

"Don was smart, though—and tough. When we were under heavy enemy fire, he slipped away—AWOL. He probably could have survived. To tell you the truth, I was surprised when they said he was killed. I thought he'd be the last man standing."

He looked at Ty who had turned pale, "I'm sorry if this is a shock to either of you."

Ronda thanked the manager for his time, shook his hand, and they left the dealership. She suddenly realized that she had forgotten to ask if he had called Tommy at home the day she heard him fervently insisting there was a mix-up in identity. She looked over at Ty's gray face and was glad she didn't. It seemed as though he had heard enough.

Ronda had to work the next day, Saturday. Ty left Friday night for LA and promised to be back on Sunday.

She arrived early. Wanting to check on Jenna's condition Ronda hoped the weekend staff at the hospital would be more understanding. Rather than go in after work and be run off again, she called first. Jenna had been transferred to a regular floor. Ronda was ecstatic.

For good measure, she asked to be transferred back to the operator and asked for Michael's floor. She had to hold for a while, but a nurse picked up the phone eventually. She asked the nurse how Michael Lawson was doing and was told that they had no one by that name. She knew that patients were discharged as soon as they could survive, so she assumed that he was stable. *Is he in prison or home on bail? Do I care anymore?*

Ronda set the tables for the morning and told the weekend cook, Manny, about Jenna. They had a couple of waitress who worked only on weekends. When Wendy came in, Ronda gave her the good news about Jenna too.

"I'm so glad to hear that," Wendy said. "I only worked with her every third weekend or so, but I really liked her. She was sweet." Ronda noticed the amount of hairspray required to hold the woman's hair in place. Wendy helped herself to a glass of orange juice.

"Yeah. Much too sweet for that monster of a boyfriend." Ronda took the coffee pot from the warmer and poured herself a cup.

"Do you believe what they said about Tommy killing him?"

"I doubt he did it purposely, if he did it at all." Ronda tried to keep her expression passive and noncommittal. "It might have been one lucky punch. Or, *unlucky*, as the case may be."

"I hope they find him," Wendy said.

"What?" Ronda couldn't believe what she was hearing.

"So if he's innocent, he can clear his name."

"I guess if there are no witnesses, it's hard to prove you're innocent or guilty. I don't blame him for not wanting to take a chance on it."

"Yeah, I guess." The girl shrugged.

Ronda couldn't just let it go. It rankled her. "Juries are tricky. Sometimes they see circumstantial evidence and they focus on that. Sometimes they just want to get home early."

"Yeah," Wendy said, but she didn't sound convinced. "So I guess Ty will be back soon and you'll be here in the meantime?" Wendy asked.

"That's right," Ronda said trying to put a cheerful smile on her face. She didn't say any more to Wendy. She just hoped that Tommy would be attending a certain graduation ceremony in a few hours.

Everything in the office was under control, so Ronda planned to work in the restaurant most of the day. Roy happened to come in. He said he was going to take Saturday off, but was offered one short run to Haymarket Square in Boston.

"I heard that boyfriend of yours gave you a hard time the

other day."

Ronda stopped wondering how information like that spread so fast.

"Ex-boyfriend, and yeah. Ed, Mark, Al, and a few other guys stood up, started walking toward him, and he took off. I was never so happy that they were looking out for me."

"We're all looking out for you, sweetie."

"At least I have some good friends."

Nate entered the restaurant, slowly, sizing up the place first.

She looked over at him and rolled her eyes. Hands in his pockets, he approached the counter slowly.

"Ronda, I just want to apologize, and then I'll be out of your hair—forever if you insist."

She turned to face him and frowned. "Make it short and sweet. I'm working." She sounded a little bitchy, but she really didn't give a fig.

"I had no right to intrude the way I did. I know you're a private person, yet there was so much going on around you. I couldn't help worrying and wondering if you were in danger. I've seen too much in this profession. I was afraid for you."

"So you've said." She didn't soften one bit.

"And the other day, I saw you kiss Ty through the window, and I had a bout of temporary jealous insanity."

The regulars sat up straighter, appearing to listen attentively.

"There are still some things I need to tell you, Ronda. Some important pieces of the puzzle concerning your neighbor. You might want to know what I found out."

She took the towel she was using to wipe the counter and threw it into the sink behind her.

"Fine. You can come to the office and tell me what you know, but then I want you gone. Understand?"

"Perfectly," he mumbled.

"Wendy, I'll be back in two minutes."

Roy called out, "We'll send a search party if it's much longer than that." Then Roy looked at the other customers at the counter and said, "Hey, I'm gettin' low on coffee."

There were some comforting chuckles as she led Nate to the office. Why did he feel like she was leading him to a firing squad?

"Ronnie, thank you for giving me a chance to explain. First of all, there's a connection between what happened to your neighbor and the two break-ins in your home."

"I thought there might be."

"I believe that Mr. Carroll just got in the way. Either he confronted one of them, or they knew he could identify whoever he saw."

"That makes *some* sense."

"What about it doesn't make sense?"

"Well, there's still nothing missing from my house. Why would he come back and still leave empty-handed?"

"I thought there might be something there, like a planted bug. He was scared off the first time, wasn't he?"

"Yeah. I came home unexpectedly."

"So he just had to finish the job. Ronda, I looked around your house carefully when you left me there. I found what I was looking for. Three microphones. One was near your front door, so they could monitor your comings and goings. One was on the stairs. They squeak. The other one was inside the kitchen. Under the cabinets, near the rug where we..."

She shook her head but didn't comment. She began playing with a paperweight.

"The stuff happening in Kennebunkport?"

"I'm sure the same guy who broke into your place was in with the group of thieves at your parents' house. The description the researchers gave matched Mr. Carroll's."

"My parents had some valuable paintings and antiques.

But, nothing was missing from their house, either."

"One painting was missing. Michael told us he was having it copied and where we could find it. The painting was recovered. Michael was beaten up for helping himself before the others had their chance to pilfer the house, and soon the rest of the perpetrators will be arrested."

"Which painting?"

"The Cézanne."

She gasped and bolted upright. "What Cézanne?"

"You didn't know the still life in their dining room was an original Cézanne?"

"Oh my God! The basket of fruit?" *Janice said my father was talking about fruit.* She fell into the chair behind the desk and took a few quiet moments before continuing. Nate didn't interrupt her thoughts.

"What about the paranormal researchers? Somebody set up that whole thing without my permission and I still don't know who or why."

"The intruders were covering their tracks by getting someone else in the house who could be blamed for whatever disappeared as soon as they left. None of the perpetrators counted on the police, or me."

Nate saw the wonder in her eyes and eased himself into the chair opposite hers. "As far as Michael's timely disappearance, you were supposed to think he was dead, and dead men don't steal paintings."

"So he was setting up the researchers."

"Creating his own fall guys. Yes. This criminal career can't be new. He made a couple of mistakes, but he isn't stupid. Another reason I was so worried about you."

"I—I had no idea." She leaned back in her chair, her eyes wide open. "How could I not know?"

"Lots of women fall for handsome con-men, Ronnie. Don't blame yourself. He must have been pretty damn good at it."

She nodded sadly. "Did Lorena ever surface?"

"Not yet."

"Do you think she's all right?"

"Probably."

"So, who's paying you?"

"Another good question. She gave me a small retainer that's run out. I hope to find her and collect the rest, but I'm doubtful." He sighed. "I'll be satisfied to know you're safe and Michael's in jail."

"So if she's innocent, what do you think happened to her?"

"The accomplices may be holding her to make Michael shut-up. Or, the other scenario is that she's waiting patiently for Michael at a rendezvous point."

"Maybe she was kidnapped from Michael's hospital room."

Nate's eyes opened wide. "What? Do you know something, Ronda?"

"There you go with that damned sixth sense of yours again."

"Might as well just accept it. I don't think it's going away." He gave just a hint of a smile.

"Okay. I tried to see Jenna at the hospital. When they wouldn't let me in to see her I detoured, very spur-of-the-moment, to see Michael. He couldn't talk but he could write with his left hand. He wrote 'Get out'."

"So, what did you do?"

"I got out."

"So, you'll listen to his good advice, but not mine?"

Ronda gave him her "I'm annoyed" look.

His expression grew more serious and he said, "I'd like to continue working on this, with your permission, as an old friend who just wants to do the right thing and make up for being a jerk."

Ronda felt both better and worse with the additional information. Tommy's situation was completely unrelated, so perhaps she could keep Nate busy elsewhere by cooperating. She would like to know the identity of these intruders and see them put away so she could relax and no longer feel threatened.

"Okay, Nate, you have to understand something, though."

"What's that?"

"By doing the investigation of my break-ins and the attack on Mr. Carroll, you will concentrate on finding the perpetrators and bringing them in, nothing else ... *and* you will accept payment from me for this, so I won't be obligated to you in any other way. I like the idea of firing your ass, if you lose sight of the boundaries."

"Sure. That's fine." He stood and put his hands in his pockets. "By the way, I'd have continued for free. I just want you to be safe, Ronnie—and happy again."

His eyes were soft and sad. She knew he meant it and her intuition said he still loved her.

Something stirred deep within. It wasn't pity. It was far more intangible. She was still in love with him too. Part of her wanted to cry. She missed him—terribly. *Damn it.* Just then, there was a knock on the door.

"Are you okay in there, Ronda?" Roy called.

She opened the door and smiled. "I'm fine," she said. "Just coming out." Waiting until Nate left the office, she locked it behind her.

At least, I hope I'm okay.

The next afternoon, Ronda was pacing back and forth behind the counter, impatiently waiting for Ty to return. She was kicking herself for not asking what time his flight was coming in. It didn't seem necessary. To Ronda, forty-eight hours seemed like such a short time two days ago.

She was so anxious and preoccupied that she was completely distracted. She knew she was in trouble when she topped off a customer's coffee, and she'd been drinking tea.

Embarrassed, she emptied the cup and started over with a fresh cup of tea. "So what's on the news today?" she asked her regulars. They probably thought she was making small talk.

Most said, "Same old, same old." No one said, "Oh, didn't you hear? A plane from LA to Boston crashed."

When the long, grueling day was over and the reinforcements showed up, she walked like a zombie into the office and stared at the burner phone.

Miraculously, it rang, and she jumped.

"Ronda?"

"Ty. Where are you?"

"I just got into Boston. I'll explain later. Can you meet me somewhere tonight?"

"Of course. Do you want me to drive down and pick you up?"

"Hell, no. There's an airport limo service I can use. It's more of a bus than a limo, but it gets the job done without putting anybody out."

"Okay. Where should I meet you?"

"Shore Inn. Portland. How's six o'clock?"

"Fine."

"I'll even spring for dinner if you're hungry," he said.

She was relieved to hear from him. She assumed he had news of Tommy, had maybe even seen him but didn't want to say anything over the phone. Maybe that's why he was late. Ronda thought up all sorts of scenarios, hoping that what actually happened wasn't as bad as her darker imaginings.

CHAPTER NINETEEN

She met Ty at the Inn and he immediately suggested that she drive him to the beach—any beach.

Heading south, Ronda decided to grab their dinner at her favorite little hole-in-the-wall seafood place in Camp Ellis where the lobster boats were docked fifty feet away and the lobster rolls were sweet, fresh and worth twice the price.

Walking to nearby Ferry Beach National Park, Ty still hadn't said anything about Tommy. They found a picnic table and he only made small talk. Following the casual dinner Ty asked if she would mind taking a long walk on the beach.

"Are you afraid the picnic tables may be bugged?" she asked, half kidding.

"No. I just have a lot of nervous energy. It helps to walk it off."

"I understand, believe me."

They strolled down to the water's edge. Ty still hadn't said anything about Tommy.

As they walked, Ty looked down at the sand. Something about the way his shoulders sagged told Ronda the news wasn't good.

Finally he spoke but so quietly she had to move closer to hear him.

"My father never showed, and he's never going to show." His voice was shaking.

"Oh, no. What have you heard?"

"Well, he didn't surface at graduation. I waited out in the quad, then went straight to my apartment, anywhere I thought he could easily find me. I was losing my mind until that friend, who he contacted before, delivered another message."

Ty glanced behind him before he continued. "He's safe, and someday he'll tell me where he is so I can go to see him, but he'll wait until things settle down." He picked up a flat rock and skipped it over the water's calm surface.

"And Marci Jo?"

"She's staying with him. She said to tell you it's time for second chances and happy endings. Lots of happy endings..."

Ronda smiled. That was definitely Marci Jo talking. She'd like to have laughed, but instead just gazed past the breaking waves toward the horizon as they strolled.

"He'll have to be missing for seven years before he's declared dead, Ronnie. I guess I understand, but I wish I could talk to him face to face."

"Oh, Ty. I'm sorry." She didn't know what else to say. She glanced up at Ty's stricken face and noticed new stress lines around his eyes and across his forehead.

"Well, I'm glad he's found a safe place," he was saying. "He was smart to stay away, but why did he ask Marci Jo to help me instead of me?" He stopped suddenly and sat on the hard sand with a thud.

Ronda wanted to say something profound and helpful, but she couldn't come up with a damn thing that would offer the level of comfort he must need.

She sat beside him and put a gentle hand on his shoulder. "We both know he's a survivor. He took the only eyewitness with him, and she's a travel agent to boot. He's probably opening a new restaurant in Central America as we speak."

He gave her a sad, resigned smile.

"So what do we do, Ty?"

"I guess I wait until I hear something. I'll keep to the same routine, work at the restaurant, live at home. Hopefully he'll find me when the time is right." He stood and brushed the sand from his pants. "So what's the private detective up to these days?"

Crossing her arms in front of her, she sighed. "He's investigating something else that has nothing to do with your father. I'm even paying him so there's no question of favors being done."

"You're sure he won't go off on a tangent? He seemed quite excited to have come up with the alternate identity."

"I don't know how much he knows about that. I don't even know how much we know about it. Nate's good to his word, and I think he'll forget it, since I asked him to."

Ty tucked his hands in his pockets. "Don't take this the wrong way, Ronnie. It's not that I don't appreciate your interest and all your help, but I don't see how this is your problem."

He had her there. She probably shouldn't get involved —but she was. "Ty, I lost my whole family, quit my job, left New York and was just floundering when I met your father. I felt like he took me in. Hell, he *did* take me in, literally. I was practically adopted by your dad when I became part of your family business, and I got a whole new lease on life."

One side of Ty's lip curled up. "I always wanted a sister."

She smiled, remembering what Tommy had said about Ty wishing he had a sibling.

"I know what it feels like to be alone. I like thinking of you as family. It's good to have someone looking out for me, especially someone as kind as you." His smile was stronger than the last one.

Ty said he had things to do. So did Ronda. She needed to talk to the funeral director about Mr. Carroll's arrangements. So they parted with a friendly hug.

The funeral home had been decorated in opulent style, about twenty years ago, she imagined. Dusty velvet drapes and antique, gold-colored fixtures.

"Mr. Bergeron will be with you momentarily," his wife said. "Make yourself comfortable."

Comfortable? In this place? While Ronda stood in the hallway, shifting from foot to foot and wondering what kind of funeral to plan for Mr. Carroll, Mr. Bergeron came through the dark red velvet drapes. He was wiping his hands on a paper towel, then he stuck out his right hand for Ronda to shake. She did so, squeamishly imagining what the funeral director might be wiping off of his hands.

"Mr. Bergeron, I'm Ronda Calhoun, Mr. Carroll's neighbor."

"Yes? How can I help you?"

"Well, I came to make arrangements for his funeral. I don't think that Mr. Carroll would want a fuss made, but I'd like something to be done for him. I'd be able to pay you in a few months, if you can wait."

"Arrangements have already been made and paid for," he said. "But, thank you."

"What? By whom?"

"By Lorena Carroll, his niece."

Ronda temporarily froze at the mention of the unusual name. "Oh, I see."

"Services will be here tomorrow, at ten in the morning."

"Thank you." Ronda smiled and hoped he hadn't noticed her shock.

Things were getting weird again, and she needed to talk to someone. There was only one person that she knew would understand. Ronda dialed the number she knew so well, took a deep breath, and left a message for Nate.

While she waited, she settled herself into her loveseat on the screen porch and patted Talon. She couldn't help thinking about the microphones Nate had found, especially the one in the kitchen.

Her mind wandered to that morning on the braided rug. She closed her eyes, leaned her head back and sighed. This time she allowed herself to remember the Nate she fell in love with. The one she trusted to do anything he wanted with her body and soul. Warm feelings flooded through her. She settled deep into the loveseat remembering his kisses, his tender touch. Her cell phone rang, and she jumped.

"What's up?" Nate asked.

"Oh, I'm not sure. Maybe nothing. I went to the funeral home just now to make arrangements for Mr. Carroll."

Nate interjected. "By the way, I should have said it before, I'm sincerely sorry for your loss. I know how close you were to him, and I know the feeling was mutual. I enjoyed talking with him that day I dropped my key off."

"Thank you." Ronda felt like crying but took a deep breath and pulled herself together. "When I asked to make arrangements at the funeral home, they said the arrangements had already been made. As far as I knew, he had no family."

"Maybe there was someone you didn't know about."

"That someone was named Lorena, Nate. Lorena!"

"Michael's fiancée?"

"I don't know. But how many people do you know who are named Lorena?"

"It could be her," Nate said, "or it could be a coincidence. Did you get her last name?"

"Carroll."

"Hmm. It could be a maiden name, I guess. Do you know what she looks like?"

"No. You wouldn't let us meet. At the time I thought it was a good idea. Now I'm not so sure. She could walk right up to me on the street and I wouldn't know her."

"Well, there is a way. When's the funeral? I could sit in the back and..."

"Would you come and sit with me? The funeral is at ten." It felt right. She needed to make peace with him. Her intuition, at last, had spoken.

They shared a moment of uncomfortable silence before Ronda continued. "I wouldn't ask, but it may prove to be seriously weird for me. I'd like to be with a friend."

"Oh, so you're considering me a friend?"

"I—I think so. I'd like to give it a try."

Ronda heard Nate sigh. "Okay, Ronnie. That's something anyway, and I won't presume more."

She hung up the phone realizing that she was looking forward to seeing him, even if she was dreading the funeral. But, it was for her friend and neighbor and she absolutely had to be there. She thought about Nate, ready and willing to go with her. At first, she had told herself it was because he could identify Lorena and collect his money, but it was more than that and she knew it.

The funeral was small and simple. Just the way he would have wanted it. Neighbors from her street and a few others, like the grocery store guy and the postman, she recognized.

A short, curvy, blond female sat in the front row, and by process of elimination Ronda determined that it must be Lorena. What niece would arrange and pay for a funeral without attending it?

When the funeral was over, "Lorena" hurried out. Ronda was talking to some of her neighbors trying to hold back her tears. The blonde rushed past and startled her, but Ronda didn't follow. She certainly didn't know what she would say to her.

Nate positioned his hand on the small of her back so gently that her skin shivered when she sensed it there. He guided her down the steps, away from the crowd.

Standing on the sidewalk, Nate said, "The woman who hired me wasn't here."

"I thought maybe that blonde who took off right away may have recognized you."

"No. I saw her too and maybe that was his niece, but she's not the woman who said she was Michael's fiancée." He kicked at the grass growing up through the cement walk. "Ronnie? I have a confession to make."

"Uh oh."

He took a deep breath. "I investigated Tommy to make sure you were safe with him. I know you were pissed off that day when I found you at his house, but I stumbled onto the alternate identity and wondered why he was using it. The more I looked into it the more concerned I became."

She leveled an intense gaze at him. "Nate. Tell me everything you know."

He sucked in a deep breath and spit it out. "Ronda, Tommy left the country because I advised him to. I only did that because I knew how you felt about him and because he was vulnerable. If I could trace his history out of curiosity, he would have been found out during a murder trial and would have served life in prison—guaranteed."

Crossing her arms, she frowned. "You'll have to stop

looking into every person I come in contact with if we're going to be friends. Can you do that?"

"Yes. Look, I'm really sorry."

"Where are they? Can Marci Jo come back?"

"She can if she wants to, but I doubt she will. They looked pretty blissful together, Ronnie."

Ronda had to smile. Two of her favorite people were finding happiness—together.

"And as far as where they are … no one knows but the two of them. We thought it would be better that way. Then nobody would have to lie to the police."

Ronda sighed, and nodded. She understood, even though she wished it didn't have to be that way.

"There's more you might hate me for, but I have to clear my conscience and you have a right to know. Out of respect for you and our possible friendship I want to be completely honest."

She braced herself. "I'm listening."

"Well, keep in mind the fact that I was going crazy when I was so far away and you were in such danger." He waited for a reaction, got none, and continued anyway.

"Ronda, I've loved you forever. After I dumped you I knew it was a mistake. I just didn't know it was the biggest mistake of my life. If anything happened to you I couldn't have handled it. I know hiring my PI buddy was an invasion of your privacy. I apologize. He was the guy you caught following you. Not too slick, but he said he helped you when Mr. Carroll was attacked. That's all I asked him to do—to keep an eye on you and help you, if you needed it."

He looked directly into her eyes. "I've been more in love with you than ever since the moment you crashed into my arms and into my life again. Please, please understand."

The expression on Nate's face beseeched her even more than his words. Softening inside, she touched his face.

"And there's one more thing. I have to get this all out, Ronnie."

She looked up at the sky and threw her hands in the air. "Go ahead."

"I knew about what happened to your family before I ran into you. I bought the beach house, hoping I could arrange to see you again. I never expected to run into you at the truck stop, though. That part was accidental. I don't expect forgiveness. I just want to start over with a clean slate. Be friends. Not lose contact. And, most importantly, I want you to be happy."

Ronda peered at him. She saw an honest man, with dark circles under his eyes, who looked like he'd really been suffering.

"Nate, I do understand." She bit her lower lip. "I think I understand a few other things too."

"Like what?"

"Like, even though you've been a pain in the ass sometimes, I've missed you." She reached for his hand and gathered it in hers. "*Really* missed you. I miss having someone in my life who loves me so much that they just want me to be happy. I know I'm alone, but I'm not a loner. I miss being part of a close family, and a partnership. I miss loving you, Nate."

Nate looked like he was going to speak, but she put a finger to his lips. "You chose to keep me safe even if it meant that I might kick you out of my life or maybe in the groin. I think I get it. As much as my parents drove me crazy with their overprotective love, at least I knew it was out of devoted concern, not lack of trust or faith in me. I think that's what you've been about."

"That's what I've been trying to tell you."

"Nate?"

"Yes?"

"I forgive you. I'd like to have a caring, give and take relationship." A couple walked by so she waited until they passed and lowered her voice. "Would you like to continue this conversation at my house?"

"More than anything."

Ronda and Nate walked the four blocks from the funeral parlor to her cottage both deep in their own thoughts. Nate had his hands in his pockets and looked at the pavement.

When she unlocked the door, she asked, "So, where did you find the microphones?"

"Here," he said tapping the side of her front door, and..." He followed her into the house. "Here." He tapped the underside of the left banister, on the squeaky stairs. "And, one more."

He led the way into the kitchen and pointed to a spot under the counter, about three feet from the braided rug. "And here," he said.

They stood on the rug together, looking at each other shyly. Shyness was something they had never experienced with each other before.

Finally Nate reached for her and she stepped forward into his embrace. Neither one of them spoke. They simply held each other, until Ronda felt him trembling. When she leaned back, she saw pain in Nate's eyes.

"What is it?"

"I don't ... I was so afraid I'd lost you for good. I still think we're a good fit, and I hope we can try again, someday. I still want to be with you, because I'm completely in love with you. I've never felt this way about any other woman."

"Maybe we should see what happens..."

Nate looked vaguely sick, and sunk to the floor, his head in his hands.

"Ronda. The PI I hired said you were with Ty at his house. He said you spent the evening with him."

"I did." She sat beside him on the rug.

"Are you two ... Do I need to be aware of anyone else in this equation?"

She saw the most tortured expression on Nate's face. "It wasn't a date. We've both lost what was left of our tiny families. We know what it's like to feel alone. We were filling up a few hours of that awful emptiness with friendship, that's all."

She sighed and shook her head. "I barely know Ty, but what I do know is that he's a good guy trying to do the right thing by his father and his employees. If it helps you at all, he thinks of me as the sister he never had."

Nate smiled and let out a deep breath. "Yeah, that does help. I'm sorry I got insanely jealous. I know he must be going through hell."

"Yeah, he is. He certainly isn't in a good place to start a relationship. His thoughts are elsewhere."

"Where are your thoughts?"

"Right here with you."

"Are you *with me?* In the sense of, us?"

Ronda curled up next to him and molded her body into his, and he put an arm around her.

"I need to ask you something before I answer that."

"Go ahead. Ask me anything."

"Okay, is there anything else you've done that might piss me off if I find out about it?"

Nate chuckled. "Uh oh. Yeah, probably one more thing." He moved so he could look at her face and reached for her hand.

She reluctantly took it and waited nervously.

Leaning his head against the cabinets, he sighed. "You're not going to like this one. I swear it will sound as if I'm insane..."

"Okay. That's the disclaimer." She took his chin and leveled it so she could look in his eyes. "Now spit it out. What did you do?"

"It's not something I did. It's who I am. I'm a shapeshifter. Once a month I become a wolf."

Her jaw dropped and she sat immobile. Nate closed his eyes tight, as if waiting for the inevitable explosion of laughter.

The only thing that exploded was "Halleluiah!"

His blue eyes opened wide.

She clapped a hand over her mouth. At last, she choked out a response. "I performed a summoning ceremony with three friends, hoping to meet immortal lovers. It worked for all three of them, but I thought I must have done something wrong, because it didn't happen for me."

"You believe me?" Nate's expression turned into a grin. "And you're okay with it? He rested his forehead against hers.

"I know how it sounds. Crazy right? Wait... I won't be in danger at the full moon, will I?"

"No. I'll remember who you are."

"Then maybe we can be crazy together."

Clasping his hands around her waist, he held her tighter. "I can't believe you're okay with this... You know the night I asked you to live with me? Remember?"

She certainly did. She nodded and smiled into his shining gaze.

"Well, that wasn't really what I wanted to ask you."

"It wasn't?"

"No. I wanted to ask you to marry me, but I'd have to tell you my secret first, and I was afraid I'd scare you to death."

Ronda chuckled and gazed past her tears at Nate's mouth curling into his sweet smile.

"Ronda, if you can forgive me for all of that, and maybe for the one or two mistakes I'll probably make in the future, I truly believe we could make a wonderful life together."

She laughed. "One or two mistakes, huh? You mean you're not going to be perfect from now on?"

"I'm afraid not. When it comes to you, I'm too emotionally involved, and when emotions get in the way, mistakes can be made. By the way, when's your birthday? I don't want to miss that and disappoint you."

"Halloween."

"Hmmm." He ran his fingers through her soft, pixie haircut. "I thought I might ask you to consider an October wedding but if that's too much excitement in one month..."

She grinned. "Please! I'll be turning forty this year. I might like to focus on something other than my birthday."

"So, you *might* like to marry me in October?"

"Well, I'll have to give it some thought."

"How long will you need to make up your mind?"

"I don't know. How long do you have?"

"I have the rest of my life. No pressure. I'll be here." He gazed into her eyes with an impish glint and swept a stray piece of hair behind her ear.

Ronda smiled. "I'd like to live in Kennebunkport. I really didn't want to sell the house."

Nate smiled, wrapped his fingers though hers and kissed her. "Anything you want."

Ronda gently placed her hand behind his head and pulled him close, bringing her mouth to his. She kissed him with all the tenderness she hoped a kiss could convey.

Returning her warmth, he loosened his tie. She glanced at the bulge below and draped her arms around his neck. He hugged her around the waist and rested his cheek on her breast. Smiling she inhaled sharply, let out a deep breath, and rested her cheek on his head. To Ronda it was as if both of them had come home.

Nate whispered, "I love you. I always will."

"I believe you, and I love you too, Nate ... more than I knew I could love—anyone." Ronda sniffed back her tears and kissed him again.

He kissed her long and slow, finally coming up for air to

ask a question. "So, if we're resuming our relationship, I need to know where you want to pick it up."

"How about where we left off?"

"Patting the rug, Nate said, "Is this a good place to pick up where we left off?"

"It's perfect." She gave him what she hoped was a "come hither" look and unzipped the back of her black dress.

ALSO BY ASHLYN CHASE

Look for these books also by Ashlyn Chase here: https://books2read.com/ap/ngobln/Ashlyn-Chase

The Goddess Gets her Guy; coming November 26, 2019

A Phoenix is Forever; Print, ebook and audio [#3, Phoenix Brothers series]

More than a Phoenix; print, ebook, audio [#2, Phoenix Brothers series]

Hooked on A Phoenix; Available in print, e, and audio [#1, Phoenix Brothers series]

Tiger's Night Out; [#2, Be Careful What you Summon series]

Never Dare a Dragon; Available in print, ebook and audio [#3, Boston Dragons series]

My Wild Irish Dragon; ebook, print, and audio [#2, Boston Dragons series]

I Dream of Dragons; ebook, print, and audio [#1, Boston Dragons series]

Wonder B*tch; Novella, ebook only

Laura's Upcycled Life; Novella, ebook only

Heaving Bosoms; ebook and print [#1, Heaving Bosoms/Quivering Thighs duo]

Quivering Thighs; ebook and print [#2, Heaving Bosoms/Quivering Thighs duo]

Thrill of the Chase; 3 Novella anthology, ebook and print

Guardian of the Angels; Novella, ebook only

Immortally Yours; 3 Novella anthology, ebook and print

Vampire Vintage; ebook and print [#1, Be Careful What You summon series]

Love Cuffs; ebook and print, Coauthored with Dalton Diaz

Out of the Broom Closet; ebook and print [#3, Love Spells Gone Wrong series]

Tug of Attraction; ebook and print [#2, Love Spells Gone Wrong series]

The Cupcake Coven; ebook and print [#1, Love Spells Gone Wrong series]

Oh My God, ebook and print, Gods Gone Wild Duo, Coauthored with Dalton Diaz

Kissing with Fangs: ebook, print, and audio [#3, Flirting with Fangs series]

How to Date a Dragon; ebook, print, and audio [#2, Flirting with Fangs series]

Flirting Under a Full Moon; ebook, print, and audio [#1, Flirting with Fangs series]

The Vampire Next Door; ebook and print [#3, Strange Neighbors series]

The Werewolf Upstairs; ebook and print [#2, Strange Neighbors series]

Strange Neighbors; ebook and print [#1, Strange Neighbors series] This series is also available as online interactive stories via the Chapters Interactive Stories App.

Thank you for reading my books! If you enjoy them, please do me a solid and leave a positive review. Reviews sell books. Sales feed authors. Well-fed authors write more books. *Thank you!*

Join the cool kids! *Sign up for my newsletter here:* https://tinyurl.com/y6lzesr7

CPSIA information can be obtained
at www.ICGtesting.com
Printed in the USA
FSHW012053210820
73212FS